Something ice-cold
ran down her spine

It wasn't until she reached for the lock that Kim noticed her apartment door was already open. She caught her breath and held it, not daring to move an inch.

One look found her apartment ransacked . . . and there was Conor Stark, rummaging around in her living room. Unaware of her, he turned and went out the terrace door.

Kim knew she should turn and run for help, even if it meant letting Conor get away, but instead she entered the apartment, picked up the phone and punched in an emergency number.

It took precious moments for the emergency operator to respond. Long enough for Conor to discover her. With narrowed eyes he advanced on her. She took a step back, hitting the wall. There was nowhere to go.

"Nine-one-one, Operator Number seven-three-two, what's the emergency?"

Kim opened her mouth, but nothing came out. She could only listen to the pounding of her heart and the operator's urgent voice sounding faraway and tinny as it called, "Nine-one-one. Is anybody there?"

ABOUT THE AUTHOR

Eve Gladstone believes that romance and adventure are constant challenges that go hand in hand. She has had a number of books published—both fiction and nonfiction—since she began her writing career. Eve lives in a New York City suburb with her husband and a compatible assortment of dogs and cats.

Books by Eve Gladstone

HARLEQUIN INTRIGUE

HARLEQUIN SUPERROMANCE

Ghostwriter

Eve Gladstone

Harlequin Books

TORONTO • NEW YORK • LONDON
AMSTERDAM • PARIS • SYDNEY • HAMBURG
STOCKHOLM • ATHENS • TOKYO • MILAN
MADRID • WARSAW • BUDAPEST • AUCKLAND

To Jim Cowen and Victor Cowen

Harlequin Intrigue edition published May 1993

ISBN 0-373-22228-9

GHOSTWRITER

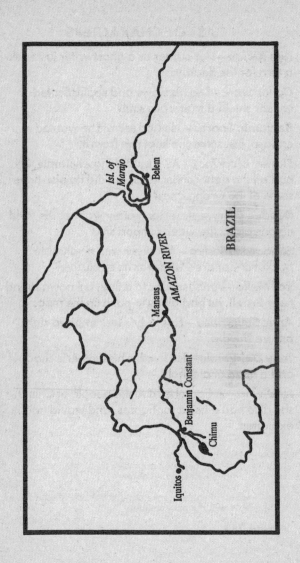

CAST OF CHARACTERS

Kim Killian—Her career as a ghostwriter just took a turn for the deadly.

Conor Stark—Did his suave and sophisticated veneer shield a traitorous soul?

Benjamin Soares—He had secrets he wanted to expose, but someone kept him from it.

Sidney Blackfoot—As a publishing dilettante, he had all the right connections, but did he also have some of the wrong ones?

Deedee Dalrymple—Her money was her life, and no one else's life was as important.

Eduoardo Moriya—A lawyer with a valuable packet of papers—why was he so elusive?

Raf Mello—Ambassador to a tiny, unknown island near Brazil, he had plans to put it on the map.

Anne Severance—This lady's luck expired right before she did.

Tony Dalrymple—He lived in his mother's shadow and a haze of alcohol.

La Divina—A figurehead to the people of Chimu, she also had a head for figures, and would not be exploited.

Chapter One

"Favor, is this Kim Killian to whom I speak?"

"Benjamin?" Kim needn't have asked. She had recognized his gravelly voice and accent at once. "You're back!" she said excitedly into the receiver. "I don't believe it. How long has it been? Two years? Two years at least. You could've warned me, you know."

"Never mind all that," Benjamin Soares said, lapsing into Portuguese. "I want to talk to you."

"Well, I want to talk to you, too. Where are you staying? Park Sheraton, as usual? I don't care how early in the morning it is, I'm going to come and get you. Now just stay put."

A little surprised at the silence that followed, Kim waited another moment. "Benjamin, you there?" The silence hung on.

"Oh damn, a disconnect," she said. "Well, he'll call back." She was about to replace the receiver when she heard a barely audible sigh. "Oh?" She broke into a smile. "Benjamin? Are you there?" Another moment of silence passed before he spoke, a moment in which alarm pulsed unexpectedly and unreasonably through her.

"I suppose you expect more money now," he said.

"What? *What* do I expect?"

He cut her off. "Worse than that, I suppose you won't be able to keep your mouth shut." His tone, a flat, implacable one she'd never heard before, certainly didn't fit the plump, bearded, kindly man she thought she knew. "Well, let me tell you, my dear, I'm prepared to sue you for libel if you so much as break the smallest comma in our contract."

Had the nuances of Portuguese escaped her? But no, you don't forget a language you grew up with. Perhaps she could blame the early hour and the fact that the call had awakened her from a deep sleep. "Benjamin, keep my mouth shut about what?"

"You know what I'm talking about. *Lucky Lady*."

"But that's history, Benjamin. It's been off the racks for nearly a year. I ghosted the book for you, you paid me and that was that." Instead of an answer, she caught his intake of breath, a click and then silence.

"Ben?"

Kim continued to grip the phone mindlessly until an urgent beeping told her to disconnect.

Now, what the devil was that all about? She had no doubt her caller was Benjamin Soares and that he had gone certifiably mad sometime during his last two years in Brazil. Probably bitten by some exotic little creature deep in the jungle while he chased after the story that continued to obsess him.

She had to call him back. She climbed out of bed, went barefoot into her living room to get her phone book, found the number of the Park Sheraton and called the hotel, fully confident she'd get through to him.

He wasn't even registered.

"Oh. Well. Hmm," she said into the receiver, tapping her fingers on the desk. "Can you tell me, did he stay at the hotel sometime during the last week, say, or is he booked for any time soon?" She had no idea where either question was leading. Nowhere, it turned out, because the hotel had no booking for Benjamin at all.

She put the receiver back in its cradle, thoroughly mystified. Benjamin wouldn't have been calling from Brazil, would he? Her only other connection to him was through Sidney Blackfoot, and why would she want to talk to Benjamin, anyway, the bad-tempered old beast? Imagine accusing her of trying to break their contract!

Sidney would know. The notion cheered her. Hearing from Benjamin, bad-tempered or otherwise, required a call to Sidney Blackfoot, publisher of *Lucky Lady*. Surely Benjamin would have contacted him first. On Saturday, Sidney could be found at his beach house in the Hamptons. She settled back in bed, and reached for the telephone just as it began to ring.

Ah, Benjamin was calling to apologize. "What happened," she asked at once, "a disconnect?"

"Kim?"

"Sidney?"

"Who else would be calling you at this ungodly hour? Listen, Kim, I don't want you to get a swelled head over this," Sidney said.

"Calling me at an ungodly hour? Never mind, we're operating on the same wavelength. I was just about to call you," she said, then paused, a little confused. "I'm to get a swelled head over what Benjamin said? A black eye maybe, but not a swelled head."

"You heard from Benjamin?"

"Well, yes, isn't that what you're calling about?"

"Then where the devil is he?" Sidney sounded hurt at being left out of this newest development. "Yesterday he gave my secretary a garbled message about wanting to see me, but never called back to set up an appointment."

"That's what I wanted to ask you. Is he in Brazil or here? He's not staying at his usual haunt, because I just checked."

"He's somewhere in town, apparently. Well, are you pleased?"

"Pleased? Hardly."

"Uh-oh," Sidney said. "I forgot about talking to you early in the morning when your head isn't on straight." He chuckled. "Swelled head."

"Look, it *is* a little early." She decided that Sidney's cheerful tone and Benjamin's accusation were too depressing to cope with all at once. "I need coffee and a shower, in that order. Let me call you back."

"Hell," he said, "even if we can't find him, I, for one, still feel like celebrating."

Celebrating? The arrival of another poorly written manuscript that wouldn't interest anyone anyway? Had the whole world, herself excepted, gone mad?

"Tell you what," Sidney said, rushing on. "Orders from the mistress of the establishment. Take the ten-something-or-other from Penn Station to East Hampton. That'll bring you here in time for lunch. I'll pick you up. Look for someone with a black mustache and a broad grin. Alice says hello and that she's laying on the champagne and caviar. And she said to come for the weekend. Oh, and don't forget your bathing suit. It's going to be plenty hot, even out here."

"The only trouble is," Kim said, nearly demolished by his run-on speech, "I have a dinner date this evening."

"Cancel it." His tone was peremptory. He was the boss, after all. "He'll more than understand. We have to plot strategy. This gives Blackfoot the leg up it needs. Ha ha ha," he bellowed. "The leg up."

"Plot strategy? What are you talking about?"

He was laughing too uproariously to answer.

"Sidney?" she cried. "Are you, by any chance, suffering from sunstroke?"

But Sidney Blackfoot had hung up and once again Kim was left staring at her telephone receiver. "Crazy," she said. "Can everyone else be going mad, or is it me?" She bounded out of bed. The train left around ten. She had calls to make, and a million small things to do. Coffee first.

Perhaps Benjamin's preoccupation with his aunt, the beautiful, brown-eyed, raven-haired Lucky Anne Severance, had finally borne fruit.

Was Lucky Anne alive after all? While packing her weekend bag, Kim remembered the sustained euphoric state she had been in while ghosting the book for Benjamin. The taste, the feel, the look of Brazil, and the personality of the woman who'd fascinated her nephew and ultimately Kim, had wound themselves into Kim's life for fully a year. At times she'd felt as if she were the young Lucky Anne, a woman alone, daredevil, breaching the code of her class, ignoring the way refined young women were supposed to conduct their lives.

Lucky Anne had escaped, danced the dream. Men fell at her feet as she dazzled in the movies, in international high society. And then, as in all glamorous lives worth citing, she had fallen in love, had borne her lover's child. There the story changed, became real and ended terribly, for Lucky Anne had retired to manage her lover's ranch on the island of Marajó in northeast Brazil. And supposedly died in a fire there shortly after her lover married another woman, DeeDee Ealing of an American lumber fortune.

Two years before, Benjamin had spoken to Kim in a far different tone from the one just used. Although his book recounted the particulars of Lucky Anne's death, he suspected privately that she might not have died in that fire after all. *Someone* had died, certainly, but he questioned whether the victim had been his aunt.

"I haven't even scratched the surface of this story," he had told Kim enthusiastically. "This is big, and," he added, fixing her with a stern look, "I won't let you get away with keeping the Dalrymples out of my follow-up book to *Lucky Lady*. It's about time somebody cut them down to size."

"Cut them down to size?" By then the argument had grown hoary with age. "You don't cut people like the Dalrymples down to size. They're indestructible! The biggest landowners in Brazil, and in the United States, and maybe the world, for all I know. They're indestructible. Benjamin, you don't want a lawsuit. I saved your neck," she reminded him, "by excising their name from the manuscript except for that one little bit about Lucky Anne managing their ranch at the time of her death. You have no proof that Anthony Dalrymple married your aunt, or plotted against her or had anything at all to do with that fire."

Benjamin gave her a rare smirk. "You'll change your mind."

"The Dalrymples could sue you for libel if you so much as whisper their name," Kim said. "Listen, Ben, they *own* any number of legislators here in the States, not to mention the clout they have in Brazil. They're too rich, too powerful. We're talking major game players here. They won't be nearly so polite as initiating a lawsuit. They'll string you from the nearest tree."

"Won't be a nearest tree. They'll have cut them all down by that time."

"They'll manage," Kim said. "The Dalrymples of this world always manage."

"Let them try. I welcome the publicity."

"You can't afford to find out just what the Dalrymples could do to you."

"I have right on my side."

"That and a dime wouldn't buy you a cup of *cafezinho* in Rio."

"You leave the worrying to me." He had chucked her under the chin and grinned in his grandfatherly way. "I'll be back, and you, my darling, are going to be in charge of the project. What a talented little genius you are." On that last flattering remark he had left for Brazil.

His telephone call not minutes before certainly belied his faith in her talent. From Benjamin's raw original manuscript she had rewritten *Lucky Lady* entirely and turned it into a publishable book. *And* had found Blackfoot Press for him into the bargain. The publisher, Sidney Blackfoot, a pilot himself, figured America supported a small market of aviation buffs and Brazil buffs who might be interested in the adventures more than thirty years before of the beautiful and glamorous Lucky Anne.

"Poetic," the critics bleated.

"Written with incandescent grace, yet full of good humor."

"Lucky Lucky Anne for having so devoted a biographer."

"A must for anyone interested in learning how to write succinctly and with clarity."

In spite of good reviews, the book unfortunately sank without a trace. Not too many Americans, after all, seemed interested in the life of Lucky Anne.

"Never mind," Sidney had said to Kim. "Poor sales notwithstanding, this book put Blackfoot Press on the map. Time will tell we were right." Sidney, who considered publishing books a deeply intellectual enterprise, could afford to be as optimistic as any heir to a large brewery fortune might be.

Kim dutifully clipped *Lucky Lady*'s notices and pasted them in her scrapbook. Nowhere in the book, or the publicity material sent out by Blackfoot's public relations department, was the name Kim Killian mentioned, not even as editor. In his effusive acknowledgments at the front of the book, Benjamin hadn't even thanked her for her so-called editorial guidance. He thanked his typist, his tailor, his airplane mechanic, his *barber,* but not Kim Killian.

But a promise was a promise and Kim kept hers. She had contracted to ghostwrite a book for Benjamin Soares. She had promised to tell no one, with the exception of Sidney and Alice Blackfoot, that she had actually written the book, and didn't even gloat over the encomiums the press threw *Lucky Lady*'s way. She hadn't contracted to ghostwrite a *bad* book, and so wrote the only way she knew how.

She had delivered the book on time, received her money promptly from Benjamin, by then far away in Brazil, and written off the experience. Benjamin would surface again, she had no doubt. Meanwhile Sidney Blackfoot kept her busy with editing projects.

Best of all, her life was beginning to get back on track. Three years before, her husband had rushed her through a divorce and married "that singer," as her mother always referred to the new Mrs. Drew Andrews. Kim had begun dating again, and memories of her marriage, or better, memories of her divorce, were beginning to have the unreality of a dream, an uninteresting, forgettable dream.

Except for her mother's occasional oblique remarks, Kim might never have been Mrs. Drew Andrews.

"I suppose you saw her on television last night," her mother would say, "and see? That could have been you." She was missing the mark by a continent. Kim wasn't a singer, and she'd never steal anyone's husband out from under her nose.

This is ridiculous, she thought. One telephone call from Benjamin Soares and every sore was in danger of opening again. She seldom thought about Drew and the two years they'd been married. The wounds had closed over, and when she suspected they might start hurting again, she knew how to hide out with a movie or a quart of double-double-chocolate ice cream. Or better yet, accept a date with an attractive, interested man. She had been pleasantly surprised to discover that this was almost as easy as it sounded.

More important, she had a small co-op apartment of her own in a Manhattan brownstone, and enough work and friends to keep her busy till the next millennium. She had examined her life and found it worth living, in spite of the damage to her ego her husband had inflicted.

Benjamin's phone call wouldn't, *couldn't* disturb her, because he was consigned to the past and she was living in the present. He'd have to come up with a Brazil-size apology before she'd touch his new book. She'd have to be firm with Sidney about that.

Chapter Two

The air-conditioned train to Long Island was halfway out of Manhattan before Kim relaxed enough to unfold the *New York Times*. Her long, light brown hair was in a neat French twist that kept it comfortably off her neck and showed her large brown eyes to advantage. She turned at once to the Saturday arts section to check the listings of upcoming concerts and exhibitions. She then read an article on a projected new gallery at the Metropolitan Museum of Art. The train ground steadily across the flat, blue-collar borough of Queens. Nearly twenty minutes went by before she reached the page devoted to literary news. And gasped at what she found there. Two inches of right-hand column space was taken up by a photograph of Benjamin Soares, his familiar face as amiable as ever.

"The Berriman Prize?" She nearly choked on the words, then realized she had spoken them to her neighbor, an elderly priest who smiled at her and went back to his crossword puzzle.

Kim eagerly digested the story announcing the award of the prestigious Berriman Prize for nonfiction literature to Benjamin Soares. *Fifty thousand dollars.* This time Kim let the whistle die aborning, for fear of offending her neighbor. No wonder Benjamin was worried. He thought she'd be the first to crow. Out loud to the press. Well, he needn't have worried. The thought would never have crossed her mind. *Never*. She was a woman of the world.

Kim read the article again and folded the paper neatly and tucked it into her canvas weekend bag. She felt a new kind of elation that in other circumstances would have had her jumping for joy.

Imagine, she had written a Berriman Prize book! For a while Kim sat very still, smiling goofily, gazing unseeing at the landscape speeding past. Then reality hit and she felt her happiness skulk away like a naughty child caught drenching herself in her mother's best perfume.

She could never tell anyone about the prize, neither her parents nor her friends. She couldn't even *dream* of Drew learning about the prize and confessing that their divorce had been the greatest mistake of his life. Except she didn't care about Drew, only that her faith in herself had been rewarded. Her happiness crept back in, a private happiness never to be shared. That was okay, too.

Lucky Lady was hers from the first word to the last. Lucky Anne had supplied her life and Benjamin the research, but the book was Kim Killian's. She had crafted every sentence, crossed every *t*, dotted every *i*. She had brought to life that beautiful, luminous woman dead these past thirty years, and perhaps that was honor enough.

Anne Severance had been the daughter of a well-known British pilot who married into the family of Brazilian rancher Maximilian Soares. Anne grew up a tomboy on the Soares *fazenda* and learned to fly when she was in her teens. She ferried planes for Great Britain late in the Second World War, where she earned her nickname Lucky Anne.

After the war, a glamorous, willful daredevil, Lucky Anne girdled the globe in a single-engine plane, greeted at every stop by wildly enthusiastic crowds. She blithely took on Hollywood, performing as a stunt pilot and actor.

She did not return to Brazil until she was in her early thirties, and there, with her father, flew tour parties into the Amazon.

Then she met Anthony Dalrymple and her world wheeled around. She was, as Kim put it, grounded by love. Her scandalous behavior with Anthony, and the birth of their son, made her a pariah within her puritanical family.

According to Benjamin Soares, Anthony callously abandoned her in Brazil to marry DeeDee Ealing, a marriage of fortunes, not of love. Benjamin also believed that his aunt and the scion of the Dalrymple empire had married and never divorced. Not long after her abandonment, Anne's body, burned beyond recognition, had apparently been found in the remains of a mysterious fire that completely destroyed the Dalrymple *vila* and nearby stables on the island of Marajó. The story of Lucky Anne ended with the report of her death. She was gone, suddenly, a woman larger than life. But a legend had begun, culminating in a Berriman Prize.

Benjamin had always been of two minds concerning his aunt's fate. Either Anthony Dalrymple had murdered her, or the body discovered had not been Lucky Anne's. As he unreasonably hoped, his aunt had escaped and was in hiding, even after all these years. Hiding was the operative word, and afraid for her life.

And so now Benjamin had a fresh platform for his favorite subject, the publicity that would attend the award.

At the Jamaica station, Kim's elderly neighbor got up and left, tipping his straw hat and giving her an amused smile. She leaned back against her seat and closed her eyes, imagining what the book jacket might have looked like: "Lucky Lady, *a Blackfoot Press book by Kim Killian. A Berriman Prize book by Kim Killian.*"

She opened her eyes. Her name *wasn't* on the cover. She'd never step up to a podium dressed to kill, to claim a prize of fifty thousand dollars.

"I wish to thank my ex, Drew Andrews, who left me so ignominiously, forcing me to write my way to fame and fortune. What more could a woman ask of a man?" No, she was a ghost and an editor, paid to live other people's lives for them on paper.

What if she'd had a few adventures of her own somewhere along the way, Kim thought. Perhaps she might have come up with as exciting a life as Lucky Anne's, written a book and won the Berriman Prize on her own.

But Lucky Anne had died young. Remembering, Kim felt a shiver lift the hairs along her arm. Testing life to the limits certainly had its downside.

Still, Kim decided with an audible sigh, perhaps it was better to have lived an exciting life and lost it than never to have done anything at all. She herself had chosen the least adventurous existence available. She was everybody's ghost, everybody's conduit to the reading public, writing about the good life instead of living it.

What made her think she had her act together? She didn't. She'd been so busy shaping other writers' work for public consumption she had forgotten the big, wide world out there. How she suddenly longed to see everything that was to be seen, do everything that could be done, go everywhere! Fly; ski the big trails! Ride a winner in the Kentucky Derby! No wonder Drew had fallen in love with "that singer." "That singer" traveled all over the world and had adventures by the score, taking her lawyer husband with her.

Perhaps the current Mrs. Andrews needed someone to ghost her autobiography. Kim thought about volunteering, but just as quickly steered herself off that road to self-pity. She was a prizewinning author!

"AMAZING COINCIDENCE, Benjamin showing up just when the prize is offered," Sidney said to Kim when he picked her up at the East Hampton station, as though their telephone conversation had never stopped. He was a slight, friendly man with dark unruly hair, kind eyes and a black, shaggy mustache Kim suspected was cultivated to give him a poetic appearance. He beamed at her, his smile informing her that the fates worked full time for Sidney Blackfoot. Perhaps they did, Kim thought, giving him a fond kiss on the cheek.

"Well, you're looking very pretty today," he said, flustered. "Cool, calm and proud of yourself, I suppose."

Kim had already forgotten about Drew and smiled at Sidney. She *did* feel confident in a cool beige linen skirt and pale pink halter top. She was ready to take on East Hampton society.

He took her arm and led her out to the parking lot. The day had turned hot. A scorching sun beamed from a cloudless, ultramarine sky, like the sky of the southern hemisphere with its heavy, almost sodden beauty and mystery. And with that image Benjamin's words and his anger came back to her. This time Kim felt a lot more apprehension.

"Amazing," Sidney went on, "that Benjamin was in the right place at the right time."

Kim shook her head to clear it of disagreeable thoughts. "I managed to reach Benjamin on the phone about a year ago, in Belém," she said. "Remember? That was when *Lucky Lady* hit the stores."

Sidney nodded. "I remember. I had thought maybe we should do a book tour when we garnered those reviews. He said he was too busy, that he was on to something big."

"And if you remember, he also said he figured on coming up sometime this summer."

"Actually, it doesn't matter how he got here or why. The point is he's here." Sidney spoke with obvious relish. "You put Blackfoot on the map, Kim. You and Benjamin." He gave her a smile, as though he would like to hug her right there in the middle of the busy parking lot. "And he'll want you as his editor. Now more than ever." He opened the door to his Jeep and handed her in.

"Forget it," Kim said. "The man I spoke to was Benjamin Soares, all right, but not *my* Benjamin Soares." Once they were on the road, she proceeded to tell him about the telephone call she'd received that morning. "He's afraid I'm going to ask for a portion of the prize money. *And* tell the world I wrote those pearly words. Why would I do that? I ghosted the book. All I am is a ghost, and nobody believes in ghosts."

Sidney turned his Jeep sharply onto the main avenue, managing to pat her hand at the same time. "Look, winning a prize like the Berriman is the last thing he expected. Suddenly he has to appear to all the world like a poet and a genius. And he must know we'd expect to reissue *Lucky Lady*. This time he wants to be in control."

"The word *macho* comes to mind. He definitely doesn't want anyone to know I wrote it. Me, a mere woman."

"He owes you his lifelong admiration. Let's give him the benefit of the doubt." Sidney turned briefly toward her and for the first time she saw worry lines crease the corners of his eyes. *He really cares about Blackfoot Press,* she thought with some surprise. *He isn't merely a dilettante.* The notion frightened her. She had given Blackfoot Press the prizewinning book it needed to be taken seriously, and he was worried that she had the power to destroy his company.

"Kim, don't blow it," he said. "We're going to reissue *Lucky Lady* and we don't need a scandal."

She wasn't hurt by his remark. She understood his fear only too well. "Me?" she said in a joking tone. "Create a scandal? Why would I do that?" Then, more seriously, she added, "I would like to point out that you didn't get the phone call. I did. Menace is the word that comes to mind."

"Forget the phone call. Think about other things. I'm going to work up a pretty effective promotion campaign for the reissue." Sidney began to describe the ad he would take out in *Publisher's Weekly.* "Congratulations, Benjamin Soares and *Lucky Lady.* Is Lucky Anne Severance still alive? Coming out this year, Soares's latest revelations about this fascinating woman, et cetera and so on. You'll have to work like a demon."

"Ben's mad at me," Kim said stubbornly. "And anyway, I'm on a deadline for you now. Remember? Delivery yesterday? And there's that biography of Eleanor Roosevelt right after."

"Eleanor will have to wait. Talk to Ben, tell him you just inherited a million dollars from an old aunt living in Pawtucket, Rhode Island. You don't need his money, the IRS won't hear of it—tell him anything. But I don't want him running to another ghost or to another publisher." He gave her a smile. "After all, you brought him to Blackfoot."

"I brought you the sane, sweet Benjamin Soares, not the current model."

"The current model is just a little overexcited, that's all, Kim. Ah, here we are, the old homestead."

The large white house loomed up suddenly, guarded by a giant red sculpture and framed by the ocean. A dozen cars, shiny, splendid ones, sat in the long, curved driveway. That meant, Kim supposed, the chic and super successful with whom she couldn't possibly have anything in common, although there wouldn't be a Berriman Prize winner among them.

"Do I know anyone here?" she asked with a sudden attack of shyness.

"Probably everyone. You know—it's the usual crowd, more or less."

She didn't know, but with the smell of salt water and the sound of sea gulls wheeling above, she found herself quivering with a kind of antic joy. How nervous she had been earlier that morning! *Funny,* she thought, *maybe I'm not nervous anymore because I'm a prizewinning author. Or because Blackfoot Press needs me as much as I need Blackfoot Press.* Whatever the reason, she bounced out of the Jeep and happily followed Sidney into his airconditioned, oversize cement monument to neo-Modernism nineties-style, ready to celebrate her almost-award, even if she couldn't mention it to anyone.

"How about dinner sometime soon?"

The question directed to Kim later that afternoon was from a distinguished white-haired gentlemen forty years her senior, who had attached himself to her the moment she stepped onto the Blackfoots' brick terrace.

"I don't think Mrs. Henderson would appreciate that," Kim said, referring to his wife.

"Never mind," Mr. Henderson said. "We have a modern marriage."

"I'm old-fashioned myself," Kim said.

"Really. I find *that* intriguing."

Kim smiled a little weakly, wondering what she was expected to say next.

But Henderson was suddenly distracted. He gestured toward the beach. "Oh, there's Conor Stark. Good, I wanted to talk to him."

Kim followed his gaze to a light-haired stranger heading quickly up to the Blackfoot house from the beach below. For a moment all action on the terrace and around the pool seemed to stop while everyone concentrated on his approach.

He smiled, taking two steps at a time to the terrace. The crowd started moving again, as though everyone had taken a collective breath and then released it. Conor Stark, whoever he was, had arrived.

He was tall and lean, even handsome in a conventional sense, with a good nose and strong jaw. Kim decided it was his smile that made him so attractive, a smile that was at once charming and intimate. His eyes were very light colored. Gray or blue, she couldn't quite tell, but they held something back. He'd be an easy man to meet and a hard one to know. He was, she thought, very levelheaded and a little removed from the party atmosphere he had just crashed.

Henderson turned apologetically to Kim. "I'll only be a moment."

"Please," Kim said, and forgot about him almost at once as she was drawn into conversation with a group of people talking politics.

Perhaps half an hour had passed before Kim found herself alone, full of political advice concerning the next election and grateful for a respite. She thought seriously of going back indoors and tucking into a book in the library.

"How does it feel to be the editor of an award-winning book?" someone whispered into her ear. She winced and swung around, to find herself face-to-face with a smiling Conor Stark.

He extended his hand at once. "I'm Conor Stark."

Rattled for no sane reason, Kim let her hand be held in his warm, strong grip for a few more seconds than necessary. "Oh, I'm..." What *was* her name? "Kim Killian," she announced with an air of triumph.

"I know," Conor said, still smiling. "Is that also an explanation of how it feels to be the editor of *Lucky Lady?*"

"Who told you I was?"

"Sid." He pointed to their host, who sat at the edge of the pool, talking earnestly to one of his guests.

"Oh." What else had Sidney been bragging about? "In that case, very happy," she murmured, "although of course I knew from the beginning we had a winner."

"I wish I'd had your prescience." He regarded her intently, then said, "The book came to the attention of Selby Press about four years ago."

Kim did not even blink. "They publish nature stuff."

"They asked me to check it over. Someone at Selby had heard about Lucky Anne and what a dynamo she was."

"You work for Selby."

He shook his head. "Consultant on nature matters pertaining to South America."

"Ah." She didn't understand, but wasn't about to let him know. She sensed a certain suppressed energy in him, a kind of potent bravado kept in check. It was as though he were aware of how out of place such concentration was in the Blackfoots' sophisticated, witty crowd. She glanced at Sidney, still at the pool edge, hoping to catch his attention. She needed him now to run interference.

"Of course I'm hired for my expertise on the Amazonian rain forest," Conor said, "not for my analysis of a writer's technique."

Kim felt his next words coming, even before Conor Stark spoke them. "However," he went on, "I decided input is input. The book was written so badly I suggested that the author either get himself a ghost or learn the English language. Selby agreed, decided the project was too much trouble against anticipated returns and rejected the book."

"Benjamin Soares speaks perfect English," Kim said, feeling the heat of protest rise in her face. "With a slight accent, that's all."

Conor lifted a brow. "Perhaps you can recommend his teacher to me. I can name any number of writers who could use him. Or her." His tone was pure irony.

Kim bridled but held her tongue. She was more worried about whether Conor had read the manuscript through and what he knew about Lucky Anne and her relationship with the Dalrymples. Those facts must be kept secret in face of all the publicity Benjamin would receive. "How did he fare on his nature facts?" she asked a little timidly, hoping by indirection to find out what Conor knew.

"Oh, he did his research."

"You gave him an *A*-plus on research, then."

"A failing grade, as a matter of fact, for insufficient attention to grammatical details and style. That's research, too."

Did he know, and was he being, for reasons of his own, equally cagey? But he couldn't know. They had been so careful during the ghosting process. "Well, lucky Blackfoot Press," she said. "You must send us other books that you reject."

"If I thought you were to be the editor, I would."

She caught something in his voice, interest that startled rather than flattered her, as if he had an agenda on which she was an item to be checked off. The feeling came to her from nowhere, but she found herself trusting in its gut truth: Conor Stark was smart, sexy and dangerous.

"Perhaps we ought to discuss the possibilities over lunch sometime," he added.

She was getting in a lot deeper than she wanted to. She felt crowded, or perhaps like a chicken bone being carefully picked clean. "If you'll excuse me," she said, with some desperation, "I have someone to see over there."

His smile this time turned enigmatic, which infuriated her. He couldn't know. She turned away, suspecting he hadn't finished with her, that more needed to be explored and revealed.

Before she could take more than half a dozen steps into the crowd, Alice Blackfoot grabbed her. "Good, you've met him," she said, tucking her arm through Kim's. "He especially wanted to meet you."

"He did?" Kim frowned. Alice was a notorious matchmaker.

"He did," she said, laughing. "You don't believe me."

Alice was a tall, slender blonde, as beautiful as her husband was dark and unremarkable.

"I'll tell you what I do believe, Alice. Conor Stark is entirely too interested in how that manuscript went from being an inarticulate mess to a prizewinner. He turned the manuscript down four years ago. And he's an expert on the Amazon."

"So he is. He works for the Americas Conservancy and spends maybe half the year in Brazil and the other half up here in the conservancy's main office."

"Oh." Kim felt a little deflated. Smart, sexy and dangerous. Was she looking for trouble where there was none? She turned and saw Conor Stark amble over to the pool. Getting down on his haunches, he greeted a woman who was clinging to the edge, a brunette with soaking-wet hair who smiled gleaming white teeth at him.

"What's the Americas Conservancy?" Kim asked, her eyes still on Conor. Was it possible to envy an unknown brunette, she wondered, just because Conor Stark was talking to her, a man Kim had met moments before and walked away from?

"You've heard of it," Alice said, "an incredibly well-funded charity established to save the world's biosphere. Conor's an expert on the flora and fauna of the Amazon."

"I'm impressed," Kim said.

"You realize that Dalrymple Enterprises is one of its chief backers."

"Uh oh." *Conflict of interest* popped into Kim's mind, but she put the thought aside for the moment.

"Incidentally," Alice said, "Conor loves *Lucky Lady.*"

"Does he? And who's the lucky lady with him? His wife?"

"He's not married." Alice squeezed Kim's arm, examining the skirt and tank top she wore. "Why don't you put on your bathing suit and go for a swim?"

A bathing beauty contest, was it? "No, I don't think so, Alice, but thanks for trying."

Alice gave her a fond smile. "For such a smart lady you're an awful fool."

Sidney came up to them, rescuing Kim, grinning his I've-got-a-treasure grin. He put an arm around her shoulder. "Met Conor Stark yet? We were lucky to get him over today. He's staying at Eastwind."

At Kim's nonplussed expression, Alice added, "That's the Dalrymple compound half a mile down the road. He's a friend of Tony Dalrymple."

Kim closed her eyes briefly. She didn't need complications, but was apparently being handed them by the score.

"Benjamin's Tony Dalrymple? Lucky Anne's son? What a coincidence."

"That's the Tony, but it's no coincidence. I play tennis with DeeDee Dalrymple, his stepmother, that's all," Alice said. "East Hampton is a small enough place, and the tennis club is decidedly exclusive. I think DeeDee has a thing for Conor. But then I would, too, given half the chance." She gave her husband's arm a warm, friendly squeeze. He beamed at her to let her know he didn't take her words seriously.

"Is that DeeDee?" Kim asked, studying the brunette hanging on to the edge of the pool.

Alice shook her head. "Conor's a very successful man in his field, but he hasn't a sou, at least compared to the Dalrymples. DeeDee likes to have him around, but she'd never seriously romance him."

Sidney, who had been standing by listening, let out a raucous laugh. "And just think, the Dalrymples have no idea they're the villains of *Lucky Lady*. Thanks to you." He placed a kiss on Kim's head.

"Exactly why do you feel lucky to have Conor Stark here?" she asked.

"He's been testifying before Congress on the damage to the Amazonian rain forest. I'm thinking of asking him to do a book for me—problems with the ozone layer, et cetera et cetera."

"And is he defending the Dalrymples in his testimony?" Kim asked quietly. "After all, he works for them if they support the Americas Conservancy. I'd call that conflict of interest. They've been involved in clear-cutting in the Amazon."

Kim glanced once more at Conor Stark. As though he felt her eyes on him, he turned and gave her his intimate smile. Despite it, she felt the first flowering of alarm in her stomach. "Have you thought about why he's really here?"

"I invited him," Sidney said.

"*Think*, Sidney."

"I am thinking. The Dalrymples are the kind of people you want in your corner, if that's what you mean."

"That's not it," Alice said quietly.

Kim threw her a grateful smile. "If Conor Stark read the original manuscript of *Lucky Lady*, then he knows what Benjamin thinks of the late Anthony Dalrymple, Sr."

"Meaning?"

"They won't want publicity on *Lucky Lady,* and certainly not on Benjamin, who has it in for them."

Sidney shrugged. "Food for thought." He didn't seem to be seriously worried about the Dalrymples.

"I've just had a sample of the revisionist Benjamin Soares," Kim reminded him. "With the Berriman Prize in his hands, we may be looking at a time bomb about to explode."

Chapter Three

DeeDee Dalrymple examined her face in the gilt Robert Adams mirror for a second or two longer, then came away clearly satisfied with what she saw there. For dinner at Eastwind, which was always formal, she wore a pale yellow flowered silk gown draped at the waist and slit at the front, so that her tanned legs showed to advantage whenever she moved. She wore baroque pearls at her ears and around her neck.

To Conor Stark, sitting across the immense drawing room in a stiff brocaded armchair, his hostess was an attractive, wealthy widow, stepmother to Tony, Jr., Conor's closest friend. He maintained friendly relations with DeeDee Dalrymple and did her bidding, not because of Tony, but because she was one of the chief benefactors of the Americas Conservancy, and the name behind the signature on his paycheck.

The ease with which Conor had gained access to the Dalrymple home never failed to fill him with a certain degree of self-congratulatory awe. The steps along the way had been as sure as the yellow brick road to Oz. The son of a construction engineer, he had come a long way, in time, place and social status, as witnessed by his presence in the Dalrymple home and even the tuxedo he wore. But purpose, and an obsessive one at that, had everything to do with success.

"Keep the goal in sight and never waver."

"Knowing you have free will, that's what separates the men from the boys."

"You can do it, kid, I know you can."

His late father had been the king of aphorisms.

DeeDee came over to the sofa and sat down, the gown opening silkily as she crossed her long shapely legs. "Well?"

"I wouldn't worry." Conor knew exactly what she referred to.

"And I suppose Sidney is crowing." Her accent, faintly British, had been acquired at an English school, during a short period when her parents had bought and refurbished a manor house outside of London.

"Sidney crowed so loud I was certain you'd hear him." The Dalrymple compound, on ten acres of valuable Hampton land, was a half mile down the beach from the Blackfoots. It included the main house, a large, weathered, brown-shingled building facing the Atlantic Ocean, and a smaller house of similar design occupied by her stepson.

"And Soares has a new exposé in hand, I suppose? Did you learn that for certain?"

"Ah." Here Conor smiled. "The winner of the Berriman Prize wasn't around, and from what I gather, no one knows where he is."

"But he's in the States."

"Apparently."

"We'll have to find him, perhaps. That is, if he's lost."

At her words, Conor felt an odd chill grip his rib cage. And the way she stared at him, with a dark impenetrable gaze, put him on edge.

"What's she like?" DeeDee reached for her drink and took a sip.

"She?" For a moment Conor was confused. Then he realized DeeDee was referring to the editor of *Lucky Lady*.

"The one we should be grateful to, after all. What's she like?"

"Pretty." His smile was careless. He found himself reluctant to talk about Kim Killian, not forgetting their verbal parrying and the wide-eyed way she'd observed him, revealing little about herself or Benjamin Soares.

That alone worried him. He had no doubt that when Kim edited *Lucky Lady,* she had advised Soares to excise all mention of the Dalrymple name. He expected DeeDee, wishing to keep the affair as private as possible, to charge him with damage control. Not her stepson, Tony, but Conor himself, who had read and rejected the original manuscript.

And then there were those rumors that Lucky Anne had survived the fire that destroyed the Dalrymple ranch near Belém, rumors DeeDee and her late husband had discounted.

"Pretty? She's pretty?" DeeDee was saying. "What the hell does pretty have to do with editing a manuscript?"

"Why don't we wait until Soares surfaces, then worry about what he's planning? We know nothing at the moment."

"My husband had every opportunity to stop him, and—" With a glance at Conor, she threw up her hands, not bothering to finish the sentence.

"The fuss caused by trying to stop Benjamin Soares would have been greater than watching the book end up on the remaindered tables," Conor reminded her. "Three thousand copies, that's all that were sold—"

"Until this, this..." She sighed, exasperated.

"Won a prize. Isn't it a gas?" Tony Dalrymple strode rapidly into the drawing room and bent over his stepmother to plant a kiss on her cheek. "Why don't we just buy Blackfoot Press and put Sidney out of business?" Like Conor, he was dressed in a well-tailored tuxedo, although his tie was slightly askew. *He's been drinking,* Conor thought. Alone in his cottage, he used liquor to build up courage to face his stepmother. It was a nightly ritual.

"Buy Blackfoot Press. That's Tony, Jr. for you." DeeDee threw Conor a conspiratorial smile, as though she and Conor had decided together that Tony would never grow up. That though his father was dead, he would forever after be Tony, Jr. "My stepson certainly knows how to throw away money."

"Might be cheaper in the long run." Tony went over to the drinks cart. He poured himself a straight Scotch, after raising an eye to Conor to ask if he wanted a refill. Conor signaled no, smiling indulgently at his friend. Then, as usual, the expected moment of depression overtook him. Tony was in harm's way, but there was nothing Conor could do about it.

"Suppose Dad had really married my mother before he married you?" Tony asked DeeDee, an ingenuous light in his dark, deep-set eyes, not the Dalrymple eyes, but the eyes of Lucky Anne Severance. "I mean, what if he really was a bigamist?"

"He didn't marry her. I'm sorry, Tony, but that makes you a bastard. I thought you were used to the idea." The words were spoken with the coolness of a much-repeated conversation in which neither party ever changed so much as a comma.

"I am," Tony said placidly, having come to terms with his history a long time before. "I know nothing about the woman. Have no curiosity whatsoever. I never even read that damned book. I was a tot when she died and I'm the little bastard who came to stay."

DeeDee was fond of telling Conor that Tony was a weakling. Afraid of his own shadow, even afraid of the servants. Perhaps that was why he had taken a liking to Conor Stark, who was impressed by no one.

The men had met in college and become buddies. Conor had entered on a full-time scholarship provided by the Dalrymple Education Fund. Tony was there because his father was the school's most important benefactor. That both fathers, Conor, Sr. and Anthony, Sr., knew one another wasn't coincidental. The Dalrymple empire included immense *fazendas*—ranches—in northeastern Brazil. Conor's father, a construction engineer, had been employed by the Dalrymples to oversee the building of a brand-new town in a corner of Amazonia.

When Conor's father died in a job-related accident in Brazil, the Dalrymples had been exemplary in their behavior toward his family, supporting them and sending both Conor and his sister to college. Conor, interested from childhood in natural history, was encouraged by generous Dalrymple grants to study in his chosen field. His feelings toward the Dalrymples had always been grateful ones. Those feelings changed suddenly and dramatically when his mother died, after Conor had already accepted a job with the Americas Conservancy.

But for now his mind was on Kim Killian. She would be privy to all that Benjamin Soares might have learned in the past two years. If Benjamin could prove that the head of the Dalrymple empire had married Lucky Anne Severance in Brazil, it would be public knowledge that the financier had become a bigamist when he married DeeDee. And if Lucky Anne were still alive, the son of that union might be the legitimate heir to the Dalrymple estate and not DeeDee.

Except that Anthony Dalrymple, Sr., had denied ever having married Lucky Anne, and even his son believed him. His estate had gone to his wife, DeeDee, although Tony was generously provided for in his own right. The law courts would have fun with this one, Conor decided, if a marriage certificate between Lucky Anne and the head of the Dalrymple empire could be found.

Tony showed no interest in proving the legitimacy of his birth, however. His current life-style suited him fine. He was unambitious, good-natured and lazy. He played tennis in the summer and skied in the winter. He thought about getting married, but never seriously. In fact, it was the differences in Conor's and Tony's life-styles, and Tony's apparent disinterest in his family's business, that allowed them to be friends.

Life was good to the product of an uncertified union between Lucky Anne Severance and Anthony Dalrymple, and Tony, Jr., knew it.

Later that evening, as Conor and Tony walked along the ocean's edge, kicking up the still-sun-warmed sand with their bare toes, Conor asked the question that had been bothering him all day.

"Aren't you at all interested in Benjamin Soares and what he might have to say about your mother?"

"No." Tony's answer was surprisingly curt.

"You'd be the legitimate heir to the Dalrymple empire if she and your father had married, and if she were alive when he died."

"My mother's dead. She died a long time ago. Dead people don't inherit estates. Listen," he said, stopping and digging his heel into the sand, "I once had a nanny who told me something I've never forgotten. You can only sit on one chair at a time. If my mother were alive, sure, things might be different, but she isn't. Anyway, just how much power and money do you think I need? I'm well-heeled,

Conor, a catch, a playboy. While we're hanging around here talking, my money is working overtime.''

"What's right is right," Conor persisted. "You could make a difference if you'd show a spark of interest in what's going on around you. Didn't your nanny tell you that, too?''

Tony shook his head in disgust, as though he thought Conor would never get the point. Despite the darkness, Conor caught the cloud that passed over his friend's eyes. "The kind of power vested in the company makes me sick," he said simply.

For a moment, Conor thought of taking Tony into his confidence, but knew he must not. He was playing a lone game, the safest kind. "Then you could be the messenger of change," he said.

Tony shook his head again. "Dalrymple Enterprises can't be changed. It can only be dismantled, destroyed, dumped into that ocean out there, except it would pollute the waters. And speaking of water, I need a drink," he added defiantly, as though expecting Conor to talk him out of it. He thrust his hands into his pockets and rushed past Conor, back toward the house.

Conor shook his head. His friend drank entirely too much, particularly when he was about to come face-to-face with unpleasantness.

Conor remained standing there, not interested in returning to the main house and DeeDee. As for Tony's words, he was surprised at the passion behind them. Time, he told himself, time. The waters wouldn't be polluted, at least not that way. He had to hold on and take everything slowly.

He thought of his father, broken and dying in a far-off land. And his mother's words years later, words that would eventually change his life forever and tie him inextricably to the Dalrymples and their empire. "Your father's papers," she said. "I brought them back with me. I never had the heart to look at them, never. They're in the safe. Perhaps one day I will.''

Conor turned and gazed back at the Dalrymple mansion. Every light was on. The place positively glowed, but it contained only coldness and disharmony. He saw Tony open the front door and step inside. Conor refrained from following his friend, understanding Tony's powerlessness and his anguish. Unlike Tony, however, Conor had every intention of seeing the Dalrymple empire cut down to size.

Chapter Four

"Sidney, how do you suppose Benjamin learned of the Berriman Prize?"

Kim, who asked the question, was alone with her hosts in the only friendly room in their concrete bunker, the wood-paneled, book-filled library. The guests had long since departed, and the Blackfoot brood were scattered throughout the house on projects of their own. The air had turned pleasantly cool. A nosy breeze from the sea made its way through open terrace doors, as though seeking a special bedtime read among the library's rare, leather-bound volumes. Through the window, the moon shone with white delicacy in a jet black sky. About five hundred yards offshore, the rigging of a yacht was dotted with party lights, and in the distance, on a barely discernable horizon, a ship headed east on an Atlantic journey.

Kim sat curled up in a soft leather side chair, comfortable with her hosts and a little drowsy but a long way from sleep. The day had been full of good vibes, the food, drink and company more fun than she'd expected. She'd had several flirtations with attractive men, a couple of which might have led to something had she been interested. And every time she'd glanced his way, she found Conor's appraising eyes upon her. He was curious about Benjamin, that was all; curious how a manuscript originally submitted in benighted English had eventually won a Berriman Prize.

"How *did* Benjamin learn of the Berriman Prize," Sidney mused. "They must have called him or sent him a letter. I haven't any idea how these things work."

"Where did they call him or send a letter?"

He shrugged. "Belém?"

"How do they know where he lives?"

He shrugged once again. "Called his agent."

"Benjamin doesn't have an agent. Remember? I'm the one who brought him to you. Benjamin said he trusted you enough to deal him a good contract. That," she added with a touch of sarcasm, "was in the days when he trusted the people he worked with. B.P. *Before* his *prize.*"

"What are you getting at?" Alice asked. She sat on the sofa stitching an elaborate floral needlepoint. "Why would it matter how Benjamin heard of the prize?"

"I've been thinking of something Sidney said before," Kim remarked. "That Ben's being here at the same time as the prize was announced was sheer good luck. I said he'd planned to be in New York about this time with his manuscript. The Berriman Prize is, for reasons known only to them, awarded in the height of summer."

"Maybe no other major literary prizes are awarded at this time of year," Alice said, "and they can have newspaper headlines to themselves."

"Still, I wonder at the coincidence," Kim said. "Benjamin heard about the prize before you did, Sidney, and certainly before I did. The important question is, where was he when he got the news?"

"Does it make a difference?" Alice asked.

"The fact that he's acting in a very peculiar manner makes a difference."

"He's incommunicado for the moment, that's all."

"The voice of reason," Sidney said, giving his wife an affectionate smile.

Kim relaxed back in her chair, suddenly not certain why she had brought up the subject. "Yes, of course, you're absolutely right. I've washed my hands of him anyway. I was just curious. And then, remember, when he called me to chew me out, Benjamin assumed I already knew about the prize. Meaning, I suppose, he had just arrived from Belém. And if so, where the devil is he?"

Sidney got out of his chair and went over to his computer.

"Sidney, you're not going to work now, are you?" Alice shook her head disapprovingly.

Without answering, Sidney switched on the computer, its blue maw instantly outshining every other object in the room.

"I like conundrums," Sidney said. "The question is, where was Benjamin when the prize was announced, and where is he now? The parameters are that Benjamin learned of the prize first, obviously. I didn't hear of it until I read the article in the *Times*. The Berriman committee did not contact me, although they contacted the newspaper. Or did Benjamin jump the gun with the announcement? Not very professional behavior all around. So, the first thing we do is locate Benjamin's telephone number in Belém." He pounded away at the computer keyboard and in a few seconds his screen obliged.

"Here we go," he said. "First object, call Belém and find out whether Benjamin is there, and if not, where he is."

"You're going to try to locate Benjamin through Brazil's telephone system?" Kim asked. "Good luck!"

"No." He grinned, punching in some numbers and handing her the receiver. "You are."

"You speak Portuguese," Alice said. "You *are* the only candidate."

Through several clicks and odd sounds, as if an ocean of wire lay between the United States and Brazil, Kim at last heard a phone ringing, presumably in Belém, not Patagonia—which did not mean it was ringing in the Soares household. "If it's nine o'clock here," she said, "it's nine o'clock there. Or do they have daylight-saving time? I don't remember. I'd have to ask my parents. Let's see, that's Spring ahead, Fall behind, which makes it maybe..."

Someone picked up at the other end. *"Allo."*

"Benjamin Soares, please," Kim said, smiling in surprise at her hosts at actually having made contact with a human voice.

"Allo?"

"Benjamin Soares, is he there?" She realized she was shouting, in Portuguese, and that the Blackfoots were grinning at her, although they did not speak the language. "I'm calling from the United States of America for Benjamin Soares."

"Allo, allo."

Sidney hastily pointed out Benjamin's number on the screen. "This what you're looking for?" he asked in a stage whisper.

"Is this—" Kim dutifully reeled off the number. "I'm trying to find Benjamin Soares."

"Allo?"

"Ben-ja-meen Soo-are-es. New York calling."

She heard voices arguing, then, *"Allo? Allo? Allo?"*

"Allo!" she said, exasperated.

The telephone was disconnected. The sound of underwater wires being gobbled up by fish resumed, followed by an ear-splitting buzz.

Kim slammed the receiver down. "Would you like to place a call to the moon next? I guarantee we'll make contact a lot easier."

"Try again," Sidney said.

"Exercise in futility."

"Nevertheless . . ."

"You're the boss. He has a housekeeper, but whether she has all her wits about her . . ." She began to punch the numbers in.

"Yes," said Sidney, as if impressed with Kim's pronouncement, "I am the boss, and I'm also the publisher of an award-winning author I don't want to lose to the competition."

"You won't," Alice said. "He needs Kim."

"You didn't get the telephone call from him that I did," Kim reminded her.

"Keep trying," Sidney said.

Several minutes later, Kim gave up. "You know, of course, that I tried the Park Sheraton, where he usually stays. I could try again."

Sidney obligingly called the Park Sheraton's number, but no Benjamin Soares was registered, nor had a reservation been made in his name.

"There's always Laurence Chasen of the Berriman committee," he said. "We play poker once in a while. Lousy poker player, although he loses gracefully enough. I could give him a try."

"Not at this time of night," Alice said. "He'd think it a little odd, getting a telephone call from Benjamin's publisher on a Saturday night, asking a lot of peculiar questions. Tackle it on Monday, when your minds are clear."

"Perhaps you're right." Sidney shut down the computer and sat there staring at it.

Kim went over to the bookshelves and was busily examining the Blackfoot collection of Dickens when Alice suddenly spoke up. "Conor Stark. He's staying with Tony Dalrymple."

"What about him?" Sidney asked.

Kim took down a bound-leather copy of *Great Expectations* and opened it carefully. She found Charles Dickens's signature on the frontispiece. She had felt a faint rush of blood to her face at the mention of Conor Stark's name, although she immediately blamed it on the sight of Dickens's autograph.

"Conor Stark doesn't know Benjamin," she said without looking up. "All he did was recommend that *Lucky Lady* be turned down. I doubt Benjamin could love him for that." Kim returned Dickens to the shelf. When she sat down again, she found Alice scrutinizing her in an interested way.

"How can you be so sure they don't really know each other?" Alice asked. "After all, Conor lives part of the year in Brazil."

Kim shook her head, smiling. "Are we talking about the same Brazil, the one that looks as if it's swallowing up the continent of South America?"

Alice smiled, too, completely tranquil. "I'm talking about a number of very specific things," she said. "The Dalrymples, for one. The Dalrymple estates in Brazil, for another, and Conor's working for the Americas Conservancy which monitors large tracts of land in Brazil, including the Dalrymple holdings. One of which is an estate once managed by Benjamin Soares's aunt, Lucky Anne Severance. You of all people should see the connection between them," she finished triumphantly.

Sidney said, "Consider Conor Stark an enemy. As the lackey of the Dalrymples and possible husband—"

"Of DeeDee? I don't think he's that foolish," Alice interjected with a glance at Kim, as though she were working on Kim's behalf.

"And possible husband of DeeDee," Sidney went on, "he's interested in the good name of the family and the company. We don't want a lawsuit slapped on us before we decide how to handle Benjamin and the rerelease of *Lucky Lady*. Well," he added, trying unsuccessfully to stifle a yawn, "I'm for an early bedtime. Where my author is, I don't know. Let's sleep on it. Coming?" he said to his wife.

Alice put her needlepoint down. "I think so. What about you, Kim?"

Kim, however drowsy, wasn't ready for bed. "I think I'll take a walk on the beach, if you don't mind. I've got a lot to think about."

"Think Benjamin Soares," Sidney said. "And where he might be holing up."

"I'll try. Maybe the salt air will do something spectacular to my little gray cells."

But her little gray cells refused to be influenced by the soft summer night. Kim stepped barefoot onto the terrace and made her way slowly down to the water's edge.

The water was warm, scalloping the sand. Small birds waded out in flocks, as though on a dare, like children playing secretly after dark, then ran back only to venture forth again. Conor Stark, she supposed, would know their names. The sand, silky underfoot, lay like a shimmering ribbon curving gently away on either side. A breeze riffled playful fingers through her hair. The night was lustrous and sweet.

She hugged her arms, imagining with an inexpressible longing that was new to her of stepping out of her skin, illicit love affairs with smart, sexy and dangerous men, wheeling at the controls of a plane through the air above an unknown jungle, living on the edge of peril and not caring about the end.

She hadn't had such thoughts since she was a teenager living a sheltered life with her parents in Brazil. There she'd been expected to behave herself, to represent the entire teenage population of the United States to her peers. And all the while she'd indulged in dreams of a world far more adventurous than the formal, privileged one in which she grew up.

Caution became an automatic part of her protected life. Bedding down with her, it was a dark companion she trusted. When she met Drew, he'd presented himself as quiet and steady. She hadn't fallen in love with him on the spot, not Drew. She'd thought him the most dependable of men, and that counted for a lot.

Since her divorce, she had neatly avoided risky entanglements. Her life was stitched together now, but she had always imagined that somewhere just beyond the edges waited someone wonderful. Smart. Sexy. Dangerous. But then, *waited* was the wrong word. Lucky ladies went out and made their lives; they didn't stand on familiar shores watching for flotsam to wash up. They fell in love, she thought, surprised at the suddenness with which his image came to her, with the Conor Starks of the world, quickly, impatiently and irrevocably.

A dog barked, startling her. Off to her right, a group of kids frolicked on the sand. The sound of music drifted over on a moon-cooled breeze. Oh hell, her mood was simply heightened by the suddenness of the Berriman Prize, she decided, and the secrets she must keep. Nothing would change, nothing at all.

She tied her sweater around her waist and headed firmly east along the beach, away from the noisy party, casting scarcely a glance at the huge lighted monoliths of other people's lives that ranged the shore. She kicked through the sand, her hands thrust into her skirt pockets. She wondered about Conor's life, and the six months each year that he spent in Brazil. She wondered about the Americas Conservancy and just how honest an institution it was. She might do a little research on it. Could come in handy one way or another, once Benjamin handed in his new manuscript. *If,* that is, he had come to the States with a manuscript.

After a while the scenery changed, houses giving way to scrub and empty beach. Kim discovered she had gone a lot farther than planned. She pulled up short at a rough slatted fence that ran down the beach from the road to the water's edge. She checked her watch and realized how late it was. The moon disappeared behind a low cloud, as if to underscore the sudden risks inherent in being alone in an unfamiliar place. Standing in the unexpected blackness, with only far-off lights out at sea to mark north from south, up from down, she experienced a nagging unease. Her first instinct was to run, not walk, back to the Blackfoots. But then the moon reappeared, casting its white, indifferent light along the beach. On a whim, she went down to the water's edge and slipped around the fence, ignoring a No Trespassing sign.

Lucky Anne Severance challenged authority, enjoyed going against the grain, was always her own person. Kim thought with a self-mocking smile that the woman would almost certainly tackle the unknown on a beach at the very civilized edge of the Hamptons.

Had Lucky Anne ever felt such heightened foreboding, such a rush of adrenaline? Perhaps defying danger could call it forth like uncorking a bottle that held a genie.

The scrub off to her left was thick, black and mysterious. From somewhere in the distance she heard a furious barking and for a long moment she held her breath, undecided whether to push on or turn back. The sound of barking grew no closer, then faded away. She went another dozen yards to a jetty of stones that stuck out into the water. On the jetty at the halfway mark a lone figure stood facing the sea, hands clenched at his sides, broad shoulders back, as though daring the ocean to rise up against him. She had burst in upon someone's personal, even painful solitude.

A breeze stirred. Her arms were bare and she shivered. She and the stranger were totally alone on that wide expanse of beach. What if her desire for adventure took a particularly nasty turn? The ocean was cold, wild and deep. From somewhere to her left an animal screeched, then pushed noisily through the underbrush.

The figure on the jetty whipped around.

Conor Stark.

Even though they were separated by fifty yards, Kim felt trapped by the way he stood there, hands still clenched, as though the energy she sensed in him was waiting for release. He was the last man in the world she wanted to see at that moment—and while trespassing on private property. She started toward the fence at a near run.

"Kim? Kim Killian?"

She glanced back, her heart pounding. He was heading quickly toward her. *"He's our enemy."* Sidney's words came to her. She reached the fence breathless, and slipped around it.

"Kim, slow down."

She had not gone more than a dozen yards when Conor caught up with her.

"Trying to get away from me? Look," he said, raising his hands and turning them so she could see his palms, "I'm perfectly harmless."

A safe, facetious answer lay on the tip of her tongue, but she held it back. Yes, he looked, if not harmless, at least safe—handsome and safe. He wore a tuxedo, tie undone and shirt open at the neck. His pants legs were rolled above his ankles and he was barefoot. His smile, she thought, was genuine, and yet she knew instinctively to freeze up, stay in control.

Kim found her voice, admitting his talent for making her tongue-tied. "Oh, hi, that *was* you. I wasn't so sure and I figured better safe than sorry. A gal can't be too cautious in this day and age." Oh, she thought, was that last line necessary, the clever retort of an award-winning author? He had the most extraordinary knack of befuddling her with a look. "Anyway, I've got to go," she continued doggedly. "I'd no idea how far I walked. What's over there, anyway? State land? Oh well, it doesn't matter." She was talking too much, afraid of sounding silly. She started home, picking up her pace, hoping somehow that he'd drop behind. Her toes dug into the sand, left wet by the advancing and contracting hem of ocean. "I realize I shouldn't have been there," she added when she saw that he had every intention of keeping up with her.

"It's part of the Dalrymple compound."

"I was trespassing then."

"Lucky the dogs didn't catch your scent. They're real killers."

"They know the boundaries of the property, I hope."

"Oh, don't worry now that you're with me." He took her arm. "I'm a personal friend. Come on, I'll see you home. Where is home, incidentally?"

"I'm staying with the Blackfoots."

"Right. I should've remembered that."

"And you?" She knew quite well what his answer would be.

"Guest of the Dalrymples. Or rather Tony Dalrymple. Thought I'd have a little walk before turning in."

She remembered DeeDee, the Dalrymple he was apparently trying to marry. Why then was he out walking so late at night?

She was apprehensive and knew it showed. And not just because of Benjamin Soares and the book. Something about Conor Stark knotted her insides and sent pinpricks of warning to her heart. "Don't bother coming back with me," she said. "I can manage."

"Wouldn't hear of it." His arm was still locked through hers. "The Stark Escort Service, best in the Hamptons."

She was aware of the feel of his jacket against her arms, the fabric silken, and of the warmth that seemed to emanate from him. Danger, she thought. She was trespassing on someone else's property, in this case DeeDee Dalrymple's. He wasn't being friendly because he liked the cut of her jib, reason told her. She said, "You're going to have a long walk back."

"That's the sort of thing we of the Stark Escort Service are prepared to put up with. Of course, you can always walk *me* back, just to keep me company, in which case I'd be obliged—"

Her laugh interrupted him. Conor might have a suspicious agenda; she didn't care. She was content to be with him, his arm through hers, on the most beautiful night the universe had ever devised. "You win," she said. "I know a determined salesman when I see one."

He pressed her arm lightly. "And to think I haven't even begun my knockout sales pitch yet."

They had not gone more than a few steps when Conor said, "There's a late-night ice-cream parlor on the main drag. You know, the kind of place mothers warn their daughters against. How about a soda, double scoop with whipped cream and chocolate sauce?"

Kim turned and eyed him skeptically, but his expression was guileless. She considered his proposal for a lot longer than she should have. Unfortunately, she hadn't forgotten Sidney's stern warning.

Kim caught the wistfulness in her voice as she told Conor no. She wished that something so innocuous as having a soda with him was a luxury she could afford. "I'm sorry," she said with an apologetic smile.

"Don't tell me you're allergic to sodas."

"The Blackfoots lock the gates at midnight."

"No, they don't."

"I'm barefoot."

"So am I."

She thought of how much she liked his voice, and how warm his smile was, and how little danger she found in either—all surface reactions, as if her brain were on hold. "I'm running out of excuses, but it's still no."

After a moment of silence, during which he gazed at her thoughtfully, he said, "Would you believe me if I told you I want to get to know you?"

She preferred to duck the question, so surprising was it, but instead Kim dug her hands into her pockets and began to head back along the beach. When he caught up to her, she said, "Conor, I don't believe a word you're saying. Obviously you have a book to sell about the Amazon and you think I have Sidney's ear. The truth is, I'm a lowly freelance editor. I don't buy books, I merely do the work handed me. You can go directly to Sidney, as a matter of fact. He has some ideas about the kind of book he'd like."

Conor laughed. "And you're obviously not buying my line, either."

"I'm afraid not." She stopped and put out her hand, which he grasped warmly. "I can go on from here, honest. Maybe it's better if the Stark Escort Service runs out of gas at this point."

His smile showed that he wasn't about to press the point. "I'd still like to get to know you. Look, I'm driving to the city tomorrow night. How about going back with me?"

"I promised Sidney."

"How about I pick you up at seven o'clock? We can have dinner on the way. I know this nice little place..."

She didn't dare trust herself one moment longer. He was the enemy; Sidney had declared him so. Conor Stark had

more on his mind than Kim. He was tied up too closely with
the opposition, for so she thought of the Dalrymples. What
she needed with both Blackfoots was a strategy session.
"You're a pretty powerful salesman," she said at last.

"You're a pretty powerful incentive."

"Conor, why do I have the feeling I'm being snowed?"

"Wrong feeling."

His words were said with such complete seriousness that
Kim had no choice but to relent, or at least to back up until she had a chance to think. "Call me tomorrow morning. I'll let you know then."

"Fair enough."

She thought, with a curious onset of nostalgia, that the
moment had been etched into her memory forever: his
words, the sweet softness of the night, the slap of waves
against the shore, the luminous path of the moon along the
sea.

She resisted the desire to reach out and push back the er-
rant lock of hair that fell over his forehead. Instead, she
reluctantly raised her hand in farewell and strode away, past
the huge beach houses, now dark-eyed and closed against
the night.

When and if he called, she'd say no. The telephone was
an effective shield against his shameless sensuality.

Chapter Five

She had, on Sunday, heard from Conor. Refusing to return to the city with him had been a little easier on the
phone, especially with Sidney to back her up. Alice,
matchmaker that she was, remained uncertain. Romance
flourished in the strangest ways, she stated, and breached
all sorts of No Trespassing barriers.

The conversation with Conor had been short. He'd
seemed disappointed and said he hoped they'd meet again
soon. Kim averred that she hoped so, too, and hung up
quickly before he could take the next, inevitable step.

The following day, Monday, Kim was still trying to clear
her head of one Conor Stark. At noon, indulging in the rare
treat of reading a mystery over a solo lunch in the Central
Park Zoo cafeteria, she realized, two chapters into the
book, that she hadn't absorbed or even understood a single word. She turned back to chapter one, but the walk on
the beach with Conor's arm through hers still intruded. She
should have gone with him, even barefoot, to the soda
parlor and indulged in a double-scoop soda with whipped
cream and chocolate sauce. She should have gone back with
him to Manhattan, and had dinner, and been tight-lipped
only about Benjamin Soares. She should have, she should
have, she should have...

"Would you mind if I sit here?"

Kim glanced up at the unexpected question, putting her finger in place on page one. "No, of course not," she said to a middle-aged woman who stood there smiling at her, holding a tray aloft. For a moment Kim thought they'd met before, but she had no idea where. Perhaps they had merely passed each other in any one of a dozen ways strangers do in New York.

Kim gestured to the seat opposite. "Please." The cafeteria wasn't crowded, although nearly all the tables near the windows, like hers, were taken.

"I'll be quiet as a mouse," the woman said. "I see you're reading."

Kim smiled and ducked at once into her book, disconcerted by her glittering, deep-set and disturbingly hypnotic eyes. The woman sat down and was silent for a while. Kim was aware peripherally of her tablemate pushing the tray aside after having removed her sandwich, napkin and cup of coffee. She returned to her reading, but had lost her place, and when she at last found it and was settling in, her neighbor spoke again.

"The truth is, I've always thought mice to be quite noisy little fellows."

Kim looked up. She would certainly get no more reading done that lunch hour. She had forty minutes to go before her appointment with Sidney at the Blackfoot Press offices, and it was with a faint sigh that she said, "You're right. One year we had a mouse that lived in our living-room ceiling. Every night we heard him running back and forth, bold as brass. My mother refused to set out traps, so he made himself right at home. Of course he was a field mouse. They're cute."

The woman laughed and picked up her sandwich, which she did not eat, but examined thoroughly as though she hadn't ordered it and was surprised to find it on her plate. She was dressed in a pale blue silk print that was clearly not off the racks. She wore her thick black hair pulled back off her face and caught into a tight bun. Her skin had a faintly weathered appearance, as though she spent much of her time outdoors, but everything about her spoke of wealth and leisure.

"I'm afraid then that I've been a noisy mouse." She spoke with a faint British accent. "Considering I've disturbed your reading."

"Never mind," Kim said, curious now. "I'm Kim Killian." She closed her book and held her hand out.

"Mrs. Emma Lambert."

Kim frowned. The name had a familiar sound. But then she decided no, it was straight out of a Gothic novel. The woman's handshake was strong and Kim noted that she wore a narrow silver ring on her left hand, a ring so simple and unobtrusive it might have been discovered in a box of candied popcorn.

"British?" Kim asked. "Your accent."

"Yes. Even when you've traveled all over the world, you never lose an accent, do you?"

"No, I guess not." Kim thought of the places she had lived with her parents, and the New York patois she had acquired in college and never managed to lose.

She speared a tomato from her salad plate, feeling faintly lost, as though something were expected of her. Clever New York talk, perhaps, but she couldn't be sure. "Beautiful day, isn't it?" she remarked at last, settling for something banal and safe.

"Very. Not too hot. I thought a walk in the park was called for, and then I became ravenously hungry." Mrs. Lambert took a delicate bite of her sandwich, then proceeded to chew as though food were the last thing on her mind. "This is a very charming place, isn't it?" Her glance encompassed the enclosed terrace with its hanging plants and cheerful decor.

"Very," Kim said. "Are you a visitor to New York?"

"Yes." Mrs. Lambert answered curtly, seemingly unsettled by Kim's remark, her brilliant eyes under heavy lids sparkling with a kind of fervor that made Kim think of gypsies. "Does it show somehow?"

Kim shook her head. "No, not really. Perhaps it's your being alone. I mean, taking a walk alone in the park, then deciding to eat."

"That sounds rather ordinary to me. Are you really so clever at deduction? Sherlock Holmes's secret great-granddaughter?"

"I was thinking that out-of-towners might not know about the dangers of walking alone in the park, even in broad daylight."

"Ah, I see. I should have taken along a friend, but then I've spent a lifetime being foolish. You are right, though," Mrs. Lambert said. "I'm a visitor to Manhattan, and you most assuredly are Sherlock Holmes's descendant."

Kim held up her book and smiled. "I like mysteries."

"And you're on your lunch hour, I imagine. I've come along to disturb what was probably your only moment of peace in a long day at some very interesting job. Am I right so far?"

"I strike you as someone who has an interesting job?" Kim was pleased at the assumption. She liked the idea of looking interesting.

"As a matter of fact, yes," Mrs. Lambert said. "And just what kind of interesting job do you have?"

"I'm what's known as a free-lance editor." Kim spoke candidly, wanting Mrs. Lambert's eyes to light up at the mention of what Kim considered a career to be proud of.

Mrs. Lambert, in the act of sipping her coffee, held the mug suspended and looked properly impressed. She nodded at the paperback. "Is that one of the books you've edited?"

Kim shook her head. "I work on nonfiction mostly. I treat myself to a mystery whenever I can."

"You are clever," Mrs. Lambert said. She looked at her watch and said, "I hope I'm not keeping you."

"No, no, I'm just about on time." Kim took a last bite of her salad and another sip of coffee, then gathered her book and bag and stood up.

"Well, it was very nice meeting you, Mrs. Lambert," she said politely, extending a hand, which her table companion grasped.

"Indeed. Do you know you're the first person I've talked to all day besides taxi drivers and doormen?" She held Kim's hand for a moment, covering it with her other palm.

For an instant Kim felt as though she had been hypnotized, so strange was her reaction to Mrs. Emma Lambert.

"Thank you for giving me your time so generously," Mrs. Lambert said, releasing her hand.

Kim then had a second disturbing reaction, that of having to say goodbye with much left unsaid to someone she knew she would never see again. But what was there to say? Mrs. Lambert smiled expectantly.

"Goodbye." Kim backed away, waving.

Mrs. Lambert took in a breath, as though about to say something. "Goodbye, Miss Killian."

Kim was on the path leading to 60th Street when she heard footsteps coming up behind her, the tapping of heels upon pavement. She whipped around and discovered Mrs. Lambert coming toward her. "Miss Killian," she said when Kim stopped and waited. "I think you know my coming to your table wasn't casual." She was a little out of breath, her eyes fierce and full of determination.

"I'm sorry?"

"I think you know."

"I'm afraid I don't know." Kim had a sudden fear that if she didn't move away quickly enough, her life would be changed forever. "If there was something you wanted me to know, why didn't you speak up when we were having lunch?"

"I should have, I suppose."

Kim checked her watch. What was happening to her? She had the typical New Yorker's fear that something dire would occur if she allowed a total stranger to ask a favor. "I'm afraid I'm going to be late for an appointment. I'm really sorry." She turned away and began heading once again for the 60th Street exit from the park.

"It's about Benjamin Soares."

The name washed over Kim. She swung around to face the woman. "Do you know where he is?" she asked quietly.

"I'd like to talk to you."

Sidney was leaving for the West Coast, with Kim his last appointment of the afternoon. Their meeting concerned the book she was editing, but he had also promised to try to locate Benjamin.

"Do you know where Benjamin is?" she asked again. "Can I meet with him? It's awfully important."

"I'd like to talk to you first," Mrs. Lambert said.

Kim frowned. Why was the woman being so intractable? She looked at her closely. The odd sense of familiarity still lingered. She needed time to think, to talk to Sidney, to gather her forces. "Where are you staying, Mrs. Lambert?"

"The St. Regis."

"Can I meet you there in an hour or so?"

"Make it for dinner. Will that suit you?"

"Yes, yes, fine. Can you tell me where Benjamin is?" Kim persisted. "The St. Regis? Is that where he's staying? Is he all right?"

Mrs. Lambert shook her head. "We'll talk later. Come to the hotel at six. We'll have a proper dinner then."

Kim could see she'd get no further. "Will you give me your room number?"

"I'll see you in the lobby at six." Mrs. Lambert waved farewell and walked quickly past Kim to the avenue, where she hailed a cab and jumped in. The cab moved downtown, making the light. Kim watched perplexed. The woman couldn't be going to the St. Regis, which was only four or five blocks away.

Where then? Kim considered hailing a cab and following her, perhaps to Benjamin. But she'd had mystery enough for one day, and Sidney was waiting. As she headed east toward Madison Avenue, she silently reviewed her conversation with Mrs. Lambert. Why had the woman tiptoed around the subject of Benjamin Soares until the last minute? Perhaps she expected Kim to hop into a cab and follow her. Mysteriouser and mysteriouser! Kim wondered whether she wasn't being set up for something.

Sidney Blackfoot had the telephone to his ear when Kim bustled into his untidy, book-filled office ten minutes later. He beckoned her to a chair, raising his eyes to the ceiling to indicate that his call was taking longer than he'd expected. Instead of sitting down, Kim went over to his desk, picked up a pencil and scribbled, *I've found Benjamin, more or less,* on his message pad.

Sidney grinned at her. "Okay, it's fine, I'll get back to you," he said to his caller and put the receiver in its cradle. "You've found him. That's more than I managed. What's more or less mean?"

"Well, that's it," Kim said. She pulled up a chair after removing a couple of books from the seat and proceeded to recount her meeting in the park.

"Ever wonder how this Lambert character found you at the Central Park Zoo? Mistook you for an exhibit, perhaps?"

"Funny," Kim said. "I'd say she or someone followed me from my apartment. Benjamin knows where I live."

"And why send an emissary?"

"Maybe she's his wife, traveling under a false name."

"I didn't know Benjamin was married," Sidney said.

"Neither did I." After a pause, Kim added, "I guess she wanted to meet me first, see if I'm in a forgiving mood."

"Maybe," Sidney said. "Maybe some people can't do things in a straightforward way, like calling you on the telephone and asking for an appointment."

"If Benjamin is sorry about what he said to me last Saturday, then calling me is the last thing he'd do. He *needs* an emissary."

Sidney said abruptly, "Damn."

"Oh, I'll meet her for dinner all right," Kim said. "I guess I ought to pick up the check. She doesn't eat much, as far as I can see."

"Put it on a credit card," Sidney said, "and bill me. The trouble is I'd like to be at that dinner."

"No," Kim said. "If she wanted to talk to you about Benjamin, you'd have heard from her yourself. You'll have to trust me."

Sidney scribbled a telephone number on his message pad and handed it to Kim. "I'll be at the Beverly Hills Hotel tonight. I want you to call me as soon as you learn something, anything, even nothing. If you manage to talk to Benjamin, forget that call he made to you. Make sure we're not going to lose him."

"I'll handle it," Kim said, feeling a rising excitement. "Let's hope it's something really simple, like he has a new manuscript or he's hired an agent and wants a huge advance and a contract fit for a king."

Sidney's trip to the coast involved several projects, Lucky Anne Severance being one of them. He was so worked up about *Lucky Lady,* he was certain he'd find all of Holly-wood fighting to make a film of her life.

"By the way," Sidney told her, "I called my contact at the Berriman committee and discovered that they had located Benjamin in Belém. They got their information about where he was through the Brazilian embassy."

"Clever," Kim said. "Why didn't we think of that? He must have taken the first plane north. Your contact didn't happen to mention whether Benjamin has heard anything new about Lucky Anne."

"He didn't mention it and I wasn't about to ask. I like my friends to think I'm in control of my prizewinning authors." He winked at Kim.

Kim grinned. "You are, you are. I'm living proof."

After settling that Kim would call Sidney that evening, they spent some time on her current project, agreeing that another editor would be hired if Benjamin and his new manuscript showed up. When Kim left his office, Sidney was already throwing books and papers into his briefcase, with his worried secretary standing by gripping some letters to be signed.

Kim treated herself to a taxi ride home. Since the day was warm, she decided to allow herself the luxury of working in her back garden, where she had planted some wildflowers that now needed weeding. Life, in spite of awards she could never collect, was looking good.

She ran up the steps to the front door of the brownstone and let herself in. Beyond the double set of highly waxed mahogany doors was a tiny lobby. She found her mailbox full and spent several minutes trying to yank magazines, letters and junk mail free. Then she had to deal with an inner door that led into the building proper. The owner of the building, a widow with three cats, lived in the front apartment. Kim's apartment was at the left rear. An elderly bachelor occupied the studio at the rear right.

   She sifted busily through her mail as she headed back, finding the usual bills, letters awarding her a million dollars, catalogs and notices of books waiting for her at the post office. She paused to read a postcard from a friend in Provence. In fact, only when she reached, key in hand, for her lock did Kim discover her front door wide open. And from inside her apartment she heard the distinct sound of her desk drawer being opened and closed. Stifling the urge to scream and run, she flattened herself against the wall, where she had a view of the interior of her apartment. In another moment her intruder came into view.

Chapter Six

Conor Stark. Something ice cold ran down her spine. Conor Stark, in person, in her living room. Walking about as if he owned the place.

Kim caught her breath and held it. The rough-textured wall scratched through the thin stuff of her summer dress, but she didn't dare move an inch. Conor didn't even seem to be aware of the incongruity of leaving a door open while he rummaged around her apartment. After a moment of apparent indecision he turned, went over to the open terrace door and stepped outside. From where Kim stood, he appeared to be casually surveying her garden.

It was only then that she discovered in a horrified glance what she hadn't taken in before. Her living room had been ransacked from top to bottom, the carpet strewn with books and magazines, gizmos saved from her marriage and even sofa cushions.

The police; she'd have to call the police. She was about to risk pushing her neighbor's buzzer when she remembered that Tad Theodore was at work. In fact, with the exception of Mrs. Weber on the third floor, every tenant in the building, including her landlady, worked days.

The telephone lay not ten feet away on her desk, to the left of her small, carpeted foyer. *Her* telephone in *her* apartment. She knew she should turn and run for help, even if it meant letting Conor Stark get away. Anyone with common sense would do just that.

But at the moment she was short on common sense and long on outrage. All she had to do was take half a dozen steps to reach her phone, dial 911 and creep back into the hallway.

Conor appeared to be concentrating deeply on her garden, as though admiring nothing more than its roses and exuberant wildflowers. Beyond gall, he was in a class by himself, as yet unnamed.

She put her bag and mail on the floor. Her footfall silenced by the Persian runner on the entry floor, Kim carefully made her way to the phone, picked up the receiver and punched in 911. She took her eye off Conor only long enough to note that the red light was flashing on her answering machine. Her messages would have to wait.

The emergency operator was a long time responding. Long enough, in fact, for Conor to turn around and discover her. A rock lodged in her throat. Then a woman's voice finally came on the line. "Nine-one-one, Operator Number seven-three-two, what's the emergency?"

Kim opened her mouth but nothing came out.

Conor advanced swiftly, eyes narrowed. She took a step back and bumped up against the wall. She could hear the operator's urgent voice sounding far away and tinny. "Nine-one-one, what's the emergency? Hello? Hello?"

In a swift movement Conor had the phone out of her hand and back in its cradle. "Kim, it's not what you think."

"Isn't it?" Her heart pounded in her chest as she grabbed the receiver. "I don't want any explanations. Save it for the police."

He gripped her wrist and pulled the receiver away. "Dammit, take it easy, I've already called the police. They're on their way." His conversational tone surprised her; he couldn't be aware of the fluttering of her heart and her palpable fear.

"You called the police to turn yourself in for breaking and entering? That's funny."

"Will you listen to me?"

"Why should I? Look at this mess." She stooped to pick up some papers, but gave up, letting them flutter to the floor. "I heard you. What were you looking for, anyway? My almost-state-of-the-art computer? My Johnny Mathis tapes? You'd do better robbing the Dalrymples."

"Your door was open when I got here. Wide open."

Conor took a step back, as though sensing she'd feel less threatened if there was some distance between them. "I knocked, called out, and you didn't answer. That worried me." As he had on the beach just a couple of nights earlier, he raised both hands, showing her his empty palms. "Check for yourself. No weapons—I come unarmed. You can search me if you want." He grinned suddenly, although the expression in his eyes was still deeply serious.

"You trashed this place. You really expect me to believe a word you say?"

"As a matter of fact, yes. And I had nothing to do with ransacking your apartment."

She gave him a level look. "I heard you open my desk drawer. I know that little squeak."

"I was trying to locate your calendar, find out where you were."

"I'm here."

"Suppose," he said, "I save my explanations for the police."

"Yes, you're right. The police. Do that."

Common sense, which she'd ignored before, told her to leave her options, and the door, open. She retrieved her bag and mail from the hallway. "I'll keep the door open until the police arrive, if you don't mind." She came back and dumped everything on her desk. The red light was still flashing on her answering machine, with all the urgency of a scream. She impatiently flicked it off. "My calendar is on my desk," she said to Conor. "No, I guess it isn't—it's on the floor."

Suddenly the meaning of his words sunk in. "Wait a minute. Let's start from the beginning. You're telling me the door was open when you got here. Who let you in the front entrance?"

"Both entry doors were unlocked. However, one look tells me even an amateur could pick them. Incidentally, I locked them after me." He let loose a heavy breath. The expression in his eyes was neither hostile nor icy, merely worried. He seemed about to say something more but stopped, casting a glance toward the terrace.

Some inner mechanism in Kim took over. She felt herself draw in tight. What was going on?

"Kim, somebody was here before me."

"All I have to do is believe you, am I right?" She cast a confused glance around the room. Her paintings, the most valuable things she owned, were still hanging, if slightly askew. Her CD player in the corner cabinet lay undisturbed; her computer was still on her desk, half buried under some files. She stormed into her bedroom. The room was a mess, but the television sat in its usual spot, as did her clock radio. Her jewelry box appeared untouched. She opened it. Her gold jewelry lay glowing against its plush red bedding. The twenty-dollar bill tucked in with her plastic packet of credit cards was safe, along with the cards. What were they looking for?

She came back into the living room. Conor was waiting for her. He hadn't even tried to get away. "If you didn't, then who did?"

From beyond the terrace doors she heard the sudden bark of a neighbor's dog. The room was warm, in spite of the air drawn in from the terrace. She was about to close the doors and turn on her air conditioner when Conor came over and put a hand gently on her arm. "I'm afraid you'll have to prepare yourself for a shock."

"A shock?" She thought of her parents in Connecticut, both retired and in good health. But that didn't mean—wait a minute. She was trying to put square pegs into round holes. What had Conor to do with her parents? Perhaps her husband, her *ex*-husband...? "What kind of shock?" She'd had enough for one day, and didn't think she could take another.

Conor drew her through the terrace door. "I'm sorry," he said quietly.

Her glance took in the long, narrow garden below. "Sorry about what?" she asked in a voice so shallow it might have been nothing more than a breath.

Conor did not respond. His hold on her arm tightened. She first noticed the state of her roses, then the border plantings of dianthus and verbena, and then, at last, just beyond the small fountain in the center of the tiny garden, the body of Benjamin Soares.

"Benjamin?" She broke away and mindlessly ran down the stone steps and along the gravel path. "My god, it's Benjamin. Why's he..."

He lay on his back in her wildflower bed, his jacket open, a thin ribbon of red trickling along his white shirt and down his chest. His head was turned toward her, his eyes open. In death, the expression on his face was totally without anger.

"Benjamin?" She bent down and took his hand, feeling its fading warmth, then drew her palm along his forehead. "Oh, Benjamin." She groaned deep in her throat. He had come to see her, after all, to apologize, to ask her to work on his next project. She thought of the prize, that ephemeral award he hadn't quite come to terms with.

A sudden thought managed to curl through her even as a backwash of tears flooded her eyes. If Benjamin intended to see her, why had he sent Emma Lambert after her earlier that day?

"Come on." Conor was at her side, reaching for her.

"It's all right. I'm okay."

She turned back to Benjamin, her clouded eyes drawn to a thin gold chain that peeked out from under his shirt. She followed its trail with her fingers. At the end, half hidden by the grass, she discovered a gold amulet of a stylized bird, clearly pre-Colombian. She let it drop back and got to her feet, brushing at her eyes with the back of her hand.

"Let's go inside," Conor said. "There's nothing you can do here."

"Oh, damn." She rushed past him and ran back into the apartment. "Where are the police? If you called, why aren't they here?" She heard the edge of panic in her voice.

"Kim, take it easy, they'll be here. I can see your mind racing," he said. "Just hold tight."

"I know I locked the door when I left this morning. Double locked it. I'm always careful. Do you pick locks, too? Double-bolt locks? What were you looking for?"

The doorbell interrupted them, ringing with long, unbroken urgency. Kim jumped, her nerves giving out. She put a hand on her desk to steady herself.

"The police. Nothing subtle about them." Conor raised a brow and Kim wordlessly pressed the buzzer to allow them into the foyer. Conor waited with her while two uniformed policemen and two detectives came down the hall, her landlady trailing anxiously behind them. So she'd been home all along.

"Everything all right, Kim?" her landlady asked.

"I'll talk to you later, Mrs. Whitefield." But then Kim changed her mind. She might as well get it over with. "I'm afraid someone was shot in my garden." A shot that no one apparently heard.

"Oh Jesus, Mary and Joseph," Mrs. Whitefield said, crossing herself. She made for Kim's apartment but was stopped by one of the policemen, who blocked her passage. "Call me if you need me," she cried as the door clicked shut. Kim immediately found herself surrounded by a cordon of men, who seemed to take up all the space in her small apartment.

The next four hours were the longest she had experienced since she accidentally locked herself in the high-school gym and had to be rescued by the school custodian.

In fact, the apartment could scarcely hold the crime-scene technicians and additional officers, who thought nothing she owned was sacred or beyond their right to photograph, dust or check over.

Kim was asked to sit down at her own tiny kitchen table by a middle-aged detective wearing a crumpled cotton jacket and khaki pants. "Detective Lee," he said, shaking her hand politely. "Mind explaining exactly what your relationship was to this Benjamin Soares?" He was soft-spoken and attentive, focusing pale gray, searching eyes on hers.

She remembered the book she had once edited by a lawyer, and his caveat, "Only answer the questions asked. Offer nothing else."

"I am—*was*—Benjamin's editor," she promptly said. She did not mention being his ghostwriter. She did not mention his phone call or Emma Lambert.

She looked past the detective and caught sight of Conor in her living room, sitting on her pale linen couch, in his hand a glass of whiskey to which he had helped himself. He had been questioned separately and she had no idea what story he'd concocted. Although she had no doubt he was deeply involved with the murder, she was, oddly enough, comforted by his being there—and that made no sense at all.

"Editor. What kind of stuff did he write?" The detective was a methodical man who kept his notebook open and jotted down almost every word she uttered, including her sighs, hesitations and coughs. He made her nervous. She kept thinking he'd read them back to her and she'd sound trivial and stupid.

"What kind of stuff did he write?" Kim repeated. "Nonfiction."

"Benjamin Soares. Name sounds familiar. Should I know him?"

"Well, maybe."

The remark cost her somewhat. Detective Lee told her that in cases that promised to be high profile, the district attorney usually stepped in.

The questions dragged on. She ceased being scared, instead feeling as if her body were still present but her brain had flown to St. Tropez for vacation. The medical examiner arrived and left. The gun used to shoot Benjamin was searched for but not found. She did not hear speculations about when he died, or what kind of gun might have been the murder weapon. Benjamin's body was removed. Conor handed her a cup of freshly made coffee that seemed to have appeared out of nowhere and which she didn't touch.

Neighbors were questioned, and Mrs. Whitefield confirmed that she had been home all afternoon, soaking in a hot bath thanks to her bad back. No, she had not heard a shot, but then her radio had been on all that time.

Kim at last was handed a card by Detective Raymond Lee and told to call him if she had forgotten anything. The crime-scene notice was taken down from her door. All that was left was a mess of fingerprint powder, disturbed books and papers, and closets that would never look the same.

At eight o'clock she found herself alone again with Conor Stark. Didn't he have anything else to do? But actually, she didn't want him to leave. She made no effort to straighten up, but collapsed on the sofa. "I'll have to have the locks changed," she said.

"I wouldn't worry about that now." He paused, and looking her straight in the eyes added, "Did they find what they were looking for?"

"No!" she answered sharply, then changed her mind and softened her next words. "I don't know. Something to do with Benjamin, I suppose."

She pulled herself off the couch and stalked over to the terrace door. Dusk had almost deepened into night. The light cast from her living room did not quite reach the spot where Benjamin had died, for which she was grateful. A slight breeze blew through the garden, bending flower heads toward her.

The faint scent of roses wafted in. Tears started to her eyes involuntarily. Except for his last words to her on the telephone, her experience with Benjamin Soares had been equable and friendly. He was a man with an obsession about a beautiful and talented woman. Kim had been happy to share that obsession for a while. Now she would never know what had happened to Lucky Anne, who had been so real to her during the year she spent writing the book. "Damn," she said. "Damn, damn."

Conor came up behind her, took her shoulders in his hands and turned her around. She knew he saw the tear that drifted slowly down her cheek. Concern darkened his eyes. "Want to tell me what's going on?" he asked softly. He rubbed gently at the tear.

"I don't know any more than you do." She stepped back, away from his touch, a little confused.

"You need a drink. Food, probably."

There was something she was supposed to do, but she couldn't quite remember what it was. She should call Sidney, make him come back and share in some of the fallout. The start of a giant headache manifested itself in the tightening of her neck muscles. Had she just perjured herself to the police by not explaining she had more than edited Benjamin's book, that she had written it from start to finish? Would they suspect her of killing Benjamin just because she had ghostwritten *Lucky Lady* and envied him the prize? The headache worsened. She pressed her hands to her skull.

"You need a drink," Conor said. He went over to her liquor cabinet, makeshift at its best. Her husband had taken most of the liquor when he'd totaled up what he felt belonged to him. She had never bothered restocking the cabinet except for a bottle of Irish whiskey. She didn't drink much, but right now a glass of whiskey sounded like a good idea.

"I'll get some ice." She gathered herself together and escaped into the kitchen as a wave of fear washed unexpectedly over her. Conor had lied to her and to the detectives. He had ransacked her apartment, discovering her liquor cabinet while he was at it. She had no doubt he was looking for something pertaining to the Dalrymples. He was, to all intents and purposes, in their pay. And she had, while working on *Lucky Lady*, learned what the Dalrymples could do to protect themselves.

Perhaps he had surprised Benjamin, discovered something incriminating about Anthony Dalrymple and killed Benjamin to protect the family and its name.

She found the aspirin bottle in her spice cabinet, took out a couple of tablets and downed them with a glass of water. When she opened the refrigerator, Kim realized she hadn't even finished her lunch salad and that the sight of food made her sick. She speedily reached for the ice-cube tray, slammed it on the counter to loosen the cubes, dumped the ice into a bowl, found the tongs and then stopped and put her hands on the kitchen counter. She remained there with her head bowed, unthinking and exhausted.

After a moment Conor came in holding her drink. "Here—a good, strong one." He gave her a long, cool look, as if he were appraising just how much she could absorb at this point. She took the drink and filled the glass to the top with ice.

"I came as a favor to Tony Dalrymple," Conor said. "He wanted your assurance that with the rerelease of *Lucky Lady,* Blackfoot Press wouldn't take advantage of Lucky Anne Severance's relationship to his father, that's all."

No, she thought, that wasn't all. Conor had taken advantage of being alone in her apartment, because he was looking for something—perhaps Benjamin's purported new manuscript, perhaps the old one.

"Why would Blackfoot Press do such a thing? The only mention of the Dalrymples in the book was to Lucky Anne's managing of the ranch in Brazil, and that she died in a fire there." She was lying, of course. Benjamin, in the original manuscript, had accused Anthony Dalrymple of using hired guns to get rid of his wife because he'd wanted to marry DeeDee Ealing.

"Speculation is what fuels book sales. You know that as well as I," Conor pointed out.

"The book won a prestigious literary prize," she said, prickling at the notion. "It doesn't need scurrilous gossip to sell it."

"My apologies. You're right."

"Apologies accepted." She took a long sip of the drink, feeling its bitter warmth flow through her. The stakes had changed radically with Benjamin's death. She had no idea why he'd wanted to see her, but he hadn't sat still for the past two years. What he'd learned almost certainly figured in what had happened to him.

Conor was watching her curiously. Still holding her glass she went back into the living room and, after circling the room restlessly, settled against the fireplace mantel.

Someone had surprised Benjamin, or perhaps Benjamin had surprised someone. Who had been looking for what? She thought of the original manuscript and Benjamin's notes, both potentially libelous to the Dalrymples. She had her own original notes tucked into a wooden milk crate in her parents' attic in Connecticut. She had returned Benjamin's manuscript and notes long before to an address in Brazil.

Conor came over and sat down on her sofa, leaning back, his legs stretched before him. He seemed quite at home. She watched him objectively over the top of her glass, her eyes narrowed. The police had seen them together. She had no doubt they thought Conor was a close friend. But he was DeeDee Dalrymple's friend, an errand runner for Tony Dalrymple. His income depended upon the kindness of a wealthy and important family. In effect, he wanted something from her and she had to learn what that something was.

"The fact that he was killed in your apartment might have something to do with you," Conor said. "You'd better think long and hard about staying here. I'm not at all sure the killer wasn't looking for you and stumbled onto Benjamin instead."

"That's ridiculous," she said, trying to keep the fear out of her voice. "Why would anyone want to kill me? As for Benjamin, I don't know what he was working on or even why he was here."

"Perhaps whoever killed him doesn't know that," Conor said quietly. "And you make a bad liar."

A sudden vision of her death crossed her mind. If she died, no one would ever know she had written *Lucky Lady*.

"Why don't we get out of here for a while?" Conor said. "Find something to eat, have a cup of coffee, talk." He smiled at her and her heart gave a funny little bounce. She thought of that walk along the beach in the Hamptons, and his remark that she hadn't quite trusted, about wanting to get to know her.

"Isn't there someone you could call?" he asked when she didn't answer him. "Someone to stay with until you get the locks changed?"

Her parents, for one. Benjamin's death would be on the evening news. "Oh Lord," she said out loud. "The photographers. The press. They'll be all over Blackfoot Press and me." As if in answer, her phone rang. "No way," she said. She wouldn't even turn on the answering machine. Let the whole world call her.

They sat without saying a word while the phone rang ten times, each ring a pointed recrimination. Then the buzzer sounded, an impatient blast, repeated twice. Conor got to his feet but she shook her head. "I'd better bolt the terrace door and pull the curtains."

Kim thought of the wooden milk crate in the attic of her parents' house and its volatile contents. She'd call them, tell them she was on her way. She'd stay overnight in her old room, that incredibly childish place full of rock posters and other memories of her high school years.

Having often spent weekends with her parents, she wouldn't even have to pack a wardrobe. "Look," she said to Conor, "maybe I'll call a friend after all. If you'll excuse me."

The doorbell was pressed again, a little more urgently this time. "Perhaps I could take you where you're going." Conor smiled again, as if he had all the time in the world. "Make sure you get there in one piece."

"No," she said hastily, "I, uh, don't think that would be a good idea."

"Ah." His eyes lit up. He understood; she had a male friend and he wouldn't be welcome. Kim let the mistake stand. She went over to the door and held it open for him.

"Rain check?" he asked, taking her hand in his for a moment.

"Of course." She gently extricated her hand. She liked his warm, dry touch, the look of concern in his eyes that seemed genuine. "You live part of the time here, part of the time in Brazil," she said.

"I'm usually down there now. I winter in the Amazon."

"Their winter or ours?"

"Theirs, going on now. I only came up for a couple of weeks for some meetings."

"Well, goodbye," she said. "And—and thanks for sticking it out with me." She didn't know what else to say. She wondered if this might be the last time they'd meet.

He hesitated a moment, as though there was something more he wanted to say, then turned and left. She swallowed a rush of disappointment, waiting until the outer door closed behind him, almost hoping he'd change his mind and come back.

Standing in her small entryway, she realized she had never been more alone. Every familiar little creak in the apartment took on a fresh, ominous note, as did the hurried footsteps of her neighbor overhead, the whine of a dog, a door slamming somewhere.

She had to get away from the mess, the noise, her speculations, the memory of the small hole in Benjamin's chest and his unseeing eyes.

She tried calling her parents, letting their phone ring the prescribed half-dozen times, but their message machine didn't kick in. Perhaps they'd gone to a movie or a neighbor's. They led a busy, independent life since their retirement. Whether or not they were home didn't matter. She'd go anyway. She had her own key, and trains left from Grand Central Station every half hour or so at that time of night.

Conor Stark was right about one thing. She had to get out of her apartment, if only for a while. Evidence of the police's intrusion lay everywhere, even on her trampled flower beds. She hurried to the terrace doors and closed the curtains without even looking down into the garden, then checked the lock. She checked the windows as well, brought the glasses into the kitchen and emptied their contents into the sink. Another look around the apartment, and with a stifled cry of impatience, she grabbed her bag. She didn't bother turning on the answering machine, or listening to her messages. She'd call Sidney when she got to Connecticut. Together they'd figure out what to do with her old notes.

She had no idea why Benjamin had been murdered or why his killers had ransacked her apartment, but she could speculate. Speculation would always lead to the Dalrymples, to the fine old name of a public-spirited family.

Lucky Lady's sudden prominence could wreck that image. If they were engaged in a cleanup operation, they'd want to destroy all evidence of Benjamin's original belief that his aunt had been murdered, possibly by Anthony Dalrymple.

In a world where innuendo, true or false, made screaming headlines, Anthony Dalrymple's memory was sacred. And for that reason alone, Kim's scrawled notes would interest the Dalrymples. The original *Lucky Lady* manuscript was safe in Brazil, and she suspected she was the only one in the States who knew where.

When she stepped into the hall, her next-door neighbor came out of his apartment immediately. "Are you all right?" he asked. He was a white-haired, rather florid interior designer with the ill-natured manner of a spoiled child. Once he had understood that she was not interested in redecorating her apartment, he rarely bothered with her.

"The police were here questioning me," he said in a petulant tone. "Wanted to know if I heard anything—a shot, quarreling, anything. I wasn't even home, but never mind. Heard anything? I told them a thing or two. This block could use some noise control, I told them. That's all I hear—screams, cars screeching, kids yelling at the top of their lungs. I mean, give me a break. Heard anything! How would I know the difference? That's asking too much, even if my apartment is rent controlled."

"Sorry to have caused you any trouble," Kim said, examining her lock carefully. The police had said a double bolt was good, but not that good. Someone had evidently broken in with no trouble at all. She double locked, anyway, and then gave her neighbor an apologetic smile. He retreated huffily into his apartment.

She found no one from the press lurking outside the brownstone building and wondered whether Conor had dispatched them. The street was a busy one, a mix of town houses, brownstones, apartment buildings and corner stores. The lingering summer dusk had at last succumbed to night, bringing with it that sense of calm and order typical of many of New York's small neighborhoods. The warm night had brought out its denizens, children and adults, and any number of playful dogs.

Traffic, as her neighbor had pointed out, was a constant stream and she had no trouble at all hailing a cab. Only when she had settled back in her seat, after asking the driver to take her to Grand Central Station, did she realize that crowds could hide a murderer, and that the murderer could be stalking her. She looked out the back window at the car behind, headlights shining directly in her eyes. Was it following her or going about its own business?

Emma Lambert's face suddenly swept before her eyes. Kim had contemplated following the woman earlier that day. She glanced at her watch. It was the date with Mrs. Lambert that she'd been trying to remember. Too late for them to meet, of course. She had missed her by a couple of hours. Kim pulled the train schedule out of her bag. There'd be time, anyway, to try to reach her, and offer abject apologies.

At Grand Central Station she purchased a ticket for Westport and discovered that she had a ten-minute wait. Time enough to try to find Emma Lambert, or at least leave a message for her.

As usual the main room was crowded, with everyone from panhandlers to tourists to late-working commuters rushing for their trains. At the far end, a stage had been set up and a rock group was performing. As she headed for the bank of telephones below the balcony bar, she was stopped momentarily by a vague peripheral view of Conor Stark ducking into the crowd around the stage. But when she turned to look, she couldn't spot him. After all, he wasn't the only tall, sandy-haired, broad-shouldered man in New York.

The phones were all in use. While she waited she searched again for the man she thought resembled Conor Stark, but he had vanished. When she at last got the St. Regis on the phone, she had only minutes to spare before her train left the station.

Emma Lambert, she was told, was not registered at the hotel, nor had she been. Kim thought of having her paged, but decided that whatever game the woman had been playing, hanging around the Hotel St. Regis wouldn't be part of it.

Benjamin was dead. Perhaps Emma Lambert had had something to do with it. No, she couldn't be a murderer,

that lovely woman with the brilliant eyes who had sat across
from her that afternoon, an afternoon light-years past. A
sense of loss overwhelmed Kim and then faded as she
sprinted for her train. She'd had enough of loss for one day.

Chapter Seven

He liked trains, the smooth, rhythmic roll beneath his feet, not a *clackety-clack* as popularized, but more *chumpeter-chumpeter*. This train, on its way northeast to Connecticut, was smoother than most, but then he'd ridden some doozies in the backwaters of South America and liked them, too.

As for his quarry, Kim Killian, she sat in the car ahead, oblivious that he was following her at a discreet distance. Conor had no idea of her ultimate destination, but he was going to stay with her all the way. Once, back there at Grand Central, he'd thought she had discovered him, but no, she'd merely rushed to the bank of telephones near the balcony and then waited for one to be free, impatiently tapping her foot. Just moments before he had stood boldly behind her, a newspaper held to his face, close enough to hear her order a round-trip ticket to Westport, Connecticut.

He'd melted away from the line before she reached for her wallet, then returned to buy a one-way ticket for himself. He figured on hiring a rental car for his return.

Keeping the Dalrymple name sacred was fine with Conor, for the time being. Benjamin's death was unfortunate. No one should die because he's in someone's way. But Conor wanted Kim Killian to be a lot more lucky. He liked her looks, her manner; hell, he even liked the way she walked, and in the last half hour he'd had plenty of time to check that out.

For now, what she knew, or what she possessed that might harm the Dalrymple name, should be in his possession with a little patience. But he'd have to take care of her, even if from a distance. When the bomb eventually blew, it would take the Dalrymple empire with it. He didn't want Kim caught in flying debris.

THE YOUNGER CONOR STARK, the youthful, innocent one, had thought everything of the Dalrymples; he owed them for his education, his future, for having had the path smoothed when his father died. Conor remembered every detail of his first meeting with Anthony Dalrymple. The head of the international corporation that bore his name had attended Conor Stark, Sr.'s funeral at Warshop, Washington, the small lumber town in which Conor had grown up.

The man who headed the Dalrymple empire was a tall, slender, impressive-looking individual with graying hair, a smooth-skinned visage and eyes of a sharp, distant blue. He arrived at the church in his black Mercedes and rushed up the church steps to where Conor, his mother and sister stood.

Dalrymple said all the right things, certain of his ability to charm even at traumatic moments. He shook Conor's sixteen-year-old hand and then clapped his shoulder. "Well, young man, you're the image of your father. He was a brave man, even foolhardy in his courage. The last time we talked, maybe a month before he died, we spoke of the dark dangers of building in such a strange, inhospitable land. But he was a pioneer." Another pat. "You can be proud of him."

Then Dalrymple had assured him that the Stark family's future was going to be taken care of, that the company always took care of the families of employees who had died on the battlefield. Conor swallowed the message whole.

Only after his mother's death did Conor learn the truth about the accident in Brazil that had killed his father.

At the time he was field director for the Americas Conservancy, living part-time in Amazonia. When his mother fell ill, he rushed back home to discover that she had died the night before.

A few days after the funeral, his sister said, "You handle all the paperwork, Conor. I can't. I don't have the heart for it." She directed him to Ralph Embers, their mother's lawyer. "I think he has a bunch of papers for you to look at, said Mom wanted him to hold on to them in case she, I mean when she..." His sister, high-strung and a little helpless, threw up her hands. "You don't mind, do you, Conor?"

No, he didn't mind. His sister had held down the fort while he pursued his dream far away. He expected to find bundled letters, old photographs, a will giving away his mother's few possessions, perhaps some pieces of jewelry—the detritus of a good woman's life, a woman whose real happiness had been cut short more than a decade before. Then he remembered his father's papers, and his mother confessing she hadn't had the heart to look through them. Even so, he envisioned a passport, visa, letters, field notes, nothing incendiary.

Ralph Embers was his mother's age, a successful, busy lawyer who was nevertheless impressed with Conor because of his ties with the Dalrymples.

His office, in the tallest building in town, a three-story red brick bit of Americana, overlooked the Warshop River. Wide windows behind the lawyer's desk held a view of the river, a wild swath that cut through town on its way down from the mountains. Dalrymple lumberjacks felled the trees upriver and let them ride down until they bumped up against the barrier strung across the narrows at the far end of town. Dalrymple Lumber, name and logo, was painted across the warehouse on the opposite bank—painted on the tin roof as well, for the eagles and planes to see. Warshop was a company town, and that company was Dalrymple Lumber.

Ralph pointed to the small metal file box on his desk. "Your mother kept her valuables at the bank, but you know you can't get into that until the estate's settled."

Estate. Conor shook his head. Her simple will had left the house and its belongings to both him and his sister. His sister had married a Seattle businessman and had no need of an inheritance, nor did he.

"She asked me to hold on to this file. Said it was for you and your sister to look through," Ralph went on.

"Probably sentimental stuff," Conor said, nevertheless feeling an unexpected surge of adrenaline at the idea of seeing his father anew via his papers. "My mother never could throw out a picture. She kept every one of my baby pictures and school drawings, as if something evil might happen if she threw them away."

"Your mother was a little old-fashioned," Ralph acknowledged. "Well, if you need my help with anything, you know where to find me."

Conor brought the file back to his mother's small, neat house on River Road. The scent of cedar permeated the front entry, bringing him back in a flash to his childhood, to the time when his father, powerful and robust, bursting with life, seemed to fill up every space in the house.

His sister had left lunch for him in the refrigerator, along with a note saying she'd be back later that day. They still had some decisions to make about the disposal of their mother's possessions. He took out a sandwich and made some coffee in the old-fashioned stainless steel pot she always used, with its familiar dents and burnt handle.

The box was fitted with a key that turned easily. Conor found himself hesitating before he lifted the lid, as though something surprising might, after all, pop up like one of those jack-in-the-boxes he'd had as a kid. When he at last pushed the lid back, he found a mess of papers, books and folders, with no order to them.

He picked up the first folder, which held an oblong envelope labeled "Life Insurance Policy" in his mother's neat script. He put it aside, feeling a pressure behind his eyes that could signal tears if he wasn't careful. He'd loved his mother, but saw her rarely. Like his father, he had chosen a career that took him abroad for long periods of time. His mother was a stoic woman he remembered as once being funny and lively. His father's death had changed all that.

He impatiently fingered through the file's contents. Photographs; scraps of paper that might have been receipts for long-ago bus fares, for all he knew; a packet of letters tied with a ribbon; and, sure enough, a couple of drawings signed by six-year-old Conor Stark. Some by his sister, too, who showed a lot more talent than he.

He found a photograph of a smiling, light-haired woman, his mother in another life, holding a baby in her arms, his chubby, dimpled face a smaller facsimile of hers. A shadow lay across the lower part of the photograph—his father's thumb, probably.

"He's no photographer," his mother had said more than once, "but he has other virtues."

For the four or five years before his death, his father had supervised construction at various Dalrymple lumber and mining sites in South America. That afternoon, as Conor went through the contents of the metal file box, a new picture of his father's last months began to emerge. His letters home had not painted a true picture of what was happening. They'd been cheerful, if anything, the correspondence of a man who was both happy with his work, yet who loved his wife and wished his family was with him.

His diary told a different story, however. A small leather book, held together with a thick cord and knotted securely, it might have been taken for an engineer's logbook. In fact, the first few pages were filled with formulas and calculations written in his father's tight, dark scrawl.

There were pages of notes concerning construction of a bridge at a logging site in the Amazonian forest. Then, halfway through, Conor found a personal note.

All is not as it seems or as A.D. wishes the world to see. Mahogany. They've got mahogany fever. And rosewood, that precious rarity. Felling trees like there's no tomorrow. At this rate, there'll be no tomorrow. Treatment of locals makes me heartsick.

Conor quickly read through the following pages. His father was beginning to question Anthony Dalrymple's avowed and well-publicized interest in preserving the natural resources of the Amazon. He had discovered several incidents that proved different.

The last entries in the diary were as clear and dreadful a guide to a man's certain rendezvous with death as Conor had ever known. Conor discovered the truth behind his father's death that day, and it turned his life around.

Hallelujah, five chaps from Congress plan to be here in two weeks, to investigate American companies' involvement in clear-cutting the Amazonian basin. U.S. Consul in Belém promised me their itinerary.

A.D. at his ranch. Took a devil of a time getting through to him. He promised to make it down here middle of the week. I told him in no uncertain terms that he can pay off the world, but I want no part of it. He laughed, promised things would improve. Oh, A.D.'s a charmer, all right. Seems to know the group of congressmen on their way here and laughs it off.

May Fabric of *Newsweek* agreed to fly down here to do cover story. I'll have a story for her she won't forget.

Then, nothing.

His father's body had been discovered crushed by a falling steel girder on the half-finished bridge. No blame was fixed for the accident. It was just one of those unfortunate things that happen in a dangerous job.

Yet Conor knew Anthony Dalrymple had ordered his father's death as easily as he might have ordered an expensive gewgaw from a Neiman Marcus catalog.

It was three years since his innocence had been shattered by his father's notes. Sitting at his mother's kitchen table in the company-owned town of Warshop, Washington, Conor Stark had made a solemn oath that he would succeed where his father had failed. He would be quiet, thorough, and he would hit suddenly. He would accomplish his mission, whatever the cost, to take on the monolithic, all-powerful yet dangerously shadowy corporation headed by Anthony Dalrymple.

The appearance of Benjamin Soares's manuscript not long after had allowed him to make points with the Dalrymples. He told them it was barely decipherable and if it ever did get published, it would never be widely read. He became their dogsbody, but with his *own* purpose.

And now the purpose had a time frame, as well. The International Dialogue on the Troposphere was scheduled for September in Geneva. IDOT was a newly organized federation of both first- and third-world countries. Conor Stark was to be keynote speaker at its first symposium. As field director for the Americas Conservancy, he was most qualified to give a paper on the devastation of the Amazonian basin.

DeeDee, upon learning that Conor was to present the keynote address, had expressed her pleasure. She was certain she had an ally in him, and that the publicity would enhance the Dalrymple name.

Conor's main chance could be summed up succinctly: whistle-blower. He intended to achieve what his father, sixteen years before, had been unable to.

"Westport." The conductor's voice startled him. Conor thought for a moment that he must have fallen asleep. He got quickly to his feet and glanced into the car ahead, his heart thumping. Kim was gone.

Damn, he'd miscalculated. He tore out of his seat and rushed to the front of the car, looked through and saw with relief that she was waiting for the doors to open.

He had to get off the train before she did. He had no idea whether she intended to hire a cab, rent a car or walk to her destination. If he was following her, he'd have to be one jump ahead.

Chapter Eight

"This is it, driver."

The gray clapboard house, curtains drawn, stood on the corner of Greentree and Blossom. Kim, peering out of the taxi window, was puzzled by how thoroughly unfriendly her parents' house seemed, now shuttered and dark.

With a sense of foreboding she stepped out of the taxi, thrust her fare at the driver, then headed for the house at a near run. Halfway up the walk, however, she saw with relief that both cars stood peacefully in the driveway. The simplest explanation of all: Ambassador and Mrs. Killian were home, asleep.

She was edgy, that was it. She hadn't calmed down in the least during the ride up from Grand Central Station, even though she knew that what had happened to Benjamin had nothing to do with her parents. She was merely experiencing a proprietary feeling for the two people she loved most dearly in the world. Odd, though, their being in bed at ten o'clock. Ordinarily she'd find them in the den, Dad working on a crossword puzzle, her mother writing to one of the dozens of friends she had the world over. The television set might be playing in the background with the sound off, because neither could decide what to watch. Of course, if she didn't live a structured life, Kim told herself as she climbed the porch stairs, there was no reason to expect them to, either.

The cat, an ancient beloved pet not given to roaming outside the house, was sitting on a wicker chair near the front door. "Come on, Lester," she said, reaching out to pet him. "Time you were home and in bed, too." Lester hissed, raised himself up, his tail huge and flaring in fright, and took off.

"Hey, Lester," she called, "it's your old pal, Kim, remember?" She might keep up a line of chatter, but a silvery sliver of dread invaded her body even before she took out her key to the front door. She'd never lose that memory of Benjamin in her tiny garden, the stain of blood on his chest. Perhaps the Berriman Prize had set in motion a chain of events that reached all the way to her parents' peaceable kingdom.

She slipped the key into the lock and jiggled it. The key refused to turn left the way it should. Wrong key, perhaps; but no, she discovered when she checked. Disoriented and with shaking fingers, Kim tried to manipulate the key in the lock, only to discover that the door had been open all along.

Her heart began to wobble in her chest. She turned the knob slowly, its metal icy under her touch. The door opened silently on smooth, oiled hinges. An encouraging scent of potpourri drifted out from its cut-glass bowl in the hall. Crickets seemed to be partying noisily on the lawn, but from inside she heard only silence. The house was pitch black.

"Mom? Dad?" She listened for a long moment and then relaxed a bit. Forgetful, that was all. They'd gone to bed and had forgotten to lock up. She'd have to read them a lecture about safety tomorrow. Meanwhile she could use a good night's sleep herself.

Without warning a soft, warm pressure moved against her leg. She jumped, moved away two steps, stifling a scream. The cat, purring heavily, moved past her.

"Lester," she whispered, "I'll get you for that."

She switched on the hall light, closed and locked the door and was about to head upstairs when she heard a thumping sound emanating from the living room, not the kind a cat makes. She raced down the hall. "Mom? Dad? Are you here? What's going on?"

The light cast from the hall into the living room revealed the source of the sound: her mother and father bound and gagged back-to-back on two wooden chairs.

"Oh no!" Kim rushed in, quickly switching on the light. The familiar room popped into view with its lively suburban air now marred by the shock of seeing her parents tied up and squirming.

Her father growled—an order to get moving; they were unharmed. She thought as relief poured over her that she'd never heard anything so welcome as a bad-tempered growl from her father. "It's okay, everything's okay," she said soothingly, "just let me get the scissors."

Edmund Killian, balding and military, usually had a twinkle in his eye, but all Kim saw now was fear and embarrassment that he hadn't been able to handle things better. As soon as his gag was removed he spat out a few curses, and stormed to phone the police when his last bond was cut.

"He'll have a heart attack," were her mother's first words when Kim removed her gag and enveloped her in a hug.

"Dad gives heart attacks, he doesn't have them," Kim said, laughing with relief.

SHE HAD NO IDEA how she was going to explain either to the police or to her parents how she had become involved in a murder and a housebreaking all in one very long, very tiring day. But she needn't have worried, because her parents tripped over themselves trying to explain what had happened. As they had been preparing to sit down to dinner, a couple of men in stocking masks and waving guns had pushed their way through the open back door.

"And they tied us up," her mother wailed, "although we did everything they wanted."

"What did they want?" Kim asked, although she already suspected.

"What did they want?" Her father seemed dumbstruck at the question. "To sell me life insurance! What did they *want?*"

"Now, Ed." Her mother shook her head. "All these years living in remote outposts of the universe and this never happened to us. Now, right here in our own backyard..."

Kim turned to her father. "It wasn't a simple robbery, was it? I mean, not that robberies are simple."

Instead of answering her question, her father softened and put an arm around her. "You all right, Kim?"

"Yes," she said, giving him a puzzled frown. "Why wouldn't I be?"

"Either you're the coolest person in town or you're hiding something. They wanted to know if we were storing anything for you—manuscripts, to be exact. Your mother, bless her soul, said, 'You mean like her notes? No, we're not storing them. Believe me, they're not even in the attic with her other stuff.' They tore up the stairs. They were after that box of notes you left with us last year. You know the one I mean."

"I should have guessed." She felt inexplicable comfort at his words. "I mean, I hope you didn't put up a struggle because of a bunch of old, meaningless notes. I never should have left them here. That was so stupid of me. And I suppose they found them.''

"I suppose they did,'' her father said. "I heard them rummaging around in the attic, slamming drawers, creating God knows what havoc. After about ten minutes they came clattering down the stairs and ran out of the house. Just a bunch of old, meaningless notes, is that what you're telling me?'' He eyed her suspiciously. "Are you in any trouble?''

Kim cast a glance at her mother, who was waiting at the window for the police. "I might as well tell you now. If you'd had the television set on you'd know anyway. Benjamin Soares was murdered this afternoon.''

Her mother whipped around. "Good Lord, where? How?''

"I might as well tell you that, too. In my garden. I think that whoever murdered him was looking for the manuscript to *Lucky Lady,* or at least my notes. And I don't know exactly why.'' Her father's arm around her shoulders tightened. "I'm okay,'' she assured him. "I wasn't there when it happened. As a matter of fact, someone else discovered the body, so at least I wasn't alone.'' She surprised herself, thinking of Conor as someone dependable when she couldn't possibly afford to trust him, not when his admitted purpose was to protect the Dalrymples.

Her mother narrowed her eyes, studying her daughter. "Exactly what *are* you doing here?''

"I called you, figuring you'd learn about Benjamin and about me and that I had better get to you first. I thought it a little weird that your answering machine was off.''

"So you came running out.'' Her mother grabbed her and gave her a pleased hug, then said, as though embarrassed to be showing pleasure at her daughter's gesture, "Where are the police, anyway? They should be here by now.''

"Listen, I'm going upstairs to see whether the thieves found my notes," Kim said. "I won't touch anything."

Mrs. Killian was already headed for the kitchen. "I'll be damned if I'm going to let all that food go to waste. Did you have dinner?"

Kim smiled. She was home.

Her favorite space in the family's large old colonial was the attic, with its pleasant musty smell and colorful debris: her schoolbooks, photo albums, souvenirs of all the places they had lived, even some old wedding presents Drew hadn't commandeered. But upon opening the door she experienced the same horror she had earlier. Twice in one day her privacy had been invaded and destroyed. Trunks were overturned, shelves emptied, and in the middle of the rubble she discovered her wooden box turned upside down, its contents gone.

Everything had been taken—slips of paper, legal pads covered with her unreadable scrawl, photostats of magazine articles, dog-eared 3 × 5 cards with cryptic references on them. The question was why anyone would think they were important. Once the book was released she had returned everything to Benjamin but her own notes, and she had kept them as she might any file, for posterity, for the tax man, to refresh her own memory. The attic was her personal repository.

"Kim?" Her mother called from down below.

"Be right there."

The police. The attic was hot and stuffy and she was afraid her headache might return. She glanced at her watch. Ten-thirty. It felt like midnight, a week later. Whoever wanted her notes had wanted them badly enough to murder for them. She shuddered, thinking of what might have happened to her parents if the intruders hadn't been satisfied with what they'd found.

She had no plausible story to tell the police and she had forgotten to call Sidney. Kim went back downstairs slowly, on heavy feet.

Her mother met her in the hall. "Someone to see you." She studied Kim, her eyes unexpectedly gleaming, a familiar look usually reserved for the men in her daughter's life.

Kim paused on the bottom step. "What did you tell them?"

"It's not the police."

Kim frowned as she entered the living room. "Then where the devil are they, Mom? You'd better try them—" She stopped, her mouth open in surprise.

Standing at the fireplace talking to her father, and looking a little tired and rumpled, was Conor Stark. Her first reaction was relief and unexpected joy that oddly enough didn't seem out of keeping with the circumstances. She hadn't been able to shake him from her mind. He seemed wedged there, and for all the wrong reasons. He was the *enemy*. She had to keep remembering that.

She came to at once, aware of her mother standing patiently beside her. "What are you doing here?" she snapped at Conor. Before he could answer she turned to her mother. "Mom, this is serious. You'd better make sure the police are on the way."

"Now, Kim, take it easy," her father said from his chair. "Conor was explaining—"

"Oh, *Conor*, is it?"

But the sound of a car drawing up in front of the house, and flashing lights visible through the curtains assured her the police had finally arrived. Her father went to open the front door.

Kim remained rooted at the entrance to the living room, scarcely aware of what was happening outside. "You have a remarkable penchant for showing up at the scene of the crime," she said to Conor. "And I suppose my father told you precisely what happened. How'd you know where to find me, anyway?''

"It took a smile and a small bribe at the taxi desk in Westport, that's all. And my driver's license to rent a car."

"That *was* you at Grand Central. Next time I'll be a little more cautious about where I go and what I do."

"This way, gentlemen." Her father led two plainclothes detectives into the living room. Good, Kim thought. Her father's ranking as a diplomat guaranteed the top men in the department. She immediately recognized Jay Bennett, who had worked with her at a local hamburger joint one summer when they were both in high school. He was paunchier now, balder, but his eyes still held the same heavy-lidded look of intelligence that she remembered.

Life in a small town was a lot easier when you knew the mayor, the police, the head of the sanitation department and the justice of the peace. Knowing the bright young head of the Westport detective squad was even better. She had only to explain Conor Stark and go on from there.

But Conor, it turned out, needed no help from her. Since the questioning was a lot more informal than it had been in New York, she was present while he freely explained who he was and his relationship to Kim.

He managed, in fact, to be so open and full of information about how he had found Benjamin that Kim was required to add very little. As for the notes that had been made away with, she could in all honesty explain what they were about. She left out Benjamin's surmise, his innuendos, his distrust of the Dalrymples, since he had been able to prove nothing, at least not so far as *Lucky Lady* was concerned.

When the police left, just past midnight, Jay had in his possession the name of Detective Raymond Lee, who had questioned Kim in New York. *Good luck,* she thought. She didn't believe for a minute that they'd be able to find out who the hoodlums were and whether they were connected to Benjamin's murder.

Benjamin was dead. The woman he had been so obsessive about, Lucky Anne, was dead. And so was Lucky Anne's lover, Anthony Dalrymple, who had died of a heart attack a year ago.

The core question remained: why had Benjamin come to see her, and had his murderer made away with information about Lucky Anne that could harm the Dalrymples?

"We're not spending the night here," her mother said to Kim as soon as they settled with Conor in the kitchen over coffee and sandwiches. "I spoke with your aunt a little while ago. She said you're to come, too."

Her mother's widowed younger sister lived a little farther north, in a large old Tudor mansion with her daughter and grandchildren. Kim didn't think she wanted to face anyone else that night. "No, thank her for me, though," she said firmly, in the I'm-a-grown-woman-and-I'll-take-care-of-myself voice her parents recognized.

"You're not staying here," her father said, ignoring the set of his daughter's lips. "I agree with your mother that what we all need is a good night's sleep far away from here."

"And you're certainly not going back to your apartment," her mother said. "Are you?"

Kim wasn't certain of the answer to that one. She could call a limousine service and be back at her apartment inside of an hour. The thieves had what they'd come for. No one was going to force her out of her comfortable, hard-won nest, ransacked or otherwise. Kim, nevertheless, groaned inwardly at what she'd have to confront when she opened the front door.

"I'm going down tonight. Come with me," Conor offered. "I rented a car."

"You think of everything," she said.

"Not everything."

"That's right," she said, unable to hide her sarcasm. "If you had, I suppose you would've beaten them to my notes. I hate to disappoint you, but they've ended up with nothing."

"And has it ever occurred to you they might be back to talk to you in person?"

"Return to the scene of the crime? They'd be a little crazy to do that."

Conor glanced sharply at her, but glossed over her remark. "The question still stands," he said. "Did they kill Benjamin because of *Lucky Lady* or because of the book he was working on?"

"I told Detective Lee and I told Jay that I've no idea what Benjamin was up to."

"I think," her father said, "we've had enough conjecture for the night. Are you coming with us, Kim?"

"I'm going back to my apartment."

"Don't be ridiculous."

"Dad, I'm being practical. The thieves, whoever they are, by now know more about me than I know about myself." She reached across the kitchen table and patted his arm. He had always been protective of her, but she couldn't help feeling as if every step back into their home was a step into the past. "I'll come by on the weekend, help you straighten up the attic."

"Kim!" Her mother looked at Conor, as though expecting him to take sides.

"I'll see that she's safely tucked away," Conor said.

Her mother gave Kim an infuriatingly conspiratorial glance. So he had managed, with a smile, to make her believe there was something between them. But it was her mother's interest that made Kim decide to go back with Conor. Of all the men she'd brought around to meet her parents, Conor won the prize for gaining her mother's instant approval. She was a hard woman to please. That didn't mean all bets were off concerning his guilt, merely that Kim believed he'd deliver her safe and sound to her apartment. He had no choice.

Her mother caught up with Kim in her old room, where she had gone to wash her face and brush her hair.

"Tell me about Conor," she said.

"Nothing to tell. I met him at the Blackfoots' out in the Hamptons." And she still hadn't called Sidney, but figured he'd know by now and would be trying to call *her*.

"I like him," her mother said. "Maybe he's not as successful as Drew, but then we don't want another Drew around, do we? An ecologist, he said. An academician. Not terribly exciting, I suppose, but safe. I do like his smile. He looks steady."

"You said that about Drew."

"I was wrong then. I'm not now."

Kim smiled, put her brush down and turned spontaneously to hug her mother. "Don't make hearts and flowers out of molehills," she said, adding a kiss to the hug. "I'm not interested in Conor Stark."

"Could have fooled me," her mother said softly. "I should have held a mirror up to your face when you first saw him. Your eyes were shining."

"From sheer puzzlement. Honest."

"Honest?" Her mother smiled gleefully. "I'd like to see you happy, Kim. I don't want you putting up walls because you were hurt once."

"There's nothing to wall off," Kim insisted. "Conor got mixed up in my life because of *Lucky Lady,* that's all. And I'm not unhappy with my life. Except for today, I've been having more fun than ever." Every part of her wanted to crow, for her mother's approval, *And I won that damn prize for Benjamin Soares,* but she didn't. "You think I'm still traveling under a cloud put there by Drew. Mom, I promise I'm not.''

"Well, I'm glad to hear it." Her mother kissed her. "But you *still* lit up when you saw Conor."

As they headed for the stairs, Kim wondered. Would Conor have noticed what her mother insisted was true?

EVEN AT ONE in the morning, the turnpike was busy. Once on the highway, Kim let out a deep breath and permitted herself to relax. She had been wound so tightly her stomach hurt.

"Everything okay?" Conor asked.

"All things considered."

She leaned back and studied Conor's profile. Straight sharp nose, strong chin, hair ruffling in the night breeze. She liked his ability to concentrate; the way he drove, with just an occasional glance into the side and rearview mirrors, keeping a safe distance from other cars. He was a careful driver, but then he probably knew what an explosive package sat next to him.

She closed her eyes. Perhaps she was relaxed because she had begun to trust him a bit. Maybe that trust was premature, even foolhardy, but she knew what intrigued her mother. Conor Stark was attractive and his manner endearing when he wanted it to be.

"Kim."

She opened her eyes and looked around. Had she fallen asleep? No, they were still on the turnpike, keeping up a steady fifty miles an hour.

"We're being followed," he said.

She sat up quickly. "Come on, you're kidding."

"A gray Cadillac. Can't see the license. Moved onto the highway with us and it's been keeping a steady pace ever since."

She turned and glanced through the rear window. There it was, two car lengths behind.

"Turn around. Don't let them know we know they're following us," Conor said in a tight voice.

She turned back, feeling the heat creep into her face. "Are you sure they're following us?"

"Watch, if you don't believe me, but out of the side mirror, please." Conor changed lanes and speeded up, passing several cars before slowing down again. The Cadillac followed and was soon back in the same lane, two cars behind.

"Okay," Kim said, trying to keep the fear out of her voice. "You win."

"One thing I'm going to insist upon," he told her. "You're not going back to your apartment."

"Fine. I'll go to a hotel."

"Bad idea. Don't you have any friends you can call?"

"Scads. That's why I have them. I don't bother them in the wee hours of the morning."

"You're coming to my place."

"In your dreams, Stark." She strained to catch sight of the Cadillac through the side-view mirror. The car was nowhere in sight. She was about to tell Conor that he was all wrong about being followed when he reached out and roughly shoved her down. "Hey, what the hell do you think you're doing?" The seat belt pulled hard against her ribs.

"Don't move unless you want a bullet through your brain."

Only the seat belt stopped her from tumbling sideways as he yanked the car left with squealing tires. The sound of the gunshot smashing the rear mirror told Kim he wasn't kidding. She didn't need a picture to tell her the Cadillac wasn't in the side mirror for a good reason. It had now pulled up alongside, intending to use her head for target practice.

Chapter Nine

"Hang on!"

Kim felt a scream bubble in her throat. Before she could do more than grab the safety belt with trembling fingers, Conor made the turn across the grass divider. The car spun along the grassy strip and landed back on the highway going north.

"Did it." His tone was exultant. "Now that's Indy 500 driving." He picked up speed. There was a squeal of tires behind them. "Uh oh, trouble." He gunned the engine. The car rocked forward, an unpredictable animal in a bullring. "They're not going to give up. Hold on to your hair."

"Never mind my hair. I just lost my fingernails. They're stuck in the safety belt."

"I'll buy you new ones. Listen, I'm getting off the highway. Stay low. Maybe we can lose them in the Bronx."

"Lost in the Bronx, great. Can I sit up now?"

"Still have your head on tight?"

"Yes."

"Then keep it on."

"What about you?"

"I don't have much choice, do I? They're a couple of cars behind." He took a sharp left and then a right, burning rubber until he hit Bruckner Boulevard, a long, ugly stretch of cement watched over by factories and ware-houses.

It was empty now at two in the morning, streetlights sending out a harsh, icy glare that made shadows look mean. "Keep down," Conor said. "They're right behind us. Damn, the rental agency handed me a clinker."

She closed her eyes and sent up a childish prayer in Por-tuguese from days long ago, an incantation her nurse had taught her in Rio.

"Watch it." The car swerved. Conor drew in a deep breath as a bullet tore the rear window, whined over Kim and exited the windshield, cracking it. A nice crack, she thought crazily, by a bullet that missed her only because Conor had insisted she stay down.

"Kim? You okay?"

She caught the tremor in his voice. The lump in her throat was the size of a balloon. "All right to sit up?" she asked at last.

"No, just hold tight. We're breaking every speed law in the books. Where are the cops when you need them?"

After another few minutes of silence broken only by an occasional curse, he turned and said in an extraordinarily calm voice, "Okay, we lost them. Or," he added, "they wanted to get lost. That doesn't mean we've seen the last of them." He took his hand from the wheel and lightly brushed his fingers through her hair. "You sure you're okay?"

She sat up, pulling the safety belt down from her chest where it had stuck. Okay? Any minute now she'd toss her mother's ham sandwiches. "Sure," she said, dusting shards of mirror off her skirt. "I like the South Bronx at this time of the year."

"Kim, I'm sorry. Want to borrow my shoulder? It's guaranteed cushioned."

"I'm okay. Let's get going. Maybe we'll meet up with some cops when they see the crack in the windshield."

"Our friends don't play games, Kim. That's no .38 they used. A 9 mm is more like it. The bullet went clean through the rear window and out the front. If they want you, they'll be at your apartment—you know that, don't you?"

"No, I don't know that. Maybe they're after you." She couldn't take her eyes from the windshield, its crack splitting her view of the deserted factories lining Bruckner Boulevard. "You're going to have some job explaining this to the car-rental agency," she said. "They'll think they rented to Bonnie and Clyde."

"Don't change the subject. You know I'm going to stick as close to you as a flea on a dog."

"Itchy. No way."

"I want you to come back with me to my place."

"My apartment, Conor. It's not negotiable."

He slowed the car to a crawl, then pulled up and stopped at the curb. He reached across her for the door handle. "You want your apartment, you'll have to call a cab."

She knew he wouldn't leave her in that quiet, shadowed place. "And to think my mother decided unilaterally that you were trustworthy."

"Kim, I'm not taking you home."

"A hotel, then."

"What in hell's the difference between a hotel and my apartment except a couple hundred dollars?"

"You come with the apartment."

"The hotel, too. I said that where you go, I go. Incidentally, I provide all my guests with brand-new toothbrushes."

Female guests, she had no doubt, then wondered why the idea upset her. "You *are* thoughtful, but I guess I'll just have to pass on this one."

"Street's mighty dark and empty."

"There's nobody around to worry about then, is there?" She visualized checking into a hotel with no luggage and Conor Stark bringing up the rear. He still grasped the door handle, his arm brushing lightly against her. She reached over, pushed his hand away and opened the door. "Maybe it *is* safer out there."

"Maybe it is. Check it out." Conor sounded serious enough, but he was clearly just testing her limits.

She'd never liked the phrase "between a rock and a hard place," but that was just where she had landed. The street was deserted, dark and dismal. Not even taxis cruised this part of town. Why was emptiness so ominous? Why were these silent streets more frightening than crowded ones? The shadows, she supposed, and what they hid. She closed the door.

Conor lived on the upper east side of Manhattan in a four-story brownstone that had been converted into co-op apartments. His apartment was on the top floor and commanded a view of the roofs of other buildings and a very busy street below.

The ordinariness of the building gave Kim some comfort. She somehow had expected, a little fearfully, to find him living in an anonymous high-rise with thick, noise-muffling carpeting and mile-long, deserted corridors. Had even imagined traveling with him to the thirtieth floor with a wide view of the city and no one around to help her if he got rough.

What she found instead was reassurance, if only because of the noisy apartment below, where a couple of people argued sporadically in Spanish.

Still, the minute they entered the warm, friendly precincts of his apartment, Kim felt so queasy she had to clutch a small table for support.

"Hey!" Conor grabbed her. "Take it easy. The decor isn't that bad, is it?"

She felt beads of perspiration break out along her forehead. "I'm okay. You can let go now." She pushed gently against his chest.

Still clearly concerned, he released her reluctantly after another moment. "Everything all right?"

"Everything's all right." She couldn't explain, either to him or to herself, what had happened to her. She suspected the finality of stepping into his apartment, mixed with a feeling that she was glad to be with him, provoked an extraordinary uneasiness. "I think," she said, "I could use some sleep."

THE NEXT MORNING Kim held a cup of coffee to her lips, studying Conor Stark in pajamas and bathrobe across the small breakfast table in his efficiency kitchen. The shower that morning had felt good; her hair was still damp and scented with the lemony shampoo he used.

"Coffee okay?" he asked into the embarrassed silence between them.

"You're the only person I've met lately who likes his coffee as strong and deadly as I like mine."

"You want to meet passionate drinkers of coffee, you should visit Brazil," he said.

"I grew up in Brazil."

"Oh yes, of course, I should have realized that."

Kim caught a sudden shift in his eyes, a light that went on and dimmed in quick succession. *But he didn't know,* she thought, *and now he's connected my speaking Portuguese with* Lucky Lady. *He knows that I worked closely with Benjamin and that I read Benjamin's original research notes. And that I wasn't just his editor, I was his writing hand. He's beginning to think I know a lot more than is good for me.*

She put the cup down carefully, and for the tenth time that morning, refolded the cuffs of the long-sleeved, over-size terrycloth robe Conor had lent her the night before.

But all he said, in a mild voice, was, "Go on. You grew up in Brazil."

Imagination, of course. She was imagining things. He'd saved her life, taken her home with him after her brush with death, held her for a moment upon closing the door and locking it. Been a proper host, offering her his bed while he slept on the living-room couch. Now she owed him her life, and maybe even her life story.

"Right." She picked up the cup again. "Started drinking coffee when I was a child, sitting in the kitchen watching the servants, downing that "awful gucky black stuff," to quote my mother. That's what comes of bringing up children in a foreign culture. They develop habits and tastes they spend the rest of their lives trying to satisfy."

"Did you travel to Brazil when you worked on *Lucky Lady?*" The question was a curveball, guaranteed to hit her off guard, but hit her nevertheless.

"No, why should I?"

He grinned, pulled apart his breakfast doughnut and handed a piece to her. "Chance to have Sidney foot the bill for a trip to Brazil. Where did Ben live, exactly?"

"You have me all wrong," she said. "And Sidney, too. I did all my traveling as a youngster. Nowadays I stay home and edit books. *Edit* them. I don't research them. That's the author's job." She popped the doughnut into her mouth, and then had difficulty swallowing it. The events of the evening before hadn't gone away with a fitful sleep. If anything they were etched more clearly.

She'd been shot at twice. In real life she'd be sitting in a police station, recounting the events and asking them to find a gray Cadillac and a couple of gunmen. But this wasn't real life. She was sitting with the Dalrymple's errand boy, wearing his bathrobe and drinking coffee at his breakfast table. The fact that she now suddenly recalled a rather fevered dream she'd had the night before, with Conor in the center of it, sent a blush to her face.

"Hey."

Kim looked up. Conor was regarding her with an openly curious expression. "You've sat there for a full five minutes, staring blankly at your coffee cup."

"Reliving my recent past," she said. "Yesterday—no, this morning. I limited my reminiscences to a car chase in the Bronx. I don't think I want to go through that again."

"Kim, you can move in here until this business gets straightened out. I'm due back in Brazil. I won't even be around."

"Oh." The word came out unexpectedly, small and sharp and sounding of disappointment. She hoped he didn't notice.

"I told you I was on my way back."

"You did, I know. Thanks for your offer, but I'm happy with my apartment, or will be as soon as I get it back in shape." She got to her feet, still holding the cup. "Look, I've got to go. I have some important stuff to do, like wade through the mess in my apartment."

"I'll go with you. I said I'm sticking like glue."

"Fleas on a dog. I thought you were leaving for Brazil."

He grinned. "Not this minute." He reached across the table and gently took the empty coffee mug from her. "Get dressed. I'll meet you in the living room at—" he glanced with an exaggerated smile at the clock "—ten-twenty on the dot."

Kim hesitated a moment, about to object, but then changed her mind, giving him what she hoped was a convincing smile. He headed for the shower. She raced to the bedroom and dressed hurriedly.

She picked up her bag and quietly left the bedroom. The bathroom door was open as she tiptoed by, catching a glimpse of Conor naked. He was at the mirror shaving. Moisture still glistened on his back and shoulders. She hurried past, feeling a faint, familiar stirring that took her back to those first, exciting days with Drew, stirrings she hadn't consciously allowed herself for a long time.

To clear her head she really needed to get away from Conor Stark. She was about to close the front door when she heard him call her name.

"Sorry, Stark," she said to herself, "but stirrings with the enemy are something I don't need right now."

RETURNING TO HER apartment, however, turned out to be a task she wasn't quite ready for. Instead she went to Blackfoot Press, found it besieged by the media, and left as soon as she learned Sidney was on his way back from Los Angeles. She promised to call him later that day, when he returned. Alice Blackfoot was also looking for her.

"I'll call her, too," Kim said, and tried to look inconspicuous as she slipped out through the reception room.

Her next stop was the New York Public Library, where she spent a couple of hours on research for her current project. The main reading room always relaxed her. Immense, high-ceilinged and hushed, with dozens of people bent over work illuminated by homely lampshades, it was a safe, consistent world. Even so, any movement close by, no matter how slight, sent off messages along her nerve endings, constant little cries for help that no one but Kim heard.

At noon she put a marker in place, got up, stretched and went quickly to the bank of telephones at the end of the hall. She called her parents at her aunt's house. They had been trying to reach her, to tell her they'd decided to spend the following night there as well. Kim hung up after assurances that she'd had no further trouble and that she'd call again that evening.

A light rain was falling when she left the library, research accomplished. She had no choice now but to quit dragging her feet. She needed her computer, and her computer meant going back to her apartment. She headed toward the bus stop as a loud thunderclap cracked the air overhead. The downtown bus swung to a halt just as the rain began to sheet down. The door opened and the polite line that had formed knotted up as everybody tried to board at once.

By the time Kim dropped her fare in the box, she was soaked. The interior was cold and damp, with every seat taken. Pushed unceremoniously toward the rear, she grabbed a strap and hung on while the bus tottered away from the curb. Jumpy enough to let the sudden downpour spook her, Kim examined the faces around her, worrying as she had all day about the motives of strangers. But all she saw were the usual assortment of passengers on buses that time of day—school kids laden with books, elderly women with shopping bags, a couple of young people buried in newspapers or plugged into their portable radios.

The downpour had been brief, but a light rain still fell when she exited the bus at her stop. The soft spray against her upturned face felt astringent and calming. She even stopped at the corner fruit market to buy some apples and a container of milk.

"Welcome rain," the store owner said as he handed over her change. "We need it."

"It's so *beautiful*," Kim said in a heartfelt voice. "I love the city when it rains, and everything looks so nice and shiny."

"You a poet?" he asked.

Berriman Prize notwithstanding, she shook her head. She thought of the healing miracle of time, and how small things like a shopkeeper's friendly remark could shift life back to normal. She continued to smile as she headed around the corner. Her apartment building was halfway down the block. Surely gremlins had been at work and she'd open the door to find her place tidied up and a pot of coffee brewing on the stove. Thick, black coffee, the kind Conor served. Thinking about how she'd like to get to know him, she didn't sense someone moving up behind her until it was too late.

Icy, sharp metal was pressed against the small of her back, passing through the thin fabric of her dress to her skin.

"Don't make a sound. Keep moving."

She thought with surprising clarity that one shouldn't be mugged on an empty street in the rain, no matter how soft and fine its spray. Her knees buckled. The bag of groceries almost slipped out of her grasp. This was what she had been fearing and had almost dared to believe wouldn't happen after all.

"Over here." He grabbed her arm and dragged her into the narrow alley between an apartment house and the corner fruit store.

"Please," she said, "please, I don't know what you want." But he was no ordinary mugger, not with a fifty dollar haircut, designer jeans and a denim shirt open at the neck revealing a long, gold chain. He pushed her, stumbling, past metal garbage cans and a soaking wet stack of old newspapers.

"Okay, right here." Shoving her back against the brick wall, he pressed his knife to her throat. "You know what I want."

The groceries slipped from her grasp, sliding down her leg in what seemed like slow motion to land at her feet. His face was close now, so close she could smell his warm breath and a faint smell of liquor. He was tall, thin, rather handsome. The word *elegant* came fleetingly to mind. His eyes were dark, yet not so dark she couldn't read the danger in them. Her nerves were on hold. All she could feel was sharp-tempered steel against her throat.

"Don't try anything, Miss Killian. One move, one scream and I'll kill you."

He knew her name. "What do you want?" The steel scraped her skin with each word. "I don't have much money."

"Your money?" He laughed in a brittle, self-deprecating way. "Is that what you think I'm doing this for? Think again." He pressed the knife so that the razor edge would slice her skin with the slightest movement. "We're bargaining here for answers, that's all."

So numb not even fear pierced the coldness that wrapped around her soul, Kim dared only lower her eyes in assent. They'd killed Benjamin and wouldn't hesitate to kill her.

"All I want is the original manuscript to *Lucky Lady*."

"I don't have it."

"You know where it is, then."

From beyond the alleyway she heard a man laugh. She heard the hopeful sound of cars grinding to a halt, but knew the light at the intersection must have changed, and that she was alone with a madman.

"Come on, I'm in a hurry."

She thought of her mother coolly directing her intruders right up to the attic for Kim's notes. Belém, on the Atlantic coast of Brazil, was a million miles away. "I said I don't have it."

The knife was pressed against her windpipe. His tone turned wheedling. "Hey, you ought to consider yourself lucky, dealing with me. Somebody else would cut the information out of you. What the hell difference does it make if you tell me where the manuscript is? It isn't doing you any good. Being dead won't do you any good, either." He laughed deep in his throat.

She had no options left, only the knowledge that Benjamin was gone and the manuscript was far away. "Benjamin Soares lived in Belém. He had the manuscript."

"Go on." The pressure of the knife lightened.

"I sent his original manuscript back when the book came out. I had no reason to keep it."

He stepped back. "There. Was that so bad? Belém? Lovely city, Belém." A look of extraordinary relief came over him. He seemed exhilarated as he backed away, still holding the knife—like a little boy who had just stolen his first apple.

"I hope you haven't lied to me."

"I haven't."

"There isn't anyplace you can hide if you did."

"I know that, too."

"Good. Don't forget it."

He reached the end of the alley and disappeared.

Kim fell back against the wall and slid to the ground. The bag of groceries was soaking wet. *She* was wet, soaked to the skin. The apples, wrapped in plastic, hadn't been touched. Then she realized the rain had stopped and a shaft of golden sunlight was lighting the building six stories above.

Oh, my God, she suddenly thought, *what have I done? I just condemned a man to death I don't even know.*

She had mailed the manuscript to Belém in care of Benjamin's lawyer, Edoardo Moriya. Her attacker had sheathed his knife and run off. He apparently had no need of precise addresses, because he had the means and contacts to find out for himself what he wanted to know.

Benjamin was dead, and she had no doubt Edoardo Moriya would be next.

Chapter Ten

Chimu, a small country between Peru and Brazil

Because the main mode of travel through much of the Amazonian rain forest is by water, there are regions that remain uncharted or poorly understood. Even the Trans-Amazonia Highway, crossing the continent, leaves dense jungle, unknown and unknowable, on either side of its red, narrow strip.

Undiscovered rivers might flow below high green canopies. Clearings sighted by plane might be small aboriginal communities or outcrops of mineral deposits. And tiny stretches of plowed land could be mistaken for just another backwater.

On most maps of South America, Chimu—twenty-five miles long and fifteen miles at its widest—appeared as a colored blip, similar to Andorra and San Marino on maps of Europe. An amoebalike shape might be discerned on enlargements of the borderlands between northern Peru and Brazil, a small, green shadow in the larger presence of the Amazonian forest.

Chimu received its sustenance from a tributary of a tributary of the Ituí, itself a headwater of the Itacuaí, which spilled into the Amazon at Atalaia do Norte. Every quarter century or so both Peru and Brazil made dilatory passes at claiming ownership of Chimu, only to have the idea languish in the files of the United Nations.

Had not the lands at the farthest edge of Brazil become suddenly valuable for their wood and ore, time might have forgotten this resolutely independent country. Cradled in the arms of Brazil, with Peru tugging at its feet, Chimu was poised, against its will, to be pulled, pushed or dragged into the undoubted excesses of the twenty-first century. But not if one woman had anything to say about it.

"No," said La Divina one Saturday afternoon in late July to Raf Mello, Brazil's new ambassador to Chimu, the first ever from that venerable country to the east. She had just refused his credentials. "We've gotten along quite well these past few hundred years without the protection of your country. I suppose we can expect an ambassador from Peru soon. Then, perhaps, a small war to determine who owns us?"

Mello tried not to smile. He knew the answer but wisely refrained from offering it. La Divina wasn't quite the mad simpleton he'd been led to expect, half witch and half matriarch. Nor was she the aging cult figure depicted in the Brazilian capitol, one who had materialized years before in Chimu as though ordered up by incantation.

She sat barefoot in a wicker chair on the narrow porch of her *palafita,* a thatched, wooden stilt house built high above the river. Dressed in a loose-fitting cotton gown, her thick, dark hair plaited and drawn over one shoulder, she was, to all appearances, extremely civilized in both her speech and behavior. And however primitive conditions were in Chimu, they weren't as primitive as he had been led to believe. La Divina was a woman of experience and taste, and he was going to have to take her seriously.

Her *palafita* in the village of Michimu overlooked the Chimu River. Fast-moving and crystalline, the river flowed rapidly past, unlike the sluggish giant to the north that began a 2300-mile journey from the mountains of Peru to spill into the Atlantic at Belém. A fine river, Chimu, one that had potential. And potential was what Mello's journey was all about.

"Now, will you have *cafezhino?* Or perhaps *caipirinha?*" She referred to a popular lime-and-liqueur drink. "That is, to speed you on your journey home."

Ambassador Mello, a big, distinguished man with a black mustache and a dark, gentle gaze, had been chosen for the job perhaps equally for his appearance as for his powers of persuasion. He was the perfect diplomat for a sensitive mission. Right now, in his tan cotton suit, he was perspiring in the tropical midday heat. But there was nothing he needed so much as *cafezhino,* a hot, black, very sweet and bracing coffee. He was surprised yet again to find so cordial an amenity thousands of miles from nowhere. He gave La Divina a white, gleaming smile.

"*Cafezhino.*"

What had surprised Mello most of all upon his arrival in Michimu, the capitol, was the makeup of its population. They were not the aborigines he'd expected, complete with bows and poisoned arrows, but a different people entirely—a people who dressed in decent cottons and whose long, Incan faces and high-bridged, narrow noses made him believe that perhaps a long time earlier they had drifted down from the chill, hostile heights of the Andes. The Chimus of the Andes had been conquered by the Incas at the time Columbus set about raising money for his infamous voyage. The Andes, Mello reflected, were not more than a couple of hundred miles to the west.

La Divina did not ring or call out for servants. She disappeared indoors and quickly made the *cafezhino* herself, on a small kerosene stove. Mello stood at the door watching her, fanning himself with a palm leaf. The aroma of coffee reminded him that the sooner he arranged things, the sooner he'd be back in Brasília, in his comfortable air-conditioned apartment, among his favorite objects and books.

"You have all the amenities," he observed, looking around the *palafita* and finding it more habitable than he'd expected. One airy room, with a hammock at the far end, it contained a couple of wicker chairs, a shortwave radio, and some ceramic crafts as decoration. The wooden floor was swept clean, and despite the noonday heat, the air circulated freely. But then he'd expected to sit on his haunches in grass huts or on uncomfortable stools, trying to make himself understood.

"You're not Chimu, are you?" he asked, the question purely rhetorical, for the woman's dark eyes and berry-colored skin made him think of Portugal.

"I am Chimu," she said, handing him the coffee in a tiny, ceramic cup, "as much as the next person."

"Ah, I see, a state of mind." He was anxious to keep on her good side, although he did not understand what she meant. He downed the coffee at once and was rewarded quickly with another cup.

"Ambassador Mello," La Divina said. She was back in her wicker chair on the porch, a *caipirinha* in her hand. "Chimu has ten thousand citizens, a thousand of whom live in Michimu. Our main occupations are fishing, logging, farming and staying out of trouble. We are extremely self-sufficient and have even managed to export some crafts to the world outside. However, we keep the lowest profile possible. We are a peaceable lot and bother no one. We'd be more than happy if you would take that message back to Brasília when you leave."

"Well, I most certainly will," Mello said affably. "But I want to learn more before I do, meet your people—"

"Not my people," she said.

"But I thought . . . La Divina?"

"The name?" She gave a wistful smile. "A euphemism, that's all. Chimus are by nature believers in omens and fortuitous events. They turn calamity into good fortune and seem to think they should be grateful to me for some small service I performed a long time ago."

"Grateful enough to have made you president for life."

"A role I don't acknowledge," she pointed out. "We have a constitution, a congress, elections. But to run against me..." She shrugged. "No one seems willing."

"I've no doubt they know precisely what they're doing."

She was silent, her eyes on the river beyond.

"But my country wishes to extend its expertise in the area of ecology, mining, forestry," he said. She drew her eyes to his with an air of impatience, but he went on doggedly. "You can't expect this small land to support your people forever. The soil is thin, poor. You must consider restraining population growth, the desiccation of your natural resources, the invasion of loggers or miners who don't respect borders. And there's the matter of education...." He was pulling out all the catchwords, but noted the expression of disdain on her face and stopped in midsentence. The thought came to him unbidden that she was one to love passionately, with the love of a mature, settled woman, not the ragged, silly heat of youth. He darted a surreptitious look at her hand and noted a wedding band.

She must have understood the turn of his thoughts, for she said, "It's true, I was married once, but am widowed now."

For a fleeting moment he caught a look in her eyes he would have to interpret as hunger; then it disappeared without a trace. He gazed out across the river to the forest beyond, a green edge easily a quarter mile away, softened by steam that rose in the noonday heat and seemed to color the very air. He heard jungle noises—birds screeching, the rub of insect bodies, the calls of monkeys and peccaries—sounds made ringing and vibrant as they echoed through the rain forest.

"Don't raise any hackles," he'd been warned. *"The environmentalists will be down on us in a second."*

"When will your helicopter return?" La Divina asked.

He smiled. "When I signal for it."

She pointed to the shortwave radio visible in the room beyond. "You may call for it now."

Raf Mello made no effort to move. He detected a softening of her tone and thought he could play it through if he was very careful.

Later that afternoon they walked along the river, to where it curved gracefully into several backwater lagoons. Narrow dirt roads connected the *palafitas* that lined the banks of the lagoons. "So you can take back your impressions to the capitol," La Divina explained as she led him through the village to observe the natives working. "You see we are quite happy without its interference."

"Never interference. Guidance," he said quietly. "The world is changing, and will continue to change with or without your consent."

"Our people know firsthand what promises and interference can do. Once, a long time ago, they were promised wealth and power if they would abandon Chimu. Many listened to the magician who conjured up this future for them. The saga of how they left, and why they returned, are now sealed in history. It will never be repeated, Ambassador Mello. Tell your government that."

Yes, they had gone and they had returned; Mello knew the story. But Chimu's value—then and now—was only guessed at. For decades it had remained unknown, unexplored, out of the way but never forgotten. The time for remembering was now.

"Many of our people have become basket weavers and ceramists," La Divina said. "We farm manioc, sugarcane, bananas, pineapples, corn. Our trees yield tropical fruits and nuts. They will not be cut down."

Rosewood, he thought, that most rare and sought after tree in the Amazon, a solitary tree difficult to harvest and more difficult to transport. And mahogany, the lure of mahogany. Until now La Divina had resisted the occasional loggers who came through, offering to cull the trees for her. She had refused, as she refused all help from outside.

He thought of the river and its rapid descent to the marketing town of Mato Grosso, a hundred miles distant.

"The thin Amazonian soil can't last forever," he said to her almost as a matter of form.

But her answer came with a smile. "The Indians of the Amazon have for thousands of years successfully used the slash-and-burn method of farming, but at Chimu we can't afford to do that any longer. We've farmed by building up our soil, using the river's vegetation to enrich tracts of land. We let nothing go to waste. We husband our resources carefully, Senhor Mello. What we take from the land we give back to the land. You must also tell that to your friends in Brasília."

"Oh, I'll tell them that and much more," Mello said gallantly, taking her hand and kissing it.

She pulled away as though scorched. "Tell them that their next ambassador might not return with such ease to what he thinks of as civilization."

"But I'm anxious to remain in Chimu, *senhora*. I believe my country wishes it and is prepared to back these wishes."

Her smile was icy. "I'm afraid, dear Senhor Mello, the Amazon rain forest is your country's adversary, not I. It's a strong, cruel soldier."

New York

CONOR STEPPED OFF the elevator into the oval entry hall. This in turn led into a larger hall as neutral as a museum lobby, suitably pilastered and marbled, with Louis XVI tables, huge Chinese urns and rococo mirrors offsetting a brocaded wall covering. The butler, tall, gray-haired and straight-backed, with the required lofty mien—"my gem," according to DeeDee—led him directly to the library. Here Conor let his guard down a fraction, for the square, high-ceilinged room ringed with a balcony and glassed-in bookshelves still held visible remnants of Anthony Dalrymple's strong masculine persona. Or perhaps Conor was still mixing up green leather sofas and Persian carpets with masculinity.

DeeDee, at her husband's huge desk, was on the telephone. A year after Anthony's death she'd made no changes, except for some artistically placed vases of plump and exotic flowers.

Her secretary and her assistant sat primly side by side in front of her. They glanced up at Conor and smiled, then withdrew their eyes.

DeeDee simultaneously kept up her phone conversation, lifted her cheek to be kissed by Conor, motioned to her secretary and assistant to leave and raised her eyebrows to her butler to shut the library door after him.

"Just a second, pet," DeeDee said in a stage whisper to Conor.

"Take your time." He disliked these peremptory summonses that DeeDee frequently issued and wished that she had stayed in the Hamptons. But DeeDee, like her breed of wealthy women, managed to be everywhere at once, and now she was in New York, flown in, he had no doubt, by Joe Turbon, her personal pilot in her very own helicopter.

Conor roamed the book-lined room, examining the spines of Anthony Dalrymple's collection of nineteenth-century French novels while listening in a halfhearted way to DeeDee's phone conversation. He gathered the person at the other end was a lawyer or an accountant. In addition to the Dalrymple fortune, she was in control of the Ealing lumber fortune. And she had no direct heirs, only Tony, whom she despised as being weak willed. That he was also the illegitimate son of Anne Severance had rankled her from the first day of her marriage to Anthony. She had passionately loved her husband, and when he died, had wailed that her life was finished.

Life is never over for the very rich, however. A daily calendar as filled with appointments as a poppy is filled with seeds had her back and running in no time at all. The trouble was, DeeDee had fixed her sights on her stepson's best friend. That was being made clearer to Conor by the day.

Conor had lifted out a leather-bound, signed copy of Balzac's *Modeste Mignon* and was reading it when DeeDee put the receiver down. "Well, your friend is coming around at last," she announced. "About time, too." Her expression and tone hardened whenever she spoke of Tony or her husband's past life with Lucky Anne Severance. She had been married to Anthony Dalrymple for almost thirty years, but Lucky Anne's name always managed to throw her into a rage. And Lucky Anne's son had the same unfortunate skill.

"Tony said not to worry, he'll take care of everything. I think perhaps he's trying to prove himself to me at last," she said. But her tone was dismissive. In her eyes, Tony could never win. DeeDee admitted to the good bones he had inherited from his mother. Tony had Anne's beauty, her elegance, her vaunted charm and insouciance. But he was Lucky Anne's son and DeeDee was unforgiving.

Conor admitted to a fascination with Lucky Anne, and yet he understood DeeDee's hatred, carried on even though Anthony was dead.

"Damn her," DeeDee spit out. "All this fuss because of a dead woman who won't stay buried."

"Then don't fuss," Conor said.

She considered his remark for a second, then brightened. "You're right. I must get on with my life. Tony is going to come through, isn't he?" She moved toward Conor and peered over his shoulder at the book he was still holding. Her perfume was soft and flowery, with a sensual undertone. She pressed familiarly against his body and began to read in perfect French, "'*Mon colonel, faîtes vos affaires en paix. Je vous comprends.*' My my, apt words." She took the book away and replaced it on the shelf. "Think we can trust Tony?"

"We?" Conor crossed the room and settled in a chair opposite the sofa. "I'm not interested in whether or not you can trust your stepson to go after that manuscript," he said. "You asked me to perform a certain service for you. I did. My part of the bargain is finished, DeeDee." He took a deep breath, anticipating her reaction. "I'm booked on a flight to Belém. I'm due back at the station by the end of this week."

A quick, willful frown crossed her face. Damn, she knew he had to get back. He had no doubt she could maliciously destroy his career. She would, anyway, once he gave his speech in Geneva. But not before. He couldn't afford to cross her before the meeting.

He went on, in spite of her frown, believing DeeDee admired his independence. She just didn't want to be inconvenienced. "As far as I'm concerned, with Benjamin Soares dead your worries are over. Sidney Blackfoot will try to make fodder out of his death in order to sell a few books and then it'll all be forgotten."

"I don't think you should go back to Brazil quite yet," she said. "What's so important down there?" Before he could answer she came over and perched on his armrest. "Actually, what's important is what I say is important." She ran a finger through his hair and down the back of his neck.

"I'd like to bow to your superior judgment, DeeDee, but unfortunately I have to get back."

"Perhaps I'll go down there after all," she said, as though the matter had been under discussion.

"Your choice," he said, his voice dispassionate. If he attempted to dissuade her, she'd be in Manaus before he was. To DeeDee, traveling meant merely issuing an order, showing up on time or late at the airport, climbing aboard the company plane and disembarking somewhere else. Moving along like a Rolls-Royce on a conveyor belt to be stopped and checked, cozened, reoutfitted and fed by ever-willing hands, she might show up at the conservancy anytime, and again might not. It was necessary to act neutral in order not to encourage her.

"You don't give a damn about me, do you?" DeeDee's voice was somnolent, a little admiring. She was issuing an invitation, not an order. "Don't tell me you have someone waiting for you there."

"Is that why you wanted to see me?"

She laughed. The telephone rang and she went over to answer it. "Yes, if you want to know the truth. Hello?" She listened to her caller for a second, then put her hand over the receiver. "I'd like you to stick around."

He shook his head.

Kim Killian had calmly walked out on him and disappeared while he was busy shaving and talking to her at the top of his lungs. She was a complication he hadn't counted on, and the trouble was she made his game with DeeDee a lot more disagreeable than it already was. Kim was an unexpected ingredient he couldn't get out of his mind, and dangerous if for no other reason.

DeeDee said into the phone, "Hold on a second." She put the receiver down and came to him. She leaned close, expecting to be kissed. Conor was aware once more of the perfume she wore, something expensive, heavy and newly unpleasant. She grasped his face between her hands and closed her eyes.

"The phone," he said, his mouth inches from hers. "Have you forgotten?"

"Does it make a difference?" she asked.

"No," he said, and moved swiftly away from her. At the library door he paused. "Not a bit of difference." He was gone, shutting the door behind him, before she could even close her mouth. Kim notwithstanding, he had no choice but to move up his departure date. He needed space between DeeDee and himself. Kim was a complication he couldn't afford, either.

Chapter Eleven

"Dad, do you still keep your connections with the State Department?" Kim said when her mother finally relinquished the phone to her husband. "I've been trying to get through to someone in Belém but with no luck."

"This about Benjamin?" His voice sounded wary, as though he expected nothing but bad news from his daughter.

"Dad, I'm in a desperate hurry. Just say yes, you'll help me or no, you won't, please, please, please."

"Why don't you leave finding Benjamin's killers to the professionals? All you're going to do is get yourself in a mess of trouble."

Exasperated more because she couldn't tell him the size of the mess she was already in than because of his stubbornness, she said, "Some innocent person in Belém might be in danger because of me. I need to find him, Dad. I have to cut through the red tape."

"Stop right there, Kim. I don't know what's happening and, frankly, I don't want to."

He paused long enough for her to think he had hung up. But no, this was her father. Fathers don't hang up on daughters. "Dad?"

"Belém, you say?" Another pause. She could almost hear him thinking. "I'll come through for you this time,

Kim, but believe me, it's the last time." She heard the sigh she knew from childhood, the one that meant he could never say no to her. "Maybe I'm crazy. Maybe I'll live to regret it. Belém. I'd say Agussi, Tom Agussi. You remember him. He used to . . ."

"Dad."

"And if he's no help, James Regan. If you'll hold your horses for two seconds, I'll give you their phone numbers."

"Dad, I'm sorry. I promise things'll be back to normal in no time."

"I'll believe it when I see it."

Tom Agussi, whom she remembered from Rio as being a small, bald man who loved to tease her, was friendly and open when she got through to him. His manner changed, however, the moment Benjamin Soares's name was mentioned. He turned guarded, telling her that Belém was no longer under his jurisdiction. With Congress breathing down the collective necks of everyone in the State Department, he couldn't take on the tracking down of people who weren't even citizens of the United States.

"Ah, the bureaucracy," she managed before she hung up. "What would we do without the bureaucracy?"

James Regan gave her the same runaround. Both men were eager to help her as the daughter of Ambassador Killian, but not so eager when a foreign national was mentioned in conjunction with Benjamin Soares's name. "Sorry," Regan said, "but nowadays we stick close to the rule book."

"What rule book?" She hung up before he could answer, deciding it wouldn't be diplomatic to let the name Dalrymple pass her lips.

Since she'd been accosted in the alley three hours had passed, the rain had stopped, a soft dusk had settled in and helpful elves hadn't straightened up her apartment.

She tried reaching Moriya again. There was no answer, at either his office or home number. She had no doubt he was next in the line of fire.

In desperation, Kim went through her address book, hoping to find the name of someone who might help, noting irritably, not for the first time, that she had never deleted Drew's office number. Drew, the world traveler, might know someone in Belém. No, if she called him she'd blurt out the business of the Berriman Prize, do a little bragging. She flipped the page. Perhaps Conor had a contact she could use. If he didn't have connections through the Americas Conservancy, no one would.

She liked the idea, maybe a little just because she wanted to talk to him. Still, discretion told her to slow down, even to brew some coffee and put together a sandwich before making the call. She wondered whether he had tried to telephone her, or had come around to the apartment. After all, she had run out on him, and he should be concerned about her safety. She was even annoyed that he had given up so easily. She made a mental note to turn on her answering machine the next time she left, and then promptly forgot about it.

In the mess in the kitchen she found a jar of instant coffee that she made palatable by adding powdered chocolate. She pieced together a cheese sandwich, washed an apple and made her way back into the living room. She would put her books back before calling Conor. Books neatly lined on shelves always had a relaxing effect on her.

But first, her excuse of a dinner and some mindless television. She cleared the coffee table, plumped the pillows on the sofa, kicked her shoes off and stretched out. She caught the end of a television sitcom and had just groggily closed her eyes when the news came on. She opened her eyes again, put down her cup of nearly-spilled mocha coffee, and the half-eaten sandwich and lay back to try to do some serious thinking.

Who besides the Dalrymples had a vested interest in *Lucky Lady?* One, Emma Lambert—whoever she was. Two, Conor Stark, who had turned the book down, who lived part of the year in Brazil and who was the Dalrymples' toady. No, strike that, she decided. Conor couldn't be anyone's toady, which must mean he had an agenda of his own. She remembered him, muscled, still wet from his shower, shaving and calling out to her as she left his apartment. On that note, still smiling, she began to slip into sleep, number three forgotten.

"Here's late-breaking news. The body of Anthony Dalrymple, Jr.—"

Kim came to at once, tensing and fixing her eyes on the television screen. A blonde, stiff-haired anchor with pale eyebrows stared into her living room. "—was found a short time ago in the foyer of his uptown, east-side apartment building. Police believe him to be the victim of a robbery attempt. Dalrymple is heir to a lumber and mining fortune worth an estimated..." A picture of the victim flashed on the screen, and the voice faded into the background. Kim was off the sofa without even being aware of it, crouching close to the TV set.

"But he's..." She stopped. The blond announcer returned. The weatherman was introduced and reported that it had rained that day. Kim got slowly to her feet and went dazedly over to the telephone. The card Detective Lee had given her sat in an empty candy dish. She picked up the receiver and punched in his number. She didn't know whether or not his being there at six in the evening was her good fortune or not.

"This Anthony Dalrymple, Jr.," she said without preliminary, "the one who was just murdered? He held a knife to my throat at around two, two-thirty this afternoon down here in the Village, and wanted to know where the original manuscript of *Lucky Lady* was."

"You're sure it was the same man?" The detective seemed reluctant to believe her.

"Yes, I'm sure. His face was inches away from mine."

"Did you report the mugging to the police?"

"No." She stopped, embarrassed, afraid of being called out for dereliction of duty.

"Why not?"

"I was unhurt. New York is a big city and I hadn't a clue who he was. I'm not sure why not."

"And what did you tell him?"

"What he wanted to know."

Detective Lee sounded a little impatient. "You *know* where the manuscript is? I'm a little confused on that point."

"The manuscript I'm talking about," she explained, "was mailed to Benjamin Soares, in care of his lawyer in Brazil. I sent it down when the book first came out. That was almost a year ago. What his lawyer did with it is anybody's guess."

"Suppose you come down to the precinct, Miss Killian, and tell the whole story to me from the beginning."

"Now?"

"I can't think of a better time."

"Right." She was still groggy. "Okay. Which precinct? Where he died or the local one?"

"Start with me."

"Where did you say that was?" She was surprised to learn the precinct was within walking distance, but then she had managed to live her life up till now without so much as an overdue library book. She hung up, stretched and went into the bathroom to throw cold water on her face. Maybe she'd have time to put the books away first, make returning to the apartment a little easier. No, maybe not. Maybe she ought to call a cleaning service. When the phone rang, she was glad of the distraction and ran to answer it, toweling her face dry. She found herself hoping Conor was her caller, but no, he'd be with DeeDee Dalrymple, consoling her over her stepson's death.

"Hell's bells, where've you been and why isn't your answering machine on?"

"Sidney." If he weren't so self-involved, he'd hear the disappointment in her voice.

"If this isn't the most incredibly lousy rotten luck."

"Getting me on the phone?"

"He died in your backyard? I suppose he didn't even have the goodness to tell you where his current manuscript is. Did he even write one? Tell me you know, Kim, just tell me that."

"Sidney, you know as much as I do. And besides, I don't have time right now. The police want to talk to me."

"What did Benjamin have to say for himself?"

"Sidney, you're a ghoul. Anyway, I said I'm as blank as you are. I'll call you just as soon—"

"And then this news about Tony, Jr. I mean, I leave town for two days and the place turns upside down. Get in here pronto, Kim. We have strategy to discuss."

"I'll call you, Sidney, just as soon as I speak to the police." He was still chattering when she hung up.

On her way out her landlady stopped her. "People keep calling me asking where you are," she said. "I'm not running an answering service."

"I'm sorry. Who keeps calling?"

Mrs. Whitefield smiled suddenly, saying the words with a certain amount of pride. "The media." She worked days in a local dress shop and claimed acquaintance with any number of celebrities who lived in the neighborhood.

"I'm really sorry," Kim said again. "What do you tell them?"

"That they have the wrong number."

"Thanks. Great idea. Sorry for any inconvenience, Mrs. Whitefield. Look, I'm off to the local precinct. They want to see me about something. Then I'm going to come back and straighten my place up."

"Stop by for tea," Mrs. Whitefield said. "I still don't know what's going on."

"Neither do I."

TONY DALRYMPLE HAD DIED in another precinct. A detective from there had been dispatched to interview Kim and was already waiting when she arrived at her local station house.

The detective-squad room was an oblong shape holding half a dozen desks. An open window at the far end looked out on some windows in a brick building across the way. A tall fan in the corner of the room blew a brisk wind across and out the window, leaving the room itself damp and tepid. The dusk had deepened sufficiently for the neon ceiling light to give everyone present a waxen cast, Kim included.

She told her story about the mugging, but could offer no excuse for not having called the police immediately. But Tony Dalrymple hadn't taken anything, only the name of a port city in Brazil where a dead man had lived, and in spite of his holding a knife to her throat, he'd left no marks. *I need a friend,* she thought, *a mentor whose shoulder I can cry on and who'd tell me to call the police.*

"Ever see this?" Detective Lee asked.

He shoved a photostat at her. Someone had made a copy of the gold necklace, with its pre-Colombian bird figure, she had seen around Benjamin's neck. "He was wearing it," she said.

"Tony Dalrymple?"

"No, I was talking about Benjamin Soares."

He took the picture back. Kim realized in no time at all that they had found the same amulet on Tony. "A cult, perhaps?" she asked in a small voice.

"What gave you that idea?"

"Nothing," she said hastily. "I mean, odd about its showing up twice in one week."

Not a cult. That didn't sound like Benjamin to begin with. The papers would make a field day of it. Blackfoot Press had a book to sell and everyone knows notoriety sells books, even Berriman Prize winners. She could already see Sidney illustrating the cover with a pre-Colombian bird artifact.

She was unable to offer them witnesses, but her statement was taken down. Clearly Detective Lee no longer thought Tony's death was the result of a mugging. With Benjamin dead in her garden, and the theft of her notes in Connecticut, Kim now seemed to be the center of a mystifying conspiracy. She half expected to be told not to leave town. Instead, she was handed Detective Lee's card once again and told to call if she thought of anything else.

A couple of men were standing to the side of the elevator when she left the squad room. Kim, happy to be out of there, scarcely noticed them. She hurried to the elevator and pushed the down button.

"Kim."

She turned and found Conor striding toward her, his face ashen. Her heart sank. Of course. Everywhere there was trouble, there was also Conor Stark. Tony Dalrymple's death would certainly bring him out of the woodwork. The elevator slid to a halt. The door opened. "Hi," she said and stepped in.

"Hey, hold it." Conor followed her in. A young man in a ripped T-shirt, arm muscles bulging like balloons, stood at the back with a lank-haired blond teenage girl. They were arguing softly in thick New York accents.

Conor bent over. "Did you really see Tony?" She was shocked at the haunted expression in his eyes and the taut lines around his mouth. Tony had been his friend, and Conor was hurting.

"How'd you know I was here?" she asked.

"Mrs. Whitefield told me. Where've you been all day?"

The elevator came to a smooth stop on the ground floor. Kim stepped out and headed straight for the street door without looking at Conor. How did he know about *Tony?*

"What the devil's gotten into you?" Conor asked, catching up and taking her arm.

"I'll tell you what's gotten into me. Fear," Kim said. "Where were you when I needed you, when your friend shoved a knife under my chin and threatened my life?"

His eyes narrowed. "Who threatened you?"

"Anthony Dalrymple, Jr. This afternoon. In a back alley. In the Village. In the rain. And you know all about it."

"No, I don't know all about it. DeeDee merely said..." He stopped, clearly aware of the mistake he had just made. "Let's go for a drink. I could use one."

Kim's first instinct was to say no, to feel hurt, annoyed, jealous and confused all at once. Conor's genuine, pleading expression, however, made her relent. That, and wondering what DeeDee had said. He had lost his friend; she had lost a stepson.

"Maybe I could use one, too," Kim said.

They settled opposite each other in a cushioned back booth of a crowded bar two blocks from the station house. The air-conditioning was turned up high, which did nothing to dispel the smell of beer and broiling hamburgers. An immense television screen showing a baseball game lit up the front of the long, narrow room. The place was obviously a police hangout. Several men sat at the bar, their guns evident even under their street clothes.

Kim reflected on her eating habits for the past couple of days: on the run and mainly bread with cheese, or bread and butter or bread and bread. Besides a glass of beer, she ordered an omelet with french fries and toast. Conor stuck to Scotch, neat.

They waited for their drinks in near silence. Kim kept her eyes glued to the televised game, being played in a near-empty stadium. She wanted to talk about the Dalrymples, stepmother and stepson; to get Conor to admit they were behind Benjamin's death and the theft of her notes. And she wanted to talk about amulets. But she wasn't quite certain where to begin.

Conor was the first to break the silence. "Want to tell me exactly what happened this afternoon? You're sure it was Tony."

"Yes, I'm sure," she said, dragging her eyes away from the screen. "Listen, I'm sorry about your friend, but he threatened me with a knife. And that if I didn't tell him the truth about where Benjamin's original manuscript to *Lucky Lady* was, he'd be back to get me."

"That wasn't Tony," he said.

"Conor," she said softly, putting her hand over his for a moment, "it was Tony."

He looked away, his mouth set. "I thought I knew him." He shook his head slowly. "I'd hate to think he was killed because someone had no more use for him."

"Someone?" Who but the Dalrymples would care about a story that had begun and ended thirty years before?

Their drinks were delivered to the table, with assurances to Kim that her omelet would be right out. Conor took a long pull at his Scotch. He set the glass down, but kept his hand wrapped around it. "DeeDee's the stepmother—*was* the stepmother of a friend," he corrected himself. "And she's a generous contributor to the Americas Conservancy. She's not a bad sort when you get to know her."

"I never even mentioned her name, and I don't want to get to know her. I don't like people who can push buttons and order a murder committed."

His eyes hardened at her remark, so much so that Kim felt as if he had retaliated by slapping her face. "Whatever you may think," he said in a quiet, flat voice, "keep it to yourself."

"Why? What do you know that I don't?" She kept her eyes level with his. "I've told you and the police everything I know."

"Tony's dead. He was my closest friend. I don't have a choice of hoping it was a mugging, unrelated to Benjamin's death. Now I have you to worry about, too."

Her omelet arrived, huge, as though a dozen eggs had been used in its preparation, with a whole acre of potatoes, cut, ribbed and fried. For several seconds Kim stared down at the plate with the oddest feeling that she didn't know where to begin or even which piece of cutlery was appropriate for the job. A side order of coleslaw, served in a small soup bowl, made its appearance, too.

"Everything okay?" the waitress asked, hovering.

"Yes, great, wonderful. Looks terrific. Thanks." The waitress left, beaming.

When Kim glanced at Conor she saw the old warmth, the humor, restored for a fleeting moment. He got up, came around the table and slid into the booth next to her.

"Come to share my dinner?" she asked, pushing the dish over to him. "Actually, I'm not hungry. Tuck in." Before she could move her hand away, he closed his own over it.

"Listen to me, Kim. My friend died and I don't know why. The trouble is, I'm out of it. The police haven't released Tony's body yet. DeeDee's talking about a small private funeral next week. I'll say goodbye to him in my own way."

"Oh, Conor," she said, "I'm so sorry."

"I'm heading back to Brazil...and I won't be around to watch over you."

"When are you leaving?"

"Originally, the end of the week, but now it's tomorrow."

The news hit her in a way she had not expected. She felt as though her breath had been punched out of her. She was struck with the notion that, flying bullets, bodies in her garden and alleyway muggings notwithstanding, the past few days had been the most exciting she had ever led. She had been sleepwalking before she'd met Conor, and now he was going away, perhaps out of her life forever.

Conor clearly read the dismay in her eyes. He put his arm around her and pulled her close. "Do I have to worry about you? Are you sure you can take care of yourself?"

"Hey," she said, feigning indifference to the heat that coursed through her at his touch, "considering how you always seem to hover at my scenes of disaster, except when I need you . . . " The sentence petered out of its own accord. "Your omelet's getting cold," she said in a shaky voice.

"Kim."

"What?"

"This." He pressed his mouth to hers in a warm, lingering kiss. She found herself leaning into him, returning the pressure of his lips with a greediness that surprised her. His arm tightened around her as their kiss deepened. It was Kim who came reluctantly to her senses almost at once. He was leaving her and she didn't believe in long, shattering goodbyes. Especially not in the corner booth of a very public restaurant, even if the world had faded away, leaving them alone. She was all too vulnerable.

"I don't want to leave you," he said when she pulled back from his arms.

She had to force the words out. "But you will."

"I have to, you know that. Tonight? There's still some of it left."

"No." The word came out sharply. "I'm sorry," she said, "but no." She almost hoped he would speak some magic word that would force her to relent.

Instead he gave her his familiar, endearing grin. "Right. *No.* If there's a word I understand, it's no."

LATER, AT HER APARTMENT, Kim worked furiously at cleaning up, making a point of reshelving her books according to subject. She didn't answer the phone when it rang. The caller would be either Sidney or her mother, and she didn't want to engage in long conversations with either one. She had no right to be furious with Conor for returning to Brazil, but she was. Or maybe that wasn't all she was furious about. She could still feel the touch of his lips, his response to her greedy return of his kiss, the rush of excitement that had raced through her.

Back to business, her mind told her. Back to reality, which in this case meant two murders and the possibility of a third, in Brazil. She thought of asking Conor to find Edoardo Moriya in Belém and to warn him of the danger he might be in, but then decided against it. Her reaction to Conor Stark had surprised and almost overwhelmed her, but she wasn't ready to trust DeeDee Dalrymple's man completely.

Kim only knew that she felt suddenly and inexplicably alone.

AROUND MIDNIGHT she tried Moriya at his home number. There was still no answer. Replacing the receiver, she remembered the phone messages she had never picked up. She hesitated briefly before turning on her answering machine. What she didn't know wouldn't have to be taken care of. But then perhaps Emma Lambert had called her. She flipped the system on and then was thankful for her rash decision.

If she hadn't, she might never have heard Benjamin's voice again, not angry this time, but hushed and upset. "Oh, where are you? Why don't you pick up? I'll call back in an hour. I must talk to you."

His was the next voice on the tape. "Kim, pick up, it's Benjamin. I must talk to you. Call me when you get back. No, not a good idea. I may not be here myself. Stay put until you hear from me."

On his third try, he said, "Never mind, I'll tell you now. I wasn't myself, dear Kim, when I called you on Saturday. A thousand pardons. I was afraid, you know, that you'd tell everyone the truth, and it couldn't be, not now so close to success." He paused. She could hear brief, shallow breaths. "She's alive. That's all I dare tell now. I'll call again, or I'll drop by." He gave a brief laugh. "Be there."

Kim shut off the machine and sat down shakily. He'd had choices and had taken the wrong one. And what if she had been home when he called? Would she have forgiven him and invited him over? Would they both have been discovered and murdered? Over what, dammit? A question about whether Anthony Dalrymple had been implicated in Lucky Anne's death a long time ago and a million miles away?

Except that Lucky Anne wasn't dead. She was alive. *Alive.*

Kim reached for her phone book, then dialed Varig Airlines to check on flights to Rio and Belém.

Chapter Twelve

July in Belém was also winter in Belém, which made it a little cooler than July in New York, but not by much. On the taxi ride in from Val de Cans Airport Kim reflected that Belém, like all subtropical coastal cities, looked beautiful at night, refreshed by a recent rain and guarded over by regal palms and giant mango trees. Daylight would reveal the contrasts, and the port of Belém provided plenty, from skyscrapers and colonial mansions to *favelas,* shanty towns without electricity or running water; from its bustle as one of Brazil's major ports to its hapless underclass.

It was nearly midnight, a day after she had made her call to Varig, when Kim arrived at the Hilton Hotel on Avenida Presidente Vargas, a broad, elegant boulevard facing the park. The trip had been long, roundabout and uneventful. She hadn't caught up on her sleep and now meant to. She didn't know if anyone was on her trail. She knew only one thing—the trail was closed until morning.

She was already in bed, half-asleep, when it struck her that if she tried Moriya's home telephone number at midnight, she'd find him in. Only then did she discover what she hadn't been able to from New York. His home number was disconnected. On a lark, she tried his office number. It rang, but no one answered.

The first thing Kim did upon awakening the next morning was dial his office again, with the same result. She realized she was on Brazil time now, meaning she'd have to keep trying him until she caught him in.

She showered, dressed in a red silk shift and put on comfortable sandals. Red for Brazil. She'd stand out more, oddly enough, in her usual somber American colors. She twirled her hair into a knot, fastened it with a comb and decided that she'd stop at the Ver-O-Pêso market to pick up a straw hat, as much for disguise as to visit one of her favorite places in Belém. The market at the city docks, where everything from herbs to crocodile teeth was vended, was a tumult of color and noise. She'd been meaning to stock up on crocodile teeth. But first things first: a pre-breakfast cup of black coffee.

She dialed Moriya again, with no success. This time she asked the operator to check his number, which turned out to be correct. She was beginning to doubt that Moriya had been Benjamin's lawyer. Lawyers had secretaries who answered telephones at nine in the morning, even in Brazil.

She supposed she could try Benjamin's number. He had lived in an apartment, watched over by an elderly housekeeper, near the Goeldi Museum. Kim couldn't very well show up and ask to go through his papers if the housekeeper were still there. She needed a lawyer for that, and Edoardo Moriya was purportedly his lawyer.

She opened her door and peered into the corridor, checking to see whether anyone might be lingering there. It was reassuringly empty, as was the elevator that took her to the lobby. Although she had locked her door, she decided to keep the key in her bag. Anyone asking for her would have to assume she was still in her room.

She found a small restaurant to the left of the lobby, decorated in the international style with hanging plants, anonymous paintings and cheerful, light wood paneling.

Kim figured that juice, a sweet roll and black coffee would get her through the next couple of hours. She stood on the threshold, gazing around the interior. There were perhaps a dozen diners, mainly travelers in business suits. She was about to step inside when someone whispered in her ear, "Don't make a move."

She whipped around, gripping her bag, ready to use it like a claw hammer.

A grin was followed by the words, "Now I know why I can't let you out of my sight. You don't take advice."

She closed her eyes. Conor Stark was smiling at her like a know-it-all Buddha. She opened her eyes. He was no mirage. A shaft of pure, utterly frivolous joy surged through her, without reason, logic or even fear. It took her another moment to collect herself. "Okay, Stark," she said, "what are you doing here and why?"

"Hey, look happy, even if you don't mean it. I wanted to ask you to have breakfast with me in New York, but you took off so quickly, I never had the chance."

"Uh huh. And you flew nine thousand miles so we could have a cup of coffee together in Belém. Good thinking."

"I wanted to have breakfast with you to tell you not to do anything foolish. But you've already gone ahead and done it."

He took her arm and led her through the open restaurant door. "Coffee black and ready to stand on its own without a cup. Am I right?"

"Ten minutes, Conor, that's all the time I've got, and I'm not kidding. How'd you find me?"

He waited until they were seated, at a small table with a view of the park across the way, and their coffee was served. "Los Angeles, my foot. You covered your tracks well, telling your landlady and your parents a cock-and-bull story about flying out to LA."

"My parents? You called my parents?" She sank back into her chair. "Are they okay?"

"Sounded that way. Said they were taking a week's cruise to Bermuda, that they needed it." He frowned. "What's wrong, Kim? What happened?"

"Nothing." It was obvious she hadn't covered her tracks very well at all, if Conor could find her so easily.

"It's all right. I didn't tell your parents what I suspected. I figured, under the circumstances, you'd be foolish enough to head for Belém." He gave her a consoling smile. "Benjamin lived here. If you were on the trail of who killed him, or on the trail of his manuscript through his heirs, this is where you'd begin. I hopped a flight to São Paulo and then came straight up to Belém. That's about the fastest route and the cheapest."

Kim groaned. She'd been so busy planning evasive action in New York, she had grabbed the first flight that popped up in front of her, and that had added seven hours to her trip. But then Conor was an old hand at traveling out here.

"I arrived early last night, checked all the first-class hotels and made a bet you'd stay at the Hilton, centrally located and efficient. You'd choose efficiency over colonial architecture anytime. I struck pay dirt at seven this morning, first call. And all I had to do was book myself in and wait for you to head for a cup of coffee."

"Good reasoning. I thought you were going back to the conservancy station."

"I am, as soon as I shake some sense into you."

"I said you have ten minutes. Eight of them are left."

"Can I take five of them to try to talk you into going back home?"

"No."

"Then we talk game plan."

"No way," Kim said. "I have no intention of throwing in with you. You work for DeeDee Dalrymple."

For an instant his eyes blazed. He looked as if, given the opportunity, he'd pick her up bodily and deposit her in the deepest part of the Pará River. "I don't work for the Dalrymples," he said in an even voice.

"They support the Americas Conservancy."

"The corporation supports it. So do hundreds of other people, rich and poor. DeeDee doesn't own the conservancy, and she certainly doesn't own me."

Kim wanted to believe him, but didn't dare. Her guard was halfway down already. "Then I've no idea what you're warning me against or why we need a game plan. I've figured all along that DeeDee wants the manuscript so she can personally destroy it and save the Dalrymple name."

"Killing Benjamin and her stepson would be a strange way of going about it."

"You have to admit you've run the odd errand for her here and there."

She thought for a moment that she had hit a nerve so raw he'd cry out in agony, but all he did was shake his head. "Kim, you don't know what's propelling me, because you've never hung around long enough to find out."

"All right," she said. "Tell me."

Their breakfast arrived and the waitress took a long time serving them, offering silver jam pots and tubs of butter. Kim carefully pulled her steaming croissant apart and began to butter it. "You don't want me to know," she said when Conor didn't answer her. "Whatever you say will skirt the truth. I can tell by the set expression on your face. You want me to spill everything on my side, which isn't much, and then you'll toss me to the crocodiles."

"I'm prepared to go to Benjamin's apartment and to ask his neighbors a few questions," Conor said. "I found his name in the phone book, and chances are his lawyer's been around talking to the landlord. Are you in it with me, or do we trip over one another looking for his lawyer?"

Kim concentrated on the way the butter melted on her croissant. He wasn't going to say any more than he had to. She'd find out one way or another. Meanwhile, she had to throw in with him. "Five minutes to finish breakfast, Conor. First stop Ver-O-Pêso."

He gave her a puzzled look. "The market?"

"I need a hat."

MORIYA'S OFFICE was in one of the older office buildings off Avenida João, sandwiched between a Victorian mansion with a red-tiled roof and a block of shops. They found his office on the third floor, its glass door shut and bolted. Conor stuck his head in the doctor's office next door and asked about Moriya.

The young receptionist said she hadn't seen the lawyer or his secretary for the past week, but seemed to think that wasn't unusual. She advised them to consult the building superintendent for more information.

They found the superintendent holed up in a tiny, cluttered office on the ground floor, surrounded by mops, pails and gray rags. The place smelled of disinfectant and Gauloises cigarettes. When queried, he shrugged and said that Moriya's secretary had quit and that the lawyer was on vacation, somewhere on the border of Peru, he thought. He did not know his home address, but supplied them with the rental agent's telephone number.

The rental agent cheerfully picked up his receiver on the first ring. He just as cheerfully refused to part with Moriya's home address, explaining it was privileged information. Conor offered to visit him in person and sweeten the privileges. The agent, not so cheerfully this time, said no and hung up.

"What we need," Kim said to Conor, "is a lawyer."

"What we need is the reason why the man can't be bribed. This smells of someone having gotten to him first."

They settled for a taxi ride to La Vicente, a middle-class neighborhood close to the center of town, to an address listed as Moriya's, according to the telephone directory they consulted. His unpretentious red-roofed house sat on a charming, well-cared for acre of land, shaded over by palm trees. The morning was sunny, benign and still drenched with dew. A scent sweet as jasmine hung in the air.

"Well," Conor said, "if he isn't home, somebody is." The windows were open, lacy curtains drawn back.

They asked the driver to wait while they went up a brick walkway lined with flowered bushes on either side.

"Note the name *Adami* on the mailbox," Kim said.

"Address is right even if the name is wrong." Conor pushed the buzzer. "Senhora Adami?" he said to the young woman who answered the door.

She seemed friendly enough. Frizzy-haired in the latest style and wearing tight shorts and a loose T-shirt, she leaned against the door frame, ready for a chat. "Edoardo Moriya? Why is everyone so interested in him all of a sudden?"

"Everyone?" Kim exchanged a glance with Conor.

"In the first place, I only met the man once, when we rented the house from him. That was about six months ago. I'd like to get hold of him, too. The ceiling leaks in the bedroom closet. He's some landlord. In the second place, I only have his office address. It's off João."

"Who else wanted to know about him?" Conor asked.

She looked closely at Conor in an interested way. "You're American," she said. "I can tell by the accent, but you speak Portuguese pretty well. You from New York maybe?"

Conor nodded.

She began to snap her fingers to a tune in her head. "New York, Times Square, Broadway. Someday I'm going to go there."

"I hope you get your wish."

"The character, this morning—his accent was very lower class. I said I didn't know an Edoardo Moriya and tried to slam the door in his face." She frowned and pursed her lips. "He didn't like that one bit. But my husband was here. He explained that Moriya had rented us the house and that we're looking for him ourselves. I wouldn't give that character the time of day."

"But," Conor said, leaning toward her, "you'll give us the time of day. What did this character look like?"

She shrugged. "A bully. Small, big shoulders. Pumps iron, my husband said. Want Moriya's office number?"

"We've already been there. Please," Kim said, pulling out a card from the hotel on which she had scribbled her name, "if you remember anything he might have said, anything at all, please give me a call. I'm at the Hilton. I'd really appreciate it."

"Okay. And if you find him, tell him the closet leaks."

"That got us exactly nowhere," Conor said when they were settled in their taxi heading back to the hotel.

"Oh, it got us somewhere else," Kim said. "That's the trouble."

"You're one step ahead of me. Go on."

"They, whoever they are, know Moriya was Benjamin's lawyer and *they're* one step ahead of *us*."

KIM HAD NOT BEEN BACK in her hotel room for more than a few minutes when the telephone rang. She picked it up, thinking her caller was Conor.

She was surprised when Edoardo Moriya's young tenant, Senhora Adami, introduced herself. "Senhorina Killian, you asked me to call you if I remembered something."

Kim's heartbeat quickened. "Great, what have you got for me?"

"Well, right after you left I called my husband, and he told me that Moriya's out of town. See, my husband runs a trucking business. Well, about a week ago, right after a bad rainstorm, he called Moriya and told him about the leak. Moriya said to go ahead, have it fixed and send him the bill. Then my *husband* went out of town. The closet hasn't been leaking, because we haven't had a bad storm since, and he forgot to tell me about what Moriya said."

"What do you mean, Moriya's out of town? For how long?" Kim asked.

"He moved to Marajó."

She needed a little more information than that. "Did he say exactly where on Marajó?" The fluvial island across the Pará River from Belém was the size of Switzerland. It was also where the Dalrymple ranch lay.

"Souré."

"And you wouldn't by any chance have the *senhor*'s address on Souré."

"I'm sorry, *senhorina,* but my husband also said Moriya talked about going prospecting in the Amazon, over somewhere on the border of Peru."

Which accounted for his office being closed. "You won't give this information to that other gentleman who came calling, will you?"

"He was a thug. Anyway, I'm going to visit my sister in Argentina. I won't be talking to anyone."

"Thanks," Kim said. "I'm really grateful."

"*Nada.*"

After disconnecting, Kim immediately dialed Conor's number, but with no response. He hadn't said he was going out. They had planned to try Benjamin's place a little later that afternoon, when they'd be certain to find his neighbor home.

Plans had changed drastically. Moriya might still be in Souré, and they had to get to him. If he had just moved, within the past week or so, he might not have a telephone. She tried anyway, but was out of luck. She tried Conor again, without success, and then phoned the lobby about flights to Souré and discovered that one was scheduled for forty minutes later.

"Okay, Conor," she said. "Your loss." She felt uncomfortable running off by herself, but booked passage anyway, grabbed her bag and ran for the elevator. The ride to the airport would normally take twenty minutes, but she had to account for traffic.

The lobby was bustling when she came down. Enough luggage was strewn around to make her think a convention was in progress. She left a message for Conor at the desk, but didn't spell out the details. Nor did she know when she'd be back. If he wanted to check out Benjamin's address by himself, he was welcome to do so. She hurried through the lobby, noting that the doorman was busy. She'd flag a taxi herself.

Avenida Vargas was crowded with shoppers, tourists and cars. Although a taxi drew up to disgorge its passengers in front of the hotel, she decided to save herself a few minutes by hailing a cab heading in the direction of the airport. She went swiftly to the corner of a busy cross street, and had no trouble signaling a taxi as it came cruising toward the intersection. Automatically she glanced at her watch. Getting through traffic would still be the hard part. She stepped off the curb.

The blow across her back at precisely that moment gave her no time for reflection. She was propelled forward, right into the path of the taxi, and stumbled trying to leap out of its way. A scream escaped her throat as she felt herself going down. The screech of wheels and the smell of burnt rubber seared into her brain.

Chapter Thirteen

Damn, he hated choices, although this one was easy. Letting the man shadowing Kim melt into the crowd was hard, though. The taxi was inches away when Conor locked an arm around her slender middle and hauled her back to the curb. Her scream, soft and shattered, vibrated in his ear. The taxi careened to a halt at the curb.

Kim collapsed against him. He pulled her close, burying his lips in her hair, wanting to rail at her and kiss her at the same time. What in hell did she think she was doing, taking off solo as if she owned the place?

"You okay?" he asked in the calmest voice he could muster, feeling her body tremble in his arms.

"I think so," she said shakily, "but don't let go."

"I've no intention of letting go. Any cuts, tears, breaks, abrasions?"

"General fright, that's all. Look." She pulled away from him, her pale face taut with the effort to stay in control. "See? Nothing wrong, not even a bumped toe. Conor, someone deliberately pushed me in front of that taxi."

"I saw the whole thing."

"You *saw* the whole thing. You have the damnedest penchant for being on the scene when I'm in trouble. Maybe if you stayed away I'd be a little safer." A deep, slow flush began to suffuse her cheeks. "Don't make me think what I'm thinking."

"Don't. I just rescued you. I don't push people in front of taxis so I can rescue them."

"You'd better have a damn good excuse for being right behind me without letting me know you were there."

A crowd had begun to gather. "What happened?" was asked and answered a dozen times. The taxi driver came running over and in a rabid display of emotion swore on his mother's grave and his father's sickbed that he wasn't at fault, that Kim had stumbled into his path.

"I was pushed," Kim said to him. "You didn't see who pushed me, did you?"

He seemed not to understand her, and at last pointed to Conor. "Him?"

Conor laughed, fished into his pocket for a cruzeiro and slipped it to him. "It's okay. Not your fault. Kim, I saw what happened. I was faced with Hobson's choice, taking after your assailant or rescuing you."

"Hobson's choice, thanks a lot."

He placed a kiss across the bridge of her nose. "I thought maybe you were fishing bait. You leave the hotel in a hurry without looking back, I figure you're either in a catatonic state or planning to trap someone."

She gave him an indignant look. "I was trying to get to Marajó. Oh, nuts," she said, checking her watch. "There's no way I can make that flight."

"Marajó? You were taking off for Marajó without so much as a wave goodbye?"

"I think," she said, giving him a wary smile, "I could use a drink."

"Come on." He took her arm and waved to the taxi driver. "I've got just the place."

They settled for the bar at Castelo Fort, a restaurant overlooking the Pará River, where Conor had spent a cou-

ple of evenings earlier that year with an American doing a
story on the conservancy.

"Were you following me?" Kim asked when they were
settled and had ordered their drinks. "You said you saw
who pushed me."

"When we parted company this afternoon, I didn't go
straight up to my room," Conor said. "After you split, I
decided I could use a cup of coffee. I was paying my tab
when I caught sight of you in the lobby. Just as I was about
to go through the street door after you, someone brushed
past me in a hurry—a small, stocky man with muscular
arms and a bullish head."

"Oh no," Kim groaned. "I was so set on finding a cab
and making the flight, I didn't try basic evasive stuff."

Conor grinned. "You'll get the hang of it."

"At this rate, I'd better."

He resumed his story. "The doorman came by just then
and opened the door. A couple of people entered, and by
the time I hit the street, I was able to catch our friend in the
act of shadowing you. You went out to the curb, and our
muscular friend stopped and spent a couple of seconds
pretending to light a cigarette. Then you changed your
mind and began to hurry down the street. He kept a respectful distance. I followed. I figured it was a simple
shadowing job, nothing more." He reached out and pushed
away a lock of hair that had fallen over her eye. "Kim,
they're planning to knock you out of the game, whoever
they are. They tried telling you to go home. Now they intend to handle your return their own way, in a pine box."

Kim took his hand. "Thanks for saving me. I'm allergic
to pine."

He closed his fingers over hers, reveling in the feel of her
skin. He wanted to grab her by the arm and drag her back
to his hotel room. *Whoa, boy,* he told himself. She was no
plaything. She was vulnerable, and had a certain fragility

due to something in her past she hadn't worked through yet. The last thing he wanted was to stomp on her emotionally.

And he needed all his resources, emotional, cognitive and intellectual, for the upcoming symposium in Geneva.

Everything else in his life would have to be put on hold.

"Thank me for what?" he said, realizing he was on automatic. He didn't want to discuss her appreciation. When they fell into bed together, appreciation would have nothing to do with it. "Thank me for letting some fool follow you and almost kill you?"

She shook her head. "For rescuing me, for trying to talk sense into me and for hanging around for whatever reason. Conor," she went on earnestly, "maybe if I hadn't been so obliging to your friend Tony, he wouldn't have died. I thought by telling him the manuscript was no longer in the States, he'd back off. Instead, Tony's dead, and by indirection I put Edoardo Moriya in danger. Anyway, I found out where Moriya moved to, the town of Souré on Marajó. I was on my way there when all this happened."

Their drinks arrived, beer for Conor and *caipirinha* for Kim. She took a long swallow instead of sipping it, then made a pleased face at its bite.

"Let me put you on a flight back home," he said. "Contacting Moriya is hack work. We'll pick up the phone and call him."

"No phone."

"Send him a telegram."

"Fine. According to Senhora Adami, he may be somewhere on the border near Peru. Send him a telegram and we'll never know whether he got it, or whether our muscular friend is on his way to Peru."

"I'll fly over to Marajó first thing in the morning, find him and deliver your message. If he's in Peru, I'll find that out and alert the gendarmes. You're not going after him."

She thought about it for a while, toying with her drink. "All right," she said, "I'm here to warn Moriya he's in danger, but I've got another mission as well."

Conor wasn't surprised, although he had no doubt chasing after Moriya was her first priority. Benjamin's death, he suspected all along, wasn't solely due to a manuscript that had made any number of rounds four years before. He couldn't get a hook into why Benjamin and Tony had been killed, but more than ancient history was involved.

"I'm a ghostwriter," she said.

"Honorable profession." Conor waited for more.

Kim put her glass to her lips, took a sip, swallowed, closed her eyes for a second, then placed her glass on the table with a decisive bang. "Okay. Okay, here it is. I wrote *Lucky Lady*. I didn't edit it, I wrote it." She leaned back and let out a deep breath. "There, I've done it. I said it out loud. I wrote *Lucky Lady*—you know, like *wrote* from word one? Only don't tell a soul, it's a secret."

It took a few seconds for the information to sink in, then Conor whistled. He should have guessed, and he was lost in admiration, so much so that he had to hold himself back from planting a kiss on her lips then and there. "You just won yourself the Berriman Prize."

"So I did." She did not look particularly happy about it.

"And it's a deep dark secret that no one on the Berriman committee knows."

"Right."

"And you don't think it's fair."

"On the contrary," she said. "I signed a contract, delivered and was paid. I have to admit it would have been nice to crow and frustrating that I couldn't."

"You amaze me," he said. "What you delivered was a literary prize, to someone who certainly didn't deserve it. You didn't tell the police, did you?"

She looked a little shamefaced. "No."

"They'd have you down for killing Benjamin because he wouldn't share the winnings with you."

"That's disgusting. I couldn't tell them! And I didn't kill him . . . or maybe I did. If I'd done a more pedestrian job, he wouldn't have won the prize, and the whole business of Lucky Anne Severance would have stayed buried. No, that's not true. Conor," she said, leaning across the table and fixing serious eyes on him, "I want to take over where Benjamin left off. I intend to find Lucky Anne Severance. She's alive and I know she's in Brazil."

"A needle in a haystack. How do you know she's alive?"

Kim pushed her drink away and grabbed her bag. "Let's rent a car first and I'll explain everything on the way. We may have missed the flight to Marajó, but that shouldn't stop us from nosing around Benjamin's apartment."

AN ENCLAVE OF APARTMENTS had been built close to the Museu Emilio Goeldi, a museum in a tropical setting that focused on the natural history of the Amazon basin. Goeldi Apartments were the latest city experiment in satellite housing, utilizing the bright colors and colonial architecture of Belém, with all the modern conveniences its upper-class tenants required. The complex was built inside a small park filled with lush mango trees and twittering birds Conor identified as palm tanagers.

"In true detective style, we'll park a few houses down," Conor said.

"Good thinking, Sherlock. I'm convinced this will be an exercise in futility, but you never know. I don't think Benjamin had any family in Belém, and as for friends . . ." She shrugged, thinking of Emma Lambert. By the time they parked and stepped out of the car, the sun had set and night had begun its stately arrival.

Benjamin's corner apartment was on the ground floor of an attached concrete building painted turquoise and white. The interior hall was mosaic and stucco and smelled nicely of fresh paint. They decided to check his apartment first, in case someone from his family was there.

"Uh oh," Kim said as they approached. The door, a handsome specimen carved from mahogany, stood wide open. "Déjà vu all over again."

Conor stuck out a hand to prevent her from going farther. "Maybe not," he said in a whisper. "Maybe it's the super, or somebody moving in or out."

They edged closer to the wall, cautiously inching toward the open door. Conor put a finger to his lips. "Listen." But all they could hear was a clock ticking, and from somewhere in the deep recesses of the apartment, water running. They waited a few minutes longer. Suddenly a door opened above them and then slammed shut. Someone came clattering down the stairs. Conor grabbed Kim and quickly shoved her into the apartment, closing the door behind them.

"Maybe that was a big mistake," he said when they found themselves in the foyer of an apartment that had been torn apart. All the lights were on, producing a harsh glare that made everything look like a bright, enlarged, detailed photograph. They stood frozen, waiting and listening. A soft breeze wafted through, but instead of the scent of flowers, something stronger and unpleasant permeated the air.

"Somehow, I don't think Benjamin usually lived like this," Kim said in a fainthearted attempt at humor.

"My guess is somebody tried to redecorate for him." Conor began to make his way toward the sound of running water, past overturned files and bookshelves. "Wonder if they found what they were looking for."

"Wait." Kim grabbed his arm and pointed to the floor. "I think we're in trouble."

"Blood." The word escaped his lips without his being aware of it. There was a stain of blood, then successive drops on the tile floor, the files, the cushions that lay scattered around. "Stay here," he ordered. "Let me handle this."

"No way. I'm right behind you."

The apartment contained two bedrooms, both in disarray, and two bathrooms. The sound of water came from the master bathroom, tiled in pale gray, with pale gray print wallpaper. Gray towels hung neatly on the towel bar.

The blood had a rusty autumn color. The fully clothed body that lay slumped in the shower stall, its blood being systematically washed away, was of a small muscular man, the kind who pumps iron.

"Your shadow, I think," Conor said. "We'd better make tracks. I don't know about the winner of the Berriman Prize, but the head of the Americas Conservancy Brazilian Station had better be miles from here before the police show up."

Kim, ashen-faced, couldn't take her eyes from the body. "I've been such a fool," she said in a controlled tone. "Benjamin told me to send the manuscript to his lawyer. That didn't mean he left it with Moriya. Maybe it was here in Benjamin's apartment the whole time. Gone now, I suppose." She went over to the shower and leaned in to turn it off.

Conor, however, wasn't in the mood for speculation, or for being discovered at a murder scene. He grabbed Kim. "We have to go *now*, Kim. You're in enough trouble already."

A look of determination crossed her face. "This has nothing to do with you. You can leave if you want to." She pulled away and began to go through the victim's pockets.

He could hear the quick, anxious breaths she took and shouldered her aside. "Looking for his ID? Who cares? Okay, move over. If I can't talk you out of it, let me do it."

"I want to know who he is."

Conor felt under the soaking clothes and eased a wallet from the man's back pocket.

Suddenly there it was, the sound Conor had been instinctively waiting for—a loud, insistent knocking on the door and a shout to open up. "Police!"

"Okay, that's it. Let's go."

"Right." Kim grabbed the wallet from him.

"Drop the wallet," Conor said.

"No way!"

"I said drop it!"

"It's covered with my fingerprints. Yours, too."

"There's no time to argue."

He grabbed Kim's arm and hauled her into the bedroom. The only way out was through the window. As they hurried across the room, he heard a key slide into the outside lock. The police weren't going to kick the door down. But then Conor had something new to worry about: the window was shut tight.

Chapter Fourteen

"Meu Deus, O que é isso?"
  "Que embrulhada!"
  "Espera, ha de sangue."
  "Ssh! Eu escuto um ruído."
  "Not the police. Security guards, from the way they talk," Conor said. "We haven't anyplace to go but out the window."

The bedroom window opened more easily than he'd expected. The problem was its screen, which opened outward with a handle stiff from disuse. Conor, trying to manipulate the handle, swore under his breath. The squeak it made with each turn was loud, harsh, unmistakable, the kind that could be heard on the far side of the moon.

"Let me," Kim said in a whisper. "My fingerprints are all over the bathroom, anyway." She began to impatiently shove at the screen, trying to rip it from its hinges. She knew she couldn't afford to be caught with the victim's wallet in her possession. She considered tossing it under the bed, but at that moment the screen gave. With an extra push the space was wide enough for them to crawl through.

In the living room, the intruders were arguing vehemently, but at last they seemed to settle their differences. She could hear them shuffling along the tile floor, following the trail of blood to its source.

"Come on," Conor said, and unceremoniously helped her through the window by giving her a shove from the rear. She landed in a low, thorny bush, the kind meant to deter break-ins. She was hard put to stifle her cry of pain and then the laugh that almost exploded when Conor landed beside her cursing.

The back of the building edged the park. "We'll pick the thorns out later," Conor said, extricating himself and then Kim with no thought to the sound of dress fabric ripping. "We can't work our way to the car directly from here. Let's just ease along the building and then make a dash through the park. We can pose as lovers in case somebody decides to ask us any questions."

"Lovers with torn clothes," Kim said grimly. "Very appropriate."

They'd gone no more than a couple of yards away when someone shouted from inside Benjamin's apartment. "Uh oh," Kim said, "they've found the open screen."

"Let's go," Conor said. "I've got a feeling these guys belong in a Charlie Chaplin movie. They'll run after us first, then they'll find the body."

"I've still got the wallet," Kim said. It was all she could do to stop herself from breaking into a run.

"You've still got the wallet. Clever. What difference does it make if you know his name or not?"

"I'd like to know who nearly killed me," she said huffily. "His name and where he lives, so I can send flowers. Poison ivy."

"Kim, he's dead."

"Let's just keep walking, shall we?"

A few apartments down, the shrubbery gave way to a path lined with big-leafed anthurium in full flower, the intense, shiny red petals bright as nail polish even in the near dusk. Back at Benjamin's bedroom windows, uniformed guards were prowling the bushes, guns drawn.

"Easy now," Conor said. He draped his arm casually across Kim's shoulder. Together they sauntered onto the path as though they were lovers out for a stroll. "Hey," he said, once they were safely out of earshot, "I could get used to this."

So could she, Kim thought. Her adrenaline, on high ever since they had entered Benjamin's apartment, was now on overload. There was really no reason for the thrilling feeling. A sense of being right in the center of her life with the most exciting man she'd ever met must account for it. Gripping a dead man's wallet in her hand couldn't.

They forced themselves to stroll casually along the path, which snaked in a leisurely fashion toward an alleyway leading out front.

"Home free," Conor said once they'd hit the alley and broken into a run. "There's a garbage can. Get rid of that wallet."

"If I have to," Kim said, "but not quite yet."

Conor threw her an admiring glance when she least expected it. "You've got guts."

"I don't think it's guts. I'm all wound up."

"Same thing."

Their car was where they'd left it, with a couple of embellishments—kids no more than thirteen years old sitting on the hood smoking cigarettes.

"Scram," Conor said.

The kids were slow in obeying, taking a few extra puffs before sauntering off.

"All we needed was a noisy confrontation," Kim said.

"Let's go." Conor unlocked the door and they scrambled inside as a police car tore down the road, squealing to a halt in front of Benjamin's apartment house. "Easy now. You and I haven't seen a thing." A couple of policemen jumped out and ran for the front door. Conor started the engine and backed carefully out of their parking spot. They rolled slowly down the street, observing every traffic rule and a few not in the codebook.

Night had fallen completely by time they were on the road heading back to the hotel. "Light, please," Kim said, opening the wallet. "Okay," she said, once Conor had switched on the overhead light, "I admit I feel guilty doing this."

"You should. The man's dead. Who he is doesn't matter anymore. At least to you and me."

"He tried to kill me. *If* I can believe you." She found a thick wad of cruzeiros in the wallet and a driver's license with a picture of the deceased and his name.

"All right," Conor said, keeping his eye on the road. "Anyone we know?"

"We don't actually *know* him," Kim said tightly. "We've heard of him, though." She'd opened a can of worms back in New York, and this was the result—a dead man's wallet in her hand.

"Any reason for keeping the name from me?"

Kim looked sharply at him. "You said he was the man who followed me out of the hotel."

"He was."

"Why would Edoardo Moriya try to shove me in front of a taxi?"

"What?" He reached over, grabbed the license and held it up to the light. "I'll be a howler monkey's uncle. Well, we won't have to look for him any longer to tell him he's in danger."

"No," Kim said. "He isn't in danger anymore." She examined the address and was puzzled to find it the same. "Nice," she said. "Either Moriya never bothered to change the address on his license, or he still lives—*lived*—in La Vicente. Despite the fact that he discontinued phone service. Senhora Adami was putting us on." She went quickly through the photographs in the wallet. "Okay, here's the answer." She slipped out a photograph of a young woman and handed it to Conor. "The *senhora* is his daughter. Problem solved. Concerning his telephone number, he probably found it a lot more convenient to relist it in his daughter's name. That phone call she made came straight from him. Only an idiot would have bought it. And I'm the idiot. Moriya didn't want to be found, and he figured on sending me on a wild-goose chase. As Benjamin's lawyer, he was some piece of goods."

"Speculation," Conor said. "We don't know who wants what in this game. If the manuscript was all they were looking for, my guess is they have it. Moriya outlived his usefulness for someone. End of manuscript, end of Moriya, end of game."

"Meaning DeeDee Dalrymple has the manuscript. Now I can get on with my search for Lucky Anne."

"You don't know what DeeDee has or doesn't have. And just how do you intend to go about your search for Lucky Anne?"

"Start at the scene of the fire, the Dalrymple ranch on Marajó. And doublecheck to find out if Moriya really moved there."

"What difference does it make, Kim? The man's dead."

"Maybe no difference. Maybe he has family there, though, and maybe they'll be a little more obliging than his daughter, like telling us what he was up to, or about Lucky Anne."

"Forget it. You were right the first time. It's a wild-goose chase. They'll be talking to the police, if 'they' even exist."

"You're right. But we're still going to Marajó, and I'll still ask."

Kim leaned her head against the backrest and let the city roll past. The day had been a long, strange one, but she was reluctant to see it end. Too many fascinating loose ends needed tying up.

"Let's head over to the docks," Conor said. "I'll spring for dinner."

"That sounds good. I suppose you're due back at the conservancy station," she added after a moment.

"They've been expecting me for the last week," Conor answered in a neutral voice.

"You've spent enough time chasing after will-o'-the-wisps."

"That have nothing to do with the job I'm being paid handsomely for."

She ought to send Sidney Blackfoot a postcard. He was paying *her* handsomely to edit a book in New York City. She had no idea when she'd get back. They drove on for a while in silence, through Cidade Velho, the old part of town. They passed, on a broad mosaic boulevard shaded by mango trees, pastel-hued houses built in colonial times, and fine French Belle Époque mansions, remnants of the Amazon rubber boom. As much as Belém might carve itself into the jungle, its girth would always be held in check by the jungle and the Pará River.

Kim had been only six years old when her father was stationed as cultural attaché in Belém. She'd often gone with her mother on shopping expeditions to Ver-O-Pêso market, wide-eyed at the variety of goods it offered. At that age, she'd been interested in curiosities, not architecture.

"What are you thinking of?" Conor asked.

"How pretty everything seems. Nostalgia for the past."

And that she would never see Conor again. He'd return to Manaus, and she'd be on her way to...wherever. Home, eventually. Home, where she'd been quite happy, without realizing what the word meant. And she a prizewinning author. With Benjamin dead, she wondered if she couldn't crow a bit about the Berriman Prize to her parents.

"When does the first flight leave for Marajó?" Conor asked.

"I'll have to check."

"When we get back to the hotel, I'll put the wallet into an envelope and address it to the Adamis. They should know what to do with it. And you, my friend, will get a good night's sleep. I'll put a call through to Manaus and weave a tale about unfortunate delays. Then I'll call the airport and charter us a plane to the island."

She felt her heart give an extra blip. "You can't give up on a really good chase, is that what you mean?"

Conor suddenly pulled over to the curb and stopped. "I mean," he said, turning to her and reaching for her hands, "I have no intention of sitting it out in Manaus wondering what in hell you're up to."

Happiness, she realized, was so brittle she didn't dare embrace it. "Is that your promise to DeeDee Dalrymple?" she asked, and then felt the heat stain her cheeks when she saw a look of anger and disappointment cross his face. He released her hands, reached out to engage the engine, but did nothing more than shake his head.

"You talk too much," he said, turning again and pulling her into his arms. His kiss, which held a promise in its short intensity, told her DeeDee was the last person on his mind.

She let the kiss happen, sliding her arms around his neck. In another moment he released her and quickly put the car in gear. "Maybe you'd better go on talking," he said in a low, husky voice.

"Right," she said. "Where were we?"

Ilha do Marajó

THE ROAD THEY TOOK in their hired Jeep from the colorful town of Souré to the Dalrymple *fazenda* was paved for most of the way. The *region do campos* had been left by ranchers in its rich, natural state. The morning was bright and sunny, cooled, like Belém, by the trade winds. They figured the drive to the ranch, through a flat, golden savanna broken by occasional lagoons, ponds and low stands of mangrove forest on the edge of the river, would take a couple of hours.

"Once in a while," Conor observed when they were well into their journey, "the Dalrymples do things right. They haven't helped junk Marajó. But then I suppose they can't. During the rainy season much of the savanna is under water. Accounting for the prevalence of water buffalo."

"Water buffalo." Kim laughed. The economy on the island was partially fueled by its huge water buffalo population, and even in Souré the curved-horned animals were allowed to roam the streets like sacred cows were in India. "Anyway, I suppose there are local preservation laws," Kim said. "This is a tight, secretive island, from everything I've heard. They certainly don't encourage visitors, or at least they don't make it easy for them to get here."

"That shouldn't have worried Anthony Dalrymple."

Conor's unexpected remark about the late chairman of the board amazed her. "I'm surprised you're so judgmental about your benefactors," she said. "Dead or alive."

"Open-eyed, realistic. As long as I've known them, they've talked long and hard about saving the environment. I don't try to look behind the meanings of words. Anyway, not when I'm the indirect recipient of their largess to the Americas Conservancy."

Kim glanced over at him. From the hard set of his lips, she might have been hearing things. "I'm beginning to detect all sorts of interesting messages here."

"Don't," he said tersely.

The abrupt silence that followed was broken by an unmistakable churning sound overhead that signaled a helicopter approaching from the west.

"Okay," Kim said, watching it idly as it headed toward Souré, "my lips are sealed."

His laugh was brief, but the sudden tension that had developed was broken. "Hey, don't seal them too much. I think I'm developing a fondness for your lips."

But Kim knew she had just been shut out of a part of his life and told to mind her own business. Fine. She would. No problem. And no trying to find out what made Conor Stark tick. The helicopter became smaller and smaller and at last was no larger than one of the flamingos that flew over the savanna.

They had inquired in Souré after Edoardo Moriya and had discovered he was unknown on the island. In spite of its size, not much happened on Marajó that wasn't common gossip in Souré. Since the news of his death hadn't been deemed of sufficient interest to make it into the media, the lawyer might not have existed.

All they could do was visit the site of a long-ago fire, evidence of which would have been obliterated by rain or the inevitable tropical growth that smothered most of the island, ask some judicious questions of anyone around and return to Belém. Conor would go his way and she'd go hers, as soon as she figured out where she wanted to go.

"After this turn," Conor said, "we end up at the border of the Dalrymple *fazenda*."

"Border? Sounds like a small country."

"It is."

Kim drew her lips together. "Of course, I should have known. You've been here before."

"That's right. I have. And why didn't I tell you? You never asked."

"I didn't ask because I figured you'd tell me."

"Impasse, Kim. We're arguing like a couple of old married folks."

"I've been married, and sometimes you don't argue, things just fall apart anyway."

He reached out and covered her hand briefly. "I wish you were over this Lucky Anne business so I could learn a little more about you."

"Obviously there are areas of our lives we'd better leave unexamined."

He was silent for a long moment, then said, "Kim," as though the mere sound of her name could break down the wall between them. After another moment, he added, "Maybe you're right."

She let a beat or two go by. "Well, what do you know about the fire that you haven't bothered telling me?"

"Nothing. I never went looking for information. Why would I? I was only on the island once, three or four years ago. Before Benjamin's manuscript came to my attention, come to think of it. I came over to the island at the invitation of a conservation group in Belém. Anthony Dalrymple held the meeting at the ranch. Period. End of visit."

"It's still a working ranch, then. I somehow figured it was abandoned."

"They raise local stock—water buffalo, and cattle with zebu or Brahma blood. Anthony Dalrymple may have walked away from the scene of Lucky Anne's death, but he certainly wouldn't have abandoned an operation as healthy as this one."

The road narrowed. Sleek tan cattle and hairless water buffalo grazed on either side. Mango and palm trees lined the road. Fields were liberally sprinkled with ponds and stands of forest.

"Here it is, Rancho Dalrymple." He turned in at an elaborate black iron gate, which had been left open.

The road led in a straight line a half mile long to a compound of low buildings roofed with red tile and shaded by umbrella trees. The Jeep no sooner came to a standstill near the front entrance of the main house when a couple of men on horses rounded the building and headed toward them. Kim and Conor learned quickly that the manager wasn't on the premises and that there was no one else around who could give them permission to look over the grounds.

Conor kept the conversation going for a while longer before shrugging. With a friendly wave of his hand he backed the Jeep around. "Vaqueros," he told Kim once they were out of earshot, "and unfriendly ones at that."

"You gave in mighty easily," Kim said, wondering at his behavior. She suspected he wanted to see the site of the fire as much as she did.

"They wouldn't budge, so why waste time? We passed an arroyo a mile before we hit the ranch road. I figure there must be a road leading out from it. We'll park and take our chances on foot. Game?"

"These shoes were made for walking."

"As a matter of fact, keep your shoes *and* your socks on. I forgot about a rather unfriendly little parasite, *bicho de pé.*"

"Foot parasite. I remember my mother going on about it when I was a kid."

They drew into the arroyo near a small pond with a couple of cattle grazing nearby. "I don't think our friends at the ranch expect us to go exploring on our own," Conor said.

"I'm not so sure," Kim told him. "They were a little too unfriendly. I think the garage in Souré has a direct linkup with the Dalrymples, and maybe everybody else on the island. We're the intruders. They'll know exactly when to expect us back in Souré."

"Listen, Kim, don't go pessimistic on me." He grasped her shoulders and scrutinized her solemnly. "If I thought you were in danger from the Dalrymples or anybody else, we wouldn't be here. We're following Lucky Anne's trail. Don't mix apples, pears and paranoia." He held her for another moment, then drew away. "Come on, the road's overgrown a bit, but it would take more than a couple of lifetimes to wipe it out completely. We can't be seen, but keep down anyway," Conor said. "I don't know where those two vaqueros rode off to or how many others are around."

Kim let Conor lead. They picked their way along a trail that wound through thick weeds and tall grass. A half hour later, they discovered the ruins of an old house and nearby stables. As they came close, a flock of birds rose frantically into the air, and after the initial rush, settled in the old mango trees that grew around the house, chirping furiously at the intruders.

"This is it," Kim said a little breathlessly.

Remarkably, the foundation and some of the stucco walls were still intact and remained uncommonly free of tangled vines that should have covered them with green and grasping fingers. Blackened beams, fallen and covered by growth, had not sufficiently rotted away to hide the *vila*'s grisly history. Kim, remaining at a respectful distance, wondered whether nature herself wanted the place as a shrine.

"Nothing could have survived the fire," she remarked at last in a hushed voice. She thought of Lucky Anne—*her* Lucky Anne, with the dark and mesmerizing eyes. The way she held life in her hands, and her love for Anthony Dalrymple. Kim felt a loss so complete it weakened her knees. "Standing here, I'm beginning to understand Benjamin's obsession with his aunt. And his desperate wish that she'd somehow escaped the fire."

Conor came over and put his arm across her shoulder. "You all right?"

"I think so."

"One person died in the fire," Conor mused. "That meant everyone else was outside of the house and the stables, either through luck or because they'd been forewarned."

"Everyone but Lucky Anne. According to what Benjamin learned, her body was supposedly found near the stables. The horses escaped the fire, which meant the first thing she probably did was free them, losing her life because of it. Or whoever set the fire had freed them, and Lucky Anne died trying to rescue horses that weren't there."

"And she didn't have to worry about her son, because he was with his father in New York."

"In New York on an extended visit."

"And that's the sanest reason to believe it was Lucky Anne who died in the fire. If the woman were alive afterward, why didn't she try to see her son, take him back, go to court if she had to? Remember," Conor said, "I knew Tony well. As far as he was concerned, his mother did die in the fire. And incidentally, he knew and didn't seem to be bothered that he was born out of wedlock."

"Hey, nowadays it's the fashion. Anyway, we'll learn why she abandoned him when we finally meet up with her," Kim said. "She had her reasons, believe me. The fact that her husband was a colossal SOB was one of them. *Lucky Lady* introduced me to a pretty sensational woman," she added, and then went on somewhat ruefully, "I suppose I always encouraged Benjamin to keep looking for her. But seeing this . . . this *devastation,* I don't know."

"Benjamin must have scoured the area pretty well," Conor said.

"So you think I'm crazy to come here."

"I didn't say that, Kim. We all have obsessions of a sort. If we don't follow through, the bad guys might take over completely." He looked around. "My guess is the locals picked through the ruins pretty thoroughly and carted away anything usable. But let's check it anyway. What was buried by ash and rubble more than a quarter century ago might be pushed to the surface again by rain or a slight shift in the earth." He scraped at the soil with his boot. "Suppose I make a survey of the rear. You start at the front."

"If this is the front."

He laughed and lifted her chin, placing a light kiss on her lips. "As long as you keep your sense of humor, all's right with the world."

Kim remained rooted to the spot for a few minutes more, while Conor made his way to the back of the *vila*. The sun was high, and the breeze had died down. The place was suddenly dead silent and spooky, as though even the insects had gone to sleep. She had to drag herself over to the foundation. Slate steps and what must have been a slate porch were still intact, although the floor of the living quarters had collapsed. She began to poke through the weeds, disturbing an ants' nest. A friendly bee decided her ear was a rose and for a while buzzed delicately around her. As she worked her way through the ruins, discovering only shards of glass and blackened shapes of no discernible origin, she sensed a ghostly aura, as though Anne Severance's spirit still walked there.

"Are you here?" she asked in a hushed voice, then drew her finger to her lips. No, Lucky Anne was *alive*. Kim was communing with mosquitoes and butterflies and bees, that was all. She came down off the porch and headed toward what seemed like a fallen beam, half-hidden in the grass, wondering if anything had been taken with it when it came down. As she moved closer, she recognized the unmistakable markings of a boa constrictor. The scream died in her throat as she tore around the house.

"Oh good, Kim, I was just about to come get you." Conor motioned to a pile of rubble. "May be worth picking through."

"Boa constrictor!" she managed. "Scared the living daylights out of me!"

"That's right, I forgot," Conor said matter-of-factly. "Island's loaded with them. Don't worry, they don't like you any more than you like them."

"Thanks for your words of comfort."

"Shards," Conor said. "What we need here is an archaeologist."

"One interested in life on a ranch in ancient Brazil thirty or so years ago." She picked up a stick and began sifting through broken glass and pieces of clay. "Someone's been through this stuff, which accounts for its being in one spot. Benjamin, maybe."

Conor got down on his haunches and reached for a piece of clay, then another. "Whoever he, she, they were, they didn't know ancient Indian pottery. Actually, Marajó once had an Indian population renowned for its ceramics."

"Inca," Kim said, as he laid some small red pieces on the ground and began piecing them together.

"You're right. It's certainly not local. Most of that is in Belém, anyway. This is Chimu."

"That's getting down to details. How do you know it's Chimu?"

"Anthony Dalrymple collected pre-Colombian art, particularly Inca. He asked me to keep my eye open for good pieces."

"For sale or swindle, I suppose. You're not supposed to take ancient works out of the country."

"I doubt he'd find that a problem," Conor said with the same irony of tone he had employed earlier. He stood up and gazed with admiration at the small blackened statue he had pieced together. "Only the head's missing," he said. "A bird form, that's certain. What do you think? If it's Chimu, we ought to take the remains with us, hand it over to the Goeldi Museum in Belém."

Kim stared at the small, headless bird lying on its side, its shape somehow familiar. Then she remembered the amulet around Benjamin's neck when he'd lain dead in her garden, a fanciful bird she'd thought was Inca in origin. Tony Dalrymple had possessed an identical piece. The sculpture lying before them was an exact replica.

Chapter Fifteen

"Well, that was a wasted trip," Kim said, once they were in the Jeep heading back to Souré for their flight to the mainland. "We have a broken statue for the Goeldi Museum that we liberated from the Dalrymple ranch, and no leads to Lucky Anne."

"What did you expect to find?" Conor asked. "A letter along with a map telling you where she is?"

"Yes, I think that's what I expected to find. Or maybe a bunch of arrows pointing us in the right direction. *Follow the red arrows to Lucky Anne*—something like that."

"Chimu," Conor said. "What does that bring to mind?"

"Ancient history. Beautiful designs. No arrows. And both Benjamin and Tony owned similar amulets from a culture that died out a long time ago."

"Tony," he pointed out, "lived on the *fazenda* as a child. Benjamin may have visited Lucky Anne at the same time."

"Maybe," Kim said, "but did you ever see Tony wear the amulet before?"

Conor, clearly stymied, shook his head.

"The truth is," Kim went on, "that first sight of the broken statue absolutely chilled me."

"Chimu today is a small, contested piece of land on the border between Peru and Brazil," Conor told her. "Both countries lay claim to it but so far the only posturing they've done is to issue warlike bulletins every generation or so. Chimu is so inconsequential and remote I doubt even *National Geographic* has covered it."

"You mean it's an independent country, not aligned with either Peru or Brazil?"

"That's how the maps read," Conor said.

"I never heard of it."

"Where'd you go to school, anyway?"

"Brazil. I suppose Chimu's a real backwater, with aborigines and poison spears," she added offhandedly. The conversation was getting them nowhere. Something far more interesting occurred to her that had nothing to do with backwaters or Chimu jewelry or aborigines with spears. Something straight out of *Lucky Lady.*

"From what I've heard, which isn't much, its denizens resemble Inca Indians," Conor said.

"Forget Chimu. Look, we'll get to Souré at about four o'clock," Kim said, her enthusiasm building with each word. "Our flight to Belém is scheduled for five. Let's see what the local registry has to say about a marriage that took place between a certain Anne Severance and a certain Anthony Dalrymple."

"That, my dear, is whistling in the wind."

"In the original manuscript Benjamin hypothesized that Anthony Dalrymple married Lucky Anne when she became pregnant. I scotched the notion to save him from a lawsuit."

"Kim, the first thing Benjamin would have done was check the marriage registry in Souré."

"But he didn't. I asked him. He said he wasn't into chasing down the obvious. Anthony Dalrymple was far too powerful. Benjamin was convinced that his aunt was in danger precisely because they'd been married. Apparently Dalrymple had never heard of the word divorce. Benjamin figured every legal trace of the marriage would have been destroyed.''

"Bad detective work," Conor said. "Let's do what he never bothered to do."

"SORRY, *SENHORINA*, it's been a wasted trip to Souré, I'm afraid." The town clerk, a young man in his twenties with a bright, interested look on his face, reached for his *cafezhino* and took a sip. Then he closed the registry with a flourish. Events more than thirty years old were obviously ancient history to him, and although he seemed to want to help, he apparently didn't know how.

"One other question," Conor said. "Do you have a record of the birth of Anthony Dalrymple, Jr.?" He gave him the year of Tony's birth.

"Wonderful!" Kim said while the clerk went through his records. "I bet Benjamin never thought of that one. If he's listed as a Dalrymple, we have proof."

"Sorry," the clerk said, closing the book.

"Try Severance," Conor said, spelling the name for him. "Mother's name Anne." The clerk took another sip of his coffee and began to go through the records again.

He shook his head.

"Well, thanks anyway," Kim said disappointedly. Benjamin was right, after all. Anthony Dalrymple had covered his tracks well.

As they turned to leave, the clerk spoke up. "Too bad my mother isn't alive to talk about the celebration, though."

Kim turned slowly. "What celebration?"

"That marriage. My mother was single then, working as a cook in the Dalrymple household. They had to roast whole cows for the celebration, dozens of them. Everyone came."

Kim exchanged a glance with Conor, then came back to the counter slowly, as though she were walking on eggs. "Who'd he marry?"

The clerk shrugged. They were back in the annals of ancient history. "That one, I suppose. The one who died in the fire. My mother loved her. Tears came to her eyes when she talked about her. Beautiful woman, she said, and kind."

The tears that started up behind Kim's own eyes had no business being there. How can you cry for someone you never knew and whose very personality, in fact, had been filtered through one man's imagination? "You know for a fact that it was a marriage celebration," she stated.

An uncertain shift in his expression was followed by another shrug. "I think so, *senhorina,* but I only heard my mother's story. Too bad you weren't here earlier today. Senhora Dalrymple was at the *fazenda.* I know because my brother works at the airfield."

"Senhora Dalrymple?" Conor gripped the counter, his knuckles white with the effort. "I thought you said she had died in a fire."

"You know, the one from New York."

"Ah, I see. But *this* Senhora Dalrymple is not here anymore."

The clerk shook his head, beginning to lose interest in the conversation.

"It was the helicopter we saw," Kim said, once they were back in the Jeep heading for the airport. "What's the current Mrs. Dalrymple doing in Brazil?"

"She owns half of it," Conor said dryly.

CONOR STARK LAY in his room at the Hilton Hotel. The television set was on. A replay of a soccer game that had taken place in Italy did not engage his attention. Kim Killian did. They had come back from Marajó to a sudden downpour and had arrived at the hotel soaking wet. They'd agreed to meet in the lobby at seven o'clock, dried out and ready for dinner.

Trying to work out the logistics of the evening ahead, Conor found himself paying special attention to possible endings. He was exploring new territory, an uninhabited jungle situated around the regions of his heart. The trouble was, these last few years his fixation on nailing the Dalrymple empire had taken up all his emotional strength. Now, when he was so close to his goal, he couldn't afford distractions, he told himself for the hundredth time, not even one as desirable as Kim. He did not want to mix taking her to bed with being unable to get her out of his mind.

He had enjoyed any number of women in his life without becoming romantically involved. He hoped any number of them had enjoyed him equally. Enjoyment without love, he was beginning to understand, had been a rollercoaster ride, fun while it lasted and out of mind when it was over. He was possibly entering a profound world he'd never been in before and the thought scared him.

Kim, he suspected, was holding back, too. She'd been hurt once. It was clear the scars hadn't healed.

He wanted to know everything about her, about the man she'd married and how much she had loved him, and whether Conor could compete with his memory. How she'd looked as a kid, as a teenager; hell, even how she'd looked in her wedding dress, on her wedding night.

The phone jangled. Kim, he figured, smiling and hitting the sound button on the television set. "Can't keep away from me, can you?" he said at once into the receiver.

"That's a fine way to greet me. I've had a devil of a time finding you, in fact."

"DeeDee." Smile erased, he stared at the soundless soccer game, a bunch of bare-legged men crashing into each other as they chased a leather ball. He felt like the ball.

"Meet me for drinks in the bar," she said curtly. "In ten minutes."

"What bar?" His mind raced. Would she know Kim was registered at the same hotel? Damn, she obviously had the manuscript; what more did she want?

"The hotel bar, Conor. You sound sleepy."

"I'm tied up this evening, DeeDee."

"Business or pleasure? Never mind, I thought you were supposed to be in Manaus."

"Hey, if I wanted to punch a time clock, I'd be sitting in a bank in New York, crunching numbers. Listen, I told you I was busy. Ask Joe Turbon to buy you a drink," he added, referring to her pilot, the man he figured was her bodyguard, and possibly a lot more.

"I'll see you in ten minutes." She hung up.

Maybe he'd gone a bit far. Keep the lady happy until the propitious time, he thought. All the better to catch her unaware. He rang Kim's room, rehearsing what he would say to her.

"It's not even six-thirty," Kim said as soon as she picked up the receiver. "Gimme a break."

To Conor she seemed elated, as though she had just been laughing or was really pleased about something. Spending the evening with him?

"I'm afraid I'm going to give you a big break, Kim. Can we put dinner off until eight?"

There was a slight hesitation, then, "Sure. Of course. Frankly, I could use a nap, and anyway I just washed my hair, and I think maybe if I—"

"Kim, she's here. She wants to see me."

"She?" Another hesitation. He could almost hear the wheels turning. "You mean DeeDee. What's she doing here?"

"Look, we know she was on Marajó. Her being in Belém shouldn't come as any surprise."

"I'm not surprised at all, Conor."

"The lady's a moneybags," he said patiently. "I'd treat any moneybags the same way—meet 'em for a drink and smile a lot, hand out."

"How much did you say a membership in the Americas Conservancy costs? Maybe I should join forthwith."

Conor did not waste time letting her remark get to him. Kim was angry enough for the two of them. In fact, he was just as pleased over her anger as he'd been a minute earlier over the elation in her voice. "It's a lot more complicated than that," he said. "I agreed to meet her. It's a good opportunity to find out what she knows about the manuscript."

"Okay," she said, caving in almost too quickly. "As a matter of fact, knowing the woman—and I don't—my guess is she'll haul you out to dinner. I really don't want to sit here waiting for you and then get an apologetic phone call canceling."

"That won't happen," Conor said. "I'll pick you up at your door at eight on the button. You and I are going out on the town and we're leaving everything behind us— DeeDee, Lucky Anne, marriage certificates and stolen shards of Chimu pottery. Got that?"

"I'm off to the marriage registry first thing tomorrow morning. If you're up and want to come along, just let me know. Bye."

The disconnection was abrupt. He thought about calling her back, but knew that DeeDee wouldn't let him go so easily. Kim was giving him a certain amount of breathing space and he decided he'd take it.

DeeDee, of course, kept him waiting twenty minutes. He sat in a corner banquette nursing a *caipirinha,* light on the *cachaca* liqueur, figuring DeeDee would come in charging. He needed a clear head. The crowded bar, called the Bahia Room, was a cozy imitation of a beachfront café complete with lush palms in the corners, and candles on each table in ceramic pineapples. A type of samba music called *pagode* played softly in the background.

"New York on the phone," DeeDee said when she arrived. "The business about Tony's funeral next week—I'm keeping it very private. No flowers, no guests—all donations to the Americas Conservancy." She paused, as though expecting congratulations for her thoughtfulness. Conor had none to give her.

She wore a pale silk dress cut to reveal her shapely legs. She looked beautiful, but her expression, as usual, was without animation or humor. She sat down next to him on the banquette, but not before placing a kiss full on his lips. "Just a smidgen of lipstick," she said in a girlish voice and proceeded to wipe his lips with her napkin. "I've heard about a new restaurant right here on Avenida Vargas with incredible fish."

Piranha, he thought. Show them a little blood and they'll eat you alive.

"I've made a reservation for seven-thirty—a bit early but I figured we'd go dancing afterward."

Conor took in a deep breath to stay his tongue, and put his drink down. "If you'll excuse me a moment, DeeDee."

She smiled. "Order me a Scotch."

He nodded, and on the way out ordered a Scotch for the lady. Then he went into the hotel lobby and dialed Kim's room.

"Yes?"

She hadn't gone out to dinner. He thought of sending champagne and caviar up to her. "Checking in. The lady wants dinner and dancing. Kim, I'm sorry. I'll make it up to you."

"Have a nice day."

The receiver clicked in his ear. Damn, he was coming out at the bad end of this business. She'd have no reason to trust him, unless he trusted her. They'd talk, he promised himself. They'd talk. He ordered steak and wine to be sent to her room. When the time came for champagne and caviar, he wanted to be on the menu, as well.

When he came back to the bar, DeeDee was halfway through her drink. "Evening's yours, DeeDee, on one condition."

She leaned her chin on her hand, a flirtatious glint in her eye. "And what's that?"

"Answer a question. What in hell are you doing in Brazil?"

She gave him a slow smile. "Chasing after you."

"If I believed that, I wouldn't ask you the next question."

"Oh, believe it," she said. "But go ahead, I'm in a delicious mood. Ask your question anyway."

"Do you have the original *Lucky Lady* manuscript in your possession?"

She scrutinized him intensely, her expression shrewd. "That's no thanks to you and your little pal."

He ignored the remark. "Did you learn anything new?"

"The manuscript had to be destroyed. It was a pack of lies. With Benjamin Soares dead, who knows what might have happened if somebody else came into its possession? And, Conor, my boy, I'm beginning to believe that Anne Severance is still alive. I think both you and your friend hold the same opinion."

"Anne Severance died in a fire thirty years ago," he said evenly, still not taking his eyes from hers.

"She should have stayed that way."

"She did."

"Benjamin Soares didn't think so."

"Did you have anything to do with his death, DeeDee?"

She gave a high-pitched laugh. Several patrons nearby turned to stare at her. "You seriously believe I set him up, or do you think I pulled the trigger myself?" Her eyes didn't leave his. When he failed to answer her question, she said, "Order me another Scotch and soda."

He signaled the waiter. "And if she is alive?" he asked.

She shrugged. "Nothing. It may be she's lying in a hospital somewhere non compos mentis. I think I ought to know, that's all. Maybe she needs money, help. After all, she's Tony's natural mother. The news media gets hold of it and I'm suddenly the Wicked Witch of the West."

Conor hid his smile behind his glass. "Well, if we hear anything, you'll be the first to know."

"I'd like to meet Kim Killian," she said. "But on second thought, it's not a good idea. You might give her a message from me, however."

"I'm not in the habit of passing on messages to virtual strangers, which Kim Killian is," he said.

She gave him a skeptical smile as she put a hand over his. "Tell her that Anne Severance is none of her business. Tell her that she ought to go back to New York. Tell her New York is a lot safer for her than Brazil. Shall we go out to dinner now?"

"HAVE A NICE NIGHT?" Kim asked in her brightest tone the moment Conor came up to her in the lobby the next morning. She had decided, during a sleepless night, that she had reacted badly. Dalrymple funds supported the Americas Conservancy. Saving the Amazon from overexploitation was certainly more important to her than having a romantic night on the town with a sexy, dangerous, fascinating man.

Conor looked tired. He hadn't shaved, and from the way he took her arm, he clearly wanted them to get out of the hotel fast. "You must have had some night," she said.

He grunted. "The lady took me to the most expensive restaurant in town, and stiffed me for the bill."

"Stiffed you?" Kim let him push her toward the door, which made her conclude that DeeDee was also registered at the hotel. "I thought a gentleman is supposed to pay for the lady."

"She's no lady. I go by the new rules. You pick the restaurant, you pay the tab."

"In other words, you still don't know if she has the manuscript. Otherwise, why the bad mood? It can't have anything to do with an overpriced dinner with the world's richest woman."

Conor stepped out into the street to hail a cab, although the doorman got there first and with a flourish, handed them in.

"Town hall," Kim directed the driver. "Think we're being followed?" she asked Conor. "You're being pretty touchy. You even wanted to beat the doorman to the taxi. He has a living to make, too, you know."

Conor shook his head. "Kim, slow down. If I didn't know you better, I'd think you were wired. I'm in a foul mood because I hurt you last night. As for what I learned, DeeDee has the manuscript. She's also convinced that Lucky Anne is alive. She knows you're in town and that you and I have been running around together. She doesn't think you know where Lucky Anne is, because if you did, you'd be there. And you know what you should do, don't you?"

Thoroughly chastened, Kim shook her head.

"If you got on the plane and went home, she'd back off." He leaned forward and told the driver to go out to the Goeldi Museum.

"If she has a tail on us," he explained to Kim, "we can shake him better if we go to the museum first. Incidentally, I know the curator of Indian artifacts. He's a pretty well-informed character and knows how to keep his mouth shut."

The pretty well-informed character at the Goeldi confirmed the provenance of the shards. Old, apparently; almost certainly ancient Chimu in design. He also filled them in on Chimu, whose inhabitants claimed to be descendants of peoples of the high Andes. Their migration records, however, were lost in history. Since they were not considered true native aborigines of the Amazon, the museum had no exhibits on life in contemporary Chimu.

The curator accepted the shards with gratitude and did not question too closely how Conor and Kim had come into their possession.

They had no luck checking the registry at the town hall, either. Records, the clerk told them with a straight face, had been destroyed in a flood more than a quarter century before. That would include birth and marriage records. If he was lying, they had no way of proving it.

They had come up empty. The only new information they had was about a small country on the border of Peru.

"Peru," Kim said as they headed back to the Hilton. "Border of. That mean anything else to you?"

"It's a dead end."

"You're not thinking, Conor. It's those late nights you've been keeping. Both Senhora Adami and the office renting agent told us Edoardo Moriya was going to the border of Peru, ostensibly for a vacation. I bet he was in Chimu."

"Perhaps," Conor said. "And perhaps he learned something in Chimu that left him dead in his dead client's apartment in Belém."

"Well," Kim said in a practical manner, "Chimu it is, then. I wonder how you get there from here."

"*You* don't. Have you forgotten DeeDee's message?"

"No, but I'm not impressed with her threats. If she wanted to see the end of me, I'm sure she'd have managed it by now. At this point, she figures we both have the same information. She certainly doesn't want me to find Lucky Anne before she does. But if I keep looking and do find her, DeeDee will be well rewarded for her patience. And,'' she added with a grin, ''I bet she hasn't figured out that Chimu's the next step yet.''

"Maybe," Conor said. "My guess is that there's a helicopter landing pad in Chimu, even if it's the tail end of nowhere. Though most Amazonian tribes live, move and trade on the river, the quickest way in and out for anyone wanting to do business with the locals is by air. We'll go to Manaus first—"

"We?" Kim asked, not at all surprised.

Chapter Sixteen

The walls of the dimly lit room melted inward, reflecting only the slats of light squeezing in through shuttered windows. The ceiling fan did nothing to alleviate the scorching heat. An overhead bulb was of such low wattage that the faces of the four people sitting around the table were barely discernible. Air-conditioned office towers and carpeted floors were more to their taste, but secrecy required the occasional meeting in more questionable parts of Brasília. The seat of government had its share.

A gray-suited man with washed-out blue eyes moved thin lips over small, even teeth. "They're preparing for the Feast of the Assumption, but the natives of Chimu still worship the mountain like their ancestors did." He gave the semblance of a smile. "They no longer have any idea why, but every year they trek to the highest point in Chimu, a hill no more than twenty meters high, ten miles out of Michimu. There they perform the ritual killing of a goat." He moved his finger along his throat. "In the old days, their victims weren't quite so innocent or expendable. This time..." He stopped and glanced at his three companions. "This time we'll oblige them with a human sacrifice."

Raf Mello shuddered at the words. The flesh around his mouth grew tight. "No!" His reaction was a mistake. He retreated into clichés, shaking his head wildly. "I'm a religious man. It's a bad omen."

Opposite Mello, hand on an unopened bottle of guava juice, a suited man who had come late to the meeting spoke for the first time. "A ritual killing. That's a stroke of genius. But we'll have to work it out to the least little detail. For instance, we could start a whispering campaign. 'They say she's a witch, that she grew out of the jungle, out of a log, that her hair is nothing more than vines of the passion fruit. La Divina must be sacrificed for the good of the country'—that sort of thing. They're primitive fools. It shouldn't take much to sway them. La Divina hasn't done enough to change their way of life or to bring them into the twentieth century."

No, she hadn't, Raf thought. That was her point. She'd told him the Americans had a saying: "If it ain't broke, don't fix it." Chimu was history preserved, and no other country—not Brazil and not Peru—would ever possess its people.

The bottle of guava juice would be warm by now, Raf realized, seeing the way the man's hand rubbed the glass sides. He glanced at the others. Their faces showed no expression. He thought of La Divina's soft, fleshy body and what she had confided to him. He could tell her everything, tell her to run and hide, but it would be no use. She thought she was safe in Chimu, but safety depended upon not being in anybody's way. A million dollars lay on her head, and no one, not even he, could save her. Chimu, a hidden land, was about to be descended upon by civilization for what lay in its forests and beneath its fields, and he was powerless to stop it.

The man spoke again. "Senhor Mello, do you have second thoughts?"

He shook his head. Eyes that could witness great cruelty without flinching bore into him. "It doesn't matter what any of us thinks,'' he said. ''The juggernaut has begun to roll.''

''I thought perhaps,'' the man continued, ''the past week in the lady's company might have brought you under her spell.''

''I've been a diplomat for a long time. I don't play foolish games.''

''Well, then, let's get to work. The road juncture west from the Porto Velho bypass is finished. My bulldozers are ready to start clearing the passage through to Chimu. This business with La Divina has taken long enough. I admire the woman's strength and courage. There's no doubt history will remember her for it.''

THE FIELD OFFICE for the conservancy was located in the central part of bustling Manaus, a colonial port town where the Rio Negro met the Amazon, twelve hundred miles from the Atlantic. The river was the town's front yard, Kim discovered; the jungle a fence surrounding it. Little remained from the turn-of-the-century rubber boom that had once made Manaus the wonder of South America. Its Belle Époque buildings had been replaced by skyscrapers and busy boulevards. As Brazil's only duty-free zone, the city had awakened from its sleepy decline, which the loss of the rubber trade had inflicted.

''If this is winter in the tropics,'' Kim said to Conor, ''I'd hate to think of what summer is like.''

''The same,'' he said. ''A little hotter and a lot wetter.''

Kim, perspiration collecting on her forehead, took in a deep, cooling breath as they entered the air-conditioned premises of the Americas Conservancy building. Behind a reception desk they entered a warren of offices divided by low partitions. Computers hummed. Soft conversation combined with the mechanical whisper of the air conditioner made Kim feel as if she were back at Blackfoot Press.

A broad table held a large map, and maps were tacked to every bit of available wall space.

"Hey, Conor, welcome back. Where the devil have you been, anyway?" A tall, ruddy-faced man came loping out of a back office to clutch Conor in a bear hug. "Listen, can you spare a minute right now? I've been sitting on something too hot to ignore...."

"Hold it," Conor said, throwing his hands up and backing away. "Whoa, just give me a few minutes. Kim, this is Rolf Jenning." Before they had a chance to shake hands, he gently pushed Kim toward his corner office, calling over his shoulder, "Be right with you, pal."

"Pleased to meet you, Kim," Rolf called back, grinning.

Conor's office was small but efficient, lined with cabinets and bookshelves and filled with lush specimen plants. His second-floor view, shaded by slatted blinds, was of busy Rua dos Andradas, with its hotels and shops.

"Thirsty?" Conor closed his office door and from a small refrigerator took out a couple of cans of soda.

"I was about to run down to the Rio Negro and imbibe half of it," Kim said, grabbing one and taking a long grateful swig.

Conor's phone jangled. He picked up the receiver and peremptorily told his caller to ring back in five minutes.

"Maybe this wasn't such a good idea, coming here," he said, hanging up. "We should have caught a flight straight from Belém to the airport at Benjamin Constant and connected to Chimu from there. As it is, I've been caught playing hookey, and you know what the penalties are for playing hookey."

"Writing your name on the blackboard a hundred times?"

"Chaos. I spend half my time here, the other half hounding the world for funds so I can spend half my time

here playing watchdog. It's never a picnic when I show up."
He looked in consternation at his desk, which was piled
high with mail and reports. "The staff isn't going to be
happy when I cut and run."

"I guess what seemed like a good idea in Belém isn't such
a good idea in Manaus."

He studied her, frowning. "I should have hauled you
over to the airport and forced you onto a plane back to the
States."

Kim bridled, although she knew he meant it out of kindness. "You can have all the second thoughts you want to,
Conor. I'm perfectly capable of finding Lucky Anne on my
own. Better than capable, I'm determined and intrepid.
And I'm not going home until I find her."

"If she's alive and not just a figment of Benjamin's
imagination."

"Right. If she's alive and not just a figment of DeeDee
Dalrymple's imagination."

"DeeDee's clever and resourceful, but she's obsessive
about her husband's old paramour. That doesn't mean she
has all the answers."

"She's looking for the woman who may be Anthony
Dalrymple's true wife and heir."

"You've got DeeDee wrong if you think she'd do Lucky
Anne any harm. Just means to pay her off, believe me."

"Right," Kim said, not bothering to hide the sarcasm in
her voice. "Sure, right. After all, who knows DeeDee better than you?" Their conversation was getting them nowhere. She had to make tracks for Chimu. The problem
was how to make the journey without Conor. He knew the
terrain and protocol, and had the contacts that would make
a difficult trip a lot easier.

But she couldn't be selfish, not when a whole ecosystem
was at stake, which was what his job was all about. She,
Kim Killian, was a mere fallen leaf in a forest of Dalrym-

ple greed, and so was Lucky Anne Severance. She'd go it alone, and that was that.

"Conor, I know what your work means to you," she began, feeling self-righteous and sorry for herself, but persisting nevertheless. "I appreciate what you've done for me, but the truth is, I really can get to Chimu on my own."

Conor's phone interrupted them, and he picked up the receiver too quickly, as if glad of the interruption. Perched on the edge of his desk, he motioned to her to take a seat.

Instead, Kim impatiently began to circle the small office, studying the maps on the walls—yellow for destruction, green for untouched forest—his books, his plaques of recognition.

When he replaced the receiver, she said, "I'm just beginning to get used to your having another life, one I don't quite understand."

His smile was indulgent. "What don't you understand?"

"This, all of it, I guess. You. For a while there I thought we were two characters in a Hitchcock movie with no past, no future and no reality."

He came over to her, brushing her hair behind her ears. "No reality? You're right. I've been having entirely too much fun." He leaned over and kissed her forehead, only to pull away when someone knocked on his door and called out to him.

"I can't keep them hanging," he told her. "I'll put in a little time with the crew, spend today clearing my desk, and if we're lucky, we'll manage to hitch a ride on the conservancy plane if it's heading west tomorrow."

"Wait," she said. "I mean it, you can't afford—"

He put his finger to his lips and opened the door. Rolf Jenning stood there. "Ten thousand acres clear-cut ten miles north of the Jutaí, and nobody moved a muscle," he said in a low, urgent voice to Conor. "Heavy equipment, a major operation and the army insisting they know nothing."

"Who?" Conor asked, his face grim.

"One guess."

Conor cast a glance at Kim, then said to her, "How about I give you the key to my apartment? Settle in, or do some sight-seeing. Careful sight-seeing," he added as a warning. "We'll never get out tonight, anyway."

"No problem," she said brightly, holding her hand out. She could use a shower, a cup of coffee and a clear head.

The sky was an unremitting blue when she stepped outside. The heat hadn't gone away. She really should just pick up and leave, she thought; hop a ride to the airport and book a flight out. Benjamin Constant was a small city at a juncture in the Amazon, near the border of Peru. As the crow flies, she'd be a couple of hundred miles from Chimu once she landed at Benjamin Constant. *Benjamin Constant.* Constant Benjamin. Odd, but she hadn't even made the connection before. She owed it to Benjamin to find Lucky Anne Severance, but she couldn't or didn't want to leave Conor without seeing him again.

He lived in a small air-conditioned apartment more sparsely furnished than the one in New York, on a side street not far from the conservancy building. It contained four rooms painted white, the furniture well constructed and of native woods. On the walls a couple of Ecuadorian wall hangings depicted colorful birds in flight, and more bookshelves held an idiosyncratic selection. The second of the two bedrooms was fitted out as an office, including the tools of his trade, a fax machine and a computer.

The apartment was cool, dry, spotless. She had the impression of its humming along, even during his lengthy absences.

She wasted no time taking a shower, and afterward rummaged in the kitchen. She found a container of coffee in the refrigerator and brewed a pot, using the late-model coffee machine on the kitchen counter. She debated getting dressed after, and suddenly very sleepy, decided to wait. She slipped into her nightgown and cotton robe. With a cup of coffee on the side table, she stretched out on the sofa, her eyes closing before she even had a chance to take a sip.

"Kim?"

Her name was gently spoken. She was slow coming awake, yet when she opened her eyes knew immediately where she was. Conor bent over her. "What time is it?" she asked, then realized the lights were on and night had fallen.

"Late enough. Ten-thirty. I'm sorry, I just couldn't get away."

She sat up, reached for her cold cup of coffee and took a sip. "Oh damn," she said. "I helped myself to a shower and figured I'd get dressed, but I was really sleepy." She gave an embarrassed laugh. "I seem to spend a lot of time in your apartments, note the plural."

"I make a perfect roommate," he said. "I'm neat, I can cook and I take messages. I've even been known to do windows."

"Great, because if there's anything I hate it's windows."

"Have you eaten?"

She shook her head. She wasn't even hungry.

"Well, I bought some native delicacies for you. Bread and cheese from the conservancy refrigerator. Unless you'd like to go to a restaurant."

"Bread and cheese will do fine," she said, following him barefoot into the kitchen. The bread, packaged in cellophane as if taken off an American supermarket shelf, sat on the table along with some cheese and a couple of cans of soda. Kim began to open and close cabinet doors, looking for dishes and cutlery.

"I've booked the conservancy plane for eight tomorrow morning," he told her. "No problem. A friend of mine is the pilot. He'll take us to Benjamin Constant. He said we can easily grab a copter to Chimu from there. He's never made the trip himself but seems certain they have a landing pad."

None of the dishes matched. It was obvious Conor didn't care about company, and maybe equally obvious he'd had no permanent woman in his life, at least not in Brazil. Then the word hit her: *we.* Her heart soared. "Are you coming along?" she asked, not daring to look at him.

"It's a bad idea, but yes, now that you ask."

She brought out the dishes and set the table. "This, of course, is woman's work. I'm a guest in your house, but here I am, deep in woman's work. Where are the napkins?"

He drew his brows together. "Beats me. You'll have to ask the cleaning lady."

She found them behind a canister of sugar mercifully not overrun with ants. "What about your crew? They can't be happy you're leaving."

"They'll manage. They always do." He opened the package of bread and put the cheese on a cheese board.

Kim folded the napkins with extra care and set them next to the plates. "Shall I make fresh coffee?"

"No, just heat up the old stuff." He made no move to help.

They were going through the motions, she thought, pretending that eating was on their minds. Something had changed between them, some providential notion that had clicked in when he'd gently called her name and she'd woken up. The very air around them was heavy with the fact that they were alone, in his apartment, with the night before them.

She was at the sink, deciding which of the identical cups in the cabinet should be used for coffee, when Conor came up behind her.

"This dinner is taking longer to prepare than a *cordon bleu* meal," he said quietly.

She turned, her back pressed against the cool porcelain. "It's not what it tastes like, it's all in the look."

He touched her face with his hand, then, as he had earlier that day, brushed her hair back. "Shut up, Killian." He pulled her close and held her, his body crushing hers. She felt a surge of such tangible pleasure that her whole being gave a wild shudder. He felt it clearly, his eyes glinting with surprise. He bent and kissed her lips, a long, intense and passionate kiss.

Yet even as the kiss deepened, a sudden, overwhelming uneasiness invaded her.

As if he felt her hesitation, Conor drew away. "What is it?" he asked.

She shook her head, turned and grabbed the mugs.

"Second thoughts?"

Sure, about Drew, about herself, about Conor and who he really was, and just how much he expected of her. "Second thoughts?" she asked, putting the cups down on the table. "Second thoughts require first thoughts." She looked at him a little defiantly. "Do you mind telling me what my first thoughts were?"

"I'm not interested in some half-baked story about a lost land where a lost lady might be. I shouldn't even be interested in you, not now, not when something I've been planning for a long time is on the point of breaking."

"Not even interested in me?" She picked up a cup, then slammed it down and ran back into the living room. "Who asked you to be interested in me? Who asked you to look me up in Belém, anyway?" she said when he followed her in.

"Kim, cool it. Let me explain."

"Your explanation will have to be a damn good one," she said. "Just where do you fit in with the Dalrymples, the conservancy and the rain forest?"

"I think I'm falling in love with you."

Kim, who had ruled her life with caution and measured responses, felt awash with new perceptions, little fire-crackers of happiness that exploded one after another. "We're talking apples and pears," she said.

"We're talking love." He pulled her close again, and with his lips above hers, said, "You feel it, too, but you're dragging your old hurt along with you. For what? For protection against me? I owe you answers, but do you know what? I want you to love me whether you approve of what I do or not." His lips closed on hers. An unfamiliar heat swept along her flesh as he lifted her and carried her to his bedroom.

Beams of moonlight flickered into the room through rattan blinds and across the white bed covers. As he slipped the straps of her gown down to reveal her breasts, she heard his intake of breath. In a moment his clothes were in a heap on the floor, and he was beside her on the bed, clutching her close and breathing her name. She released a whisper of delight as his mouth closed over hers.

Her body was alive with sensations and needs she did not recognize. Forgotten was doubt and suspicion. She ached for his touch, experiencing a love that was brand-new and had no anchor in her past. In a few urgent, heated mo-ments he was in her and her frenzied cry broke the silence of the night.

Later, as she held him cradled in her arms, shadows played a game along the sleek walls of the room and sleep was a distant void she couldn't tumble into yet. She needed to relive the moments just past. Conor had given her back something she had not even realized was lost, and the wonder of love stilled her blood and made every fiber of her being rejoice.

He stirred once and murmured something unintelligible. She smiled at him. She knew so little about him and yet knew this—he talked in his sleep. Somehow that little bit of intimate knowledge illuminated the dark corners. She closed her eyes as his arms tightened about her, and in a brief, happy moment was asleep.

Chapter Seventeen

The twin-engine plane took off smoothly from Eduoardo Gomez Airport outside of Manaus. The pilot, a smiling, talkative fellow that Conor apparently knew well, invited Conor to join him in the cockpit.

"Do you mind?" Conor asked Kim.

Yes, she did mind. Morning had come in a glow for them both, and she had almost reluctantly dragged after him to the airport. Suddenly her emotions were inextricably mixed in with her priorities and she wasn't being allowed to bask in her raw happiness. They should be sitting side by side, holding hands and exchanging endearments.

"No, of course not," she said, giving him an unguarded look of pure desire she meant him to catch.

"That's what I like about you," he said, bending over and kissing her. "The willingness to share."

"That's been my life." She sat back in the seat as he made his way up front and let the truth of the previous night's magic wash over her. Conor loved her, and in a way that was brand-new. His love was without Drew's selfish edge, which had always made her feel as if a benediction was being conferred upon her. No, Conor's love was fresh, full of wonder and selfless. Her old hurt had vanished without a hint of it ever having shadowed her heart.

The morning sky was a clear, heavy blue, the sun a pale orb above the monotonous green horizon. The forest canopy was split by the wide, brown river that moved sluggishly toward its wedding outside of Manaus with the pure, black waters of the Rio Negro. The world, for as far as she could see, was a hazy green.

An occasional clearing appeared on the river's edge, each with a couple of rush-roofed houses and an open patch of cultivated land; the water was spotted with boats, both small and large, and occasionally a vessel of oceangoing size.

The journey via air to Benjamin Constant would cover about seven hundred miles in a little more than an hour and a half. From there, they'd arrange for a helicopter to take them directly to Chimu.

And if Lucky Anne was not in Chimu, they'd have dealt their last card. Kim was puzzling over possibilities when Conor came back and sat down next to her. "We're making a detour to observe some clear-cutting near the mouth of the Jutaí River. The Trans-Amazonia Highway is under construction there, opening up more and more land for exploitation."

The change in plans disconcerted Kim. They were supposed to be racing to Lucky Anne's rescue, and every minute counted. But she thought of the night before, when the world and all its troubles had seemed very distant indeed. "Couldn't it wait?" she asked, but gently. "I mean, we're supposed to be rushing to Lucky Anne's rescue."

"I have to see this for myself, Kim. I promise we'll rescue Lucky Anne, if she needs rescuing."

She was impressed with the look of determination in his eyes, a look that had nothing to do with Lucky Anne. Love was compromise and the setting of priorities and covering hurts with bandages. This called for all three. "Yes, of course, I know you will. Does clear-cutting mean Dalrymple mischief?''

He nodded. ''They claim permission from the government, and I'm sure they have it. But that doesn't mean it's right.''

''Wise-use ecology. Isn't that a new term in the ecology lexicon?'' Kim asked, remembering an article she'd read recently.

''Just another euphemism for 'stay out of my way, I'm coming through with bulldozers.''' He was silent for a while, then said casually, ''Ever heard of the International Dialogue on the Troposphere?''

Kim said no. ''Is that a formalized group or just a lot of people hanging around talking about the trouble the world is in?''

''It's a symposium being held in Geneva on the destruction of forests worldwide. A prestigious event, incidentally, with countries great and small as sponsors. We want to come out of the symposium with a general agreement over measures to be taken. Incidentally, I've been asked to give the keynote address.''

She turned to Conor, astonishment curling through her. He would never fail to surprise her. ''How come you've never said anything to me before about keynote addresses?''

He leaned over, clearly touched by her reaction, and brushed her cheeks with his lips. ''We've been on the same side all along, Kim. There's been something I haven't been able to tell you, a hand grenade with the pin already pulled. I'm going to throw it in Geneva. You,'' he said, reaching for her hand, ''can write the prizewinning book about it under your own name.''

His words were light, but beneath them Kim noticed a new note that frightened her, one both earnest and tough.

"It's okay," he said. "I know exactly what has to be done. And I know how to get out of the way after." Then, with a smile almost of relief, he went on, rushing his words as though afraid he'd regret telling her if he stopped to think about it.

"I'm going to lower the boom on the Dalrymple empire. And on the sacred memory of Anthony Dalrymple. I can't say whether he murdered Lucky Anne, but I know as clearly as I breathe that he ordered my father's murder here in the Amazon some sixteen years ago, because my father was going to blow the whistle on him and his business empire. And unfortunately, Anthony's death last year hasn't changed a thing. I'd been hoping Tony would take over, but he didn't want any part of it. Poor drunken Tony! Yet in the end, he needed to prove himself to DeeDee, after all. And died because of it."

"Are you telling me DeeDee had her own stepson murdered? Or murdered him herself?"

"I don't know," he said. "I do know that DeeDee tolerated Tony as long as her husband was alive. She discarded a lot more in her life than fur coats and living-room furniture. If she had no more use for Tony, or if he was in her way somehow, I wouldn't put it past her."

"You're scaring me," Kim said.

"I want you scared. We're going up against a monolith that considers us as insignificant as . . ."

"A flea on a dog," she finished for him.

"A flea on a dog is never insignificant, not to the dog. Maybe you have a point there."

At that moment, the plane banked and swept in low over an immense clearing in the rain forest.

Conor leaned over her. "Everything gone," he said. "A whole ecosystem, an interdependency of insects, birds and animals, some maybe gone forever."

He left her to return to the cockpit, where he was going to photograph the ruin. When he returned, he told her everything he knew about the Dalrymples and what he hoped the outcome of his speech might be.

A SMALL, PRETTY colonial town not far from the Peruvian border, Benjamin Constant supported a surprisingly busy airport.

"Who the devil was Benjamin Constant, anyway?" Kim asked as they made their way into the terminal, a stucco barn that, without air-conditioning, was close and hot.

"A constant reminder that we're doing all this for your friend Benjamin," Conor replied. They stepped up to the departures counter and he told the clerk sitting there, "I'm looking for a helicopter pilot named Antonio Silva." Conor turned to Kim. "Apparently Silva claims to have made the trip there with La Divina."

"La Divina?" Kim asked. "Who's that?"

Conor shrugged. "Someone who seems to fly in and out of Chimu from time to time. A witch, a seer—you never know around these parts."

"Over there, *senhorina.*" The clerk pointed to a photograph tacked to the bulletin board behind him. "La Divina. Beautiful lady. Silva took the picture himself. I sometimes think he's in love. But he's married and she lives in Chimu."

"Doesn't look like a witch to me," Kim said, stepping around the counter to examine the photograph, a small one showing a pilot with his arms around an attractive woman *d'un certain âge,* with dark braided hair, wearing a long, loose gown.

"How many pilots fly out of here, anyway?" Conor asked the clerk.

"It depends. No Silva listed for today. I'll call the controller."

But Kim heard the conversation as though it were merely background noise. She reached up and removed the photograph from the bulletin board, her mouth open in astonishment. "La Divina, Omigod. Conor, I've found Emma Lambert."

He came over and reached for the photograph. "La Divina is Emma Lambert—good detective work. Who in hell is Emma Lambert?"

"Emma Lambert is Lucky Anne Severance, thirty years older and just as beautiful. I recognize her now from the old photos used in the book. I met her, Conor, at the cafeteria at the Central Park Zoo. I actually met her!" she said, her excitement increasing with every word. "I talked to her, and wondered why she seemed familiar. And her name. I remember wondering about it. Emma Lambert— her paternal grandmother. She borrowed her paternal grandmother's name! And to think I let her walk away from me. She's alive! She's alive and *living in Chimu!* And maybe in big trouble."

"Take it easy, Kim. Obviously the lady knows what she's doing."

"Suppose Edoardo Moriya knew about her—from Benjamin—and told DeeDee. And once he told her, she was finished with him—he had *totally* outlived his usefulness." Kim shivered. "DeeDee isn't trying to protect the family name. She's trying to find the first Mrs. Anthony Dalrymple, who is really the heir to the Dalrymple empire."

They were distracted when a small, rotund gentleman wearing a crushed white linen suit came quickly toward them and introduced himself as the assistant flight controller. "Senhor Stark," he said, shaking Conor's hand, "a small problem. The pilot scheduled to fly you out was delayed on a trip over the border. I took the liberty of arranging for another pilot, Hector Ramos. He is well recommended.''

"Guaranteed he knows the way?" Conor asked. "No foul-ups?"

"He flies here regularly and I've never heard any complaints."

"Fine with me."

The pilot was waiting for them at the helicopter, a shiny new six-passenger Huey. Tall, broad-shouldered, with a gap-toothed smile, Hector Ramos was dressed in army fatigues, already sweaty on a day that had begun hot and was not improving any. He held a map in his hands, and spread it out on the ground. "Michimu," he said without further delay. "We follow the Ituí River about sixty miles and then veer west a hundred miles. Small place, well hidden, but we'll get there." He punched at the map, but when Conor bent closer, he smiled, flicked his finger at the spot he'd identified as Michimu and quickly folded the map.

"You've been to Chimu," Conor said.

"Sure. La Divina, she's a regular customer. Place is getting civilized. They even have an ambassador from Brazil." He laughed and spat on the ground.

"Okay," Conor said, "let's get a move on."

"Strap yourselves in," the pilot said. "I wouldn't want anything to happen to you."

Kim, fastening the safety belt, wondered why she felt so queasy. The heat perhaps, or maybe the gap-toothed grin.

"You look a little green around the gills," Conor said as the propellers started up. "Ever been in a chopper before?"

"No, but I'm okay."

"You won't find your congenial airline pilots out here in the rain forest," he said to her in English, "giving you weather conditions and a comic routine."

"I'm okay," she reiterated. "I just wish he'd get a move on. And I hope he knows what he's doing."

Ramos started the engine. The propellers swung noisily into action and in another moment they were airborne. Kim leaned back against her seat, gripping the armrests. They were headed on a rescue mission to a backwater country where anything could happen, and it suddenly struck her that the most dangerous implement she carried was a nail file.

The aircraft traced the Ituí, veered west and then followed ever-narrowing rivers, some disappearing under heavy forest canopy. Occasionally the pilot pointed something out to them, small launches or canoes or clearings on the riverbanks, his words lost in the chopper noise.

"How much longer?" Kim impatiently asked Conor.

"Take it easy. He's looking for the proverbial needle in a haystack. Michimu might not even be visible until we're directly over it."

Then, suddenly, the helicopter lurched and nosed downward. Kim felt the sickening fear that had been riding with her from the moment they left Benjamin Constant boil in her throat.

"What's going on?" Conor shouted, unbuckling himself and starting forward.

The helicopter was flying perilously close to the canopy, so close Kim figured no more than a couple dozen feet separated the craft from the tangle of green forest.

"A little engine trouble, nothing to worry about," the pilot called back. "Sit down and buckle in."

"Tell you what," Conor said, "ditching in the middle of nowhere isn't a good idea. I saw a clearing a good fifteen miles back. I suggest you turn around and head there."

The pilot turned and threw a smile back at Kim. "Tell your friend to sit down," he shouted to her.

"I said turn back."

Kim knew then that the script had changed, that Hector Ramos had no intention of taking them to Chimu. She grabbed Conor's hand and shook her head, telling him to sit down. His face was white with fury. She saw him glance at a tool kit strapped to the back of the pilot's seat. A wrench, a hammer and several screwdrivers were clearly visible.

"You're not expecting trouble, are you?" she asked.

"I'm not sure what I expect."

Suddenly Ramos turned and smiled at them, then pointed to a clearing dead ahead with a look of triumph in his eyes. Chimu. Kim felt relief so pure, tears started in her eyes.

"I think we're both spooked, that's all," she said to Conor.

"Don't bet the rent money just yet," he told her.

"What's happening?" She glanced out the window. The space they were heading to seemed no larger than a two-car garage.

"Beats me. Doesn't sound like there's a damn thing wrong with the engine, and if we've reached Chimu, it's not only a backwater, it's a playpen in the middle of the jungle."

The helicopter came down, its propellers sending a current of air whirling through the surrounding greenery. Instead of cutting the engine, however, the pilot lifted himself from his seat and turned swiftly toward them. "Welcome to Michimu." He held a 9 mm Beretta in his right hand, pointed straight at them.

Conor cursed under his breath. "What the hell's going on?"

"Delivering my cargo on time."

"Something tells me," Kim said in English, between clenched teeth, "we're not in Chimu."

Ramos tensed. "Speak Portuguese."

"And something tells me," Conor said, still in English, "that he doesn't want to mess up his chopper with our blood." He switched to Portuguese. "Who's paying you to get rid of us?"

Ramos's eyes narrowed. He grinned. "Do yourself a favor—leave quietly and I'll let you go. Just disappear into the trees. I'll say I took care of everything. See what a good guy I am?" Then, as though in an afterthought, he turned to Kim. "Hey, you, I think you're too pretty to die out there. Maybe you go first," he added to Conor. "The lady will follow."

"If that's what you want." Conor shrugged and threw a smile at Kim. He made a move toward the exit. "Sorry, Kim, but there's no other way."

Ramos laughed. "That's what I like—cooperation."

Kim could scarcely hear the men's words under the roar of the propellers. She glanced at the tools behind the pilot's seat. She knew what Conor's move meant. Ramos couldn't watch them both at the same time.

She unlocked her safety belt and edged toward the tool kit.

"Don't make a move." Ramos turned toward her, rage blanching his face. Conor kicked out swiftly and caught Ramos in the stomach. Ramos fell backward and the gun went off, the bullet tearing the roof. He was on his feet in seconds, but Conor lunged at him. Kim grabbed the wrench. The two men fell back against the controls, Conor trying to wrest the gun away. With a deep groan, Ramos pushed Conor back and freed his gun hand.

Now. Kim swung, hitting Ramos on the side of the head. The gun exploded a second time. For a split second all action stopped but for the propellers overhead. Then a scream burst out and seemed to reverberate around the cabin. Her first thought was that Conor had been hit. She dropped the wrench and rushed toward the two men, who were still locked together in combat.

"It's okay, Kim, it's okay."

Ramos fell back against his seat, the Beretta slipping from his grasp, his shoulder bloodied from a bullet wound. The welt on his head, where she'd hit him, had turned an angry red, and a thin line of blood oozed from it. If he'd been fastidious about not having blood in the chopper, she thought wildly, he was going to be pretty upset now.

Conor picked up the Beretta. "Nice work, Ramos. You shot yourself *and* the control panel. Next time try your foot instead of your shoulder." The propellers ground to a stop. He turned to Kim. "Let's get out of here."

Ramos sat slumped in his seat, breathing heavily, his hand against his shoulder. Blood oozed through his fingers. *This is real,* Kim thought, *not adventure-by-numbers.* She was afraid of him, afraid of the malevolent way his deep narrowed eyes watched her, afraid and yet unable to bear the thought of leaving him alone with his life bleeding away.

"We're leaving you here," Conor said in a cool voice. "Somebody will happen by, if you're lucky." He stopped, drew his arm across his forehead and shook his head at Kim. "All right, I know, dammit. You're scared but you're also Mother Teresa. There's got to be a first-aid kit here somewhere."

"In the provisions trunk, in the back," Ramos said, his eyes wary. He clearly expected nothing from them.

"Here, let me." Kim found bandages and an antibiotic, and while Conor threw some provisions into his backpack, she took care of Ramos's wound.

"You're going to have to leave everything behind that you can't carry in your shoulder bag," Conor told her.

She gave a resigned sigh. "Just don't forget my bug spray."

"For Amazon bugs you need Uzis. And speaking of Uzis..." He rooted around and came up with a box of cartridges.

"That's about the best I can do," Kim said, standing back and handing the rest of the antibiotic and bandages to Ramos.

He nodded dumbly. "What's going to happen to me?"

"I'll send a search party from Michimu," Conor said, swinging out of the helicopter. "You can pass the time trying to get your radio to work. I've taken the map."

Once they were clear of the helicopter, he hoisted his backpack. "Flashlight, compass, mosquito netting, machete, gun, cartridges and a couple of candy bars. Ramos wasn't planning an overnight trip. I feel sorry for the bastard, but I'm not about to carry him on my back."

The rain forest around the chopper was a curtain of impenetrable green. For the first time, she was glad Conor had insisted she outfit herself for the trip in khaki pants, jacket, heavy boots and a sun helmet.

Kim cast a glance back at Ramos. He sat unmoving, watching them. "Okay," she said to Conor, "I know what was on his mind when he told you to get out first, but how about leaving him some water?"

"Let's get a move on," Conor said. "There's a canteen sitting right at his feet. Don't feel sorry for him. He knows this spot and he knows exactly what to do. He also knows just how itchy my finger is on the Beretta." He spread the map on the ground. "Well, we're in luck. This really is a map showing Chimu. See this hatch mark? I suspect it's the X that marks the spot we're standing on. That means Chimu is maybe ten miles away, due west." He rooted around in his backpack and handed her the bug spray. "First this, and then put on the mosquito netting. This won't be a walk through the Garden of Eden, although I can guarantee snakes."

"Snakes?" Kim grabbed his arm. "Wait! You didn't tell me about snakes!"

"I didn't tell you about Ramos, either. Take your choice. Look, Kim, just keep close behind me and your eyes on the ground. There will be snakes—mostly harmless, I hope, if you don't try to start up a conversation with them. I've got the machete. And I don't recommend we hang around one minute longer than we have to. This little landing strip is here for a reason. I've got a suspicion about its uses."

"Drugs?"

He shrugged. "A Huey helicopter flying out of a provincial town with seating for six strikes me as being... excessive."

"Snakes in trees," she said. "Boa constrictors, vipers, tarantulas. *Anacondas*. They squeeze you to death." Her feet felt rooted to the ground. She considered the possibility of awaiting rescue with Ramos. After all, they had the gun. Then, suddenly, she saw a bright multicolored beetle sitting on a broken branch, poised as though to attack. She backed away. "Ugh, what's that?"

Conor was several steps ahead of her, but came back to investigate. "Take it easy. Meet *Acrocinus longimanus,* the harlequin beetle."

"Is he dangerous?"

"Only when he's mad. Natural history lesson over. Let's move."

A narrow path that had been cut through the forest was already overgrown with the young vines and plants that seemed to spring from the earth with every drop from the moisture-laden leaves above. Every fallen branch looked like a snake, and Kim suspected that every snake looked like a fallen branch. But the *thwack* of the machete, and the glances and smiles that Conor threw her, were reassuring. Conor and she were a team, she realized in exultation.

If only they got out of this alive.

"During the rainy season, this could be inches under water," Conor said. "Whoever built that helicopter landing site had something in mind. I'd guess there's a river nearby, not shown on the map, and a camp somewhere in the general vicinity."

"Great! Maybe we can get help."

"Not great. Anybody pitching camp around here wouldn't want unexpected company. Just stay low and keep your eyes on the ground. And stick right behind me."

From the high canopy, they heard noisy flocks of parrots. Closer at hand was the steady hum of a forest thick with insects, or the smooth slide of snakes through the undergrowth and along the bark of trees.

It was a hidden universe, heavy with heat, a sinister, wonderful place filled with odd rustlings and screeches, broken by the sound of Conor's machete thrusting aside the tangle of strangler vines. Kim thought of monkeys and sloths high in the canopy watching their progress, of natives with poisoned spears behind every tree. She had never imagined that her quest for Lucky Anne would end in a remote forest in Amazonia.

"How'd Ramos find out about us?" she asked after a while.

"I should have known better," Conor said. "I opened my mouth about Chimu at the conservancy. Somebody connected there."

"Maybe your friend, the pilot who took us to Benjamin Constant."

"Maybe."

"As soon as they discover the helicopter missing, they'll be on to us," Kim said.

"Worse, they'll make their way to Chimu."

They walked on, as silently as possible. After a while the path took a sharp turn north. "Say goodbye to civilization," Conor told her. "We're leaving the trail."

"*This* is civilization?"

"As we currently know it."

"Let's hope you read that map right."

"We're on compass power now, due west."

After an hour of steady work, they had progressed less than a mile. "Better stop and sip some water," Conor said, handing her the canteen. "The heat can really wipe you out."

"I'm already wiped out." Kim was soaked through. She found it difficult to take in a deep breath. The air was drenched and heavy, a potent mixture of rotting leaves and the sweetness of mimosa. They found bromeliads clinging to tree trunks, and the vines of passion flowers, which added spots of bright red to the tedium of green. But after the first half hour, she had had all the jungle she ever wanted.

"Wait." Conor touched her arm and listened. Through the trees came the low, unmistakable drone of a motor.

"A plane?" Kim asked. "Is that good or bad?"

Conor shook his head. "Not a plane. Earthbound. Heavy equipment, I'd guess a mile away. The forest acts like a voice box." He consulted his compass. "Due west. Come on, we're in luck. Maybe we can pick up a lift into Michimu."

"Maybe we're in Chimu now."

"Maybe. And maybe we're fifty miles off course."

They connected with a surveyor's path a couple of hundred yards later, orange ribbons fluttering like flamingo flowers along a straight gouge that had been cleared by a bulldozer.

"Mahogany trees knocked down and pushed out of the way as if they were matchsticks." Conor reacted by plunging ahead as though ready to take on the bulldozers by hand.

Kim hurried to catch up to him. "They're clearing a road, aren't they?"

"Probably. They've marked off the route. Americans, I guarantee it. Orange ribbons! Straight lines! Just push your way through. Come on." His voice was tight with anger.

"Conor, hold it." Kim had to run to keep up with him. "We have to find Lucky Anne. Keep your temper, okay? These guys, whoever they are, are just doing their job."

He pulled away, charging along the open cut, his shoulders tense. Kim hurried after him. Perhaps he was wrong. Perhaps they were in Chimu and—and what? Perhaps Chimu was hostile territory and perhaps the Chimus weren't benign, friendly people. And perhaps La Divina wasn't Emma Lambert and Emma Lambert wasn't Lucky Anne Severance.

"Watch out for snakes," Conor said. "They like nothing better than fallen logs and branches."

"Thanks," Kim said, not trying to hide her annoyance. "How about jaguars or man-eating lions?"

But Conor was already yards ahead of her and rushing on toward the sound of heavy earth-moving equipment. The light in the distance had shifted, Kim noted. The forest now had a distinct sky blue edge; sunlight filtered through the green shade that for a while had turned time and distance and reality upside down and inside out. Then they came out into full sunshine again, to earth the color of ocher churned up as far as the eye could see.

"My God, it's immense," Kim said, staring at a huge piece of equipment that seemed to be heading straight for them.

"I want you to get behind that tree over there," Conor ordered, "and don't show yourself."

"What are you going to do?"

Conor slipped his backpack off and handed her the gun. "Just stay put."

"What am I supposed to do with this?"

His grin was strained. "Cover me. And if you have to, act like you know how to use it."

"Hey, wait a minute, this isn't the wild West."

"It is now." He walked swiftly toward the giant bulldozer and stopped in its path, not twenty feet away. The driver slowed down and came to a grinding halt a yard from where Conor stood.

"Hey, what the hell do you think you're doing?"

The words were in English, spoken with a midwestern accent. The man in a hard hat running toward Conor seemed to materialize from nowhere. Clearly a member of an American crew, he wore yellow overalls printed with the Dalrymple logo.

"Suppose you tell me what's going on," Conor said.

"American? Where the hell did you come from?" The man in the hard hat turned and scanned the edge of the forest. Kim jumped back behind a tree without being spotted. "What is this? You alone?"

Conor raised both hands to show he was unarmed. "I didn't come to give you a hard time, I just want some answers."

"What are you, a damned environmentalist? How'd you get here, anyway?"

"That doesn't matter," Conor said bluntly. "Where's the road going?"

"West, not that it's any of your business."

Several other men came slowly down the road, their hands clenched around crowbars and other heavy implements. Without speaking, they circled Conor.

Kim, her heart banging in her chest, hoisted the gun. She didn't have to kill anybody, she only had to hang tough and shoot a volley over their heads. Being an editor had its advantages, one of which was that she'd learned a great deal about guns while working on a book about firearms. Kim wasn't a good shot, but she knew the range of the gun she was holding, and the sizable kick it would give.

One of the men reached out and knocked off Conor's helmet. "Pick it up," he ordered.

Conor swung.

A couple of other men came running. That was everybody, she hoped. Kim stepped out from behind the tree and fired the shot above their heads. The sound echoed sharply and a dozen huge, white-winged birds rose into the air. Monkeys twenty or thirty meters up in the canopy began screeching their commentary on the scene below.

"Back away," Kim called, "or I'll pick you off one by one."

"Jeez, what is this? The middle of the Amazon, we got Tarzan and Jane."

Grabbing his helmet, Conor came running toward her. "Okay, okay" he said, "I saw red."

"What do we do now?" Kim asked, still pointing the Beretta. She looked toward the men in hard hats. They were backing away slowly, their hands in the air.

"Don't ask me! You're doing fine."

"Why didn't you ask them to point the way to Chimu?"

"I didn't think of it. Sometimes my anger is the worst part of my valor."

His last words, however, were lost in the start-up of the earth mover. It began to head straight toward them at a surprising clip.

"Let's go," Conor said, grabbing his backpack.

Kim fired a shot at the front tire. A mosquito biting a giant, she thought, but she might as well make a point. Then she turned and raced after Conor. If they met up with any snakes, she had the gun.

A surge of astounding energy charged through her. "Hey, we do make quite a team!" she shouted once they had melted back into the forest.

He waited for her to catch up and then spun her into his arms. "What else can you do that I don't know about?"

She grinned and kissed him.

THE RIVER THAT CAME unexpectedly into view after another couple of miles had carved its way through a narrow gorge. On the bank they discovered a small village of thatched huts, looking soft and pink in the fading daylight.

"Javari," Conor told her, preceding her into the village. "They'll offer us a drink made of manioc. Take it and smile."

"I'll smile. Unless they tell you Chimu is around the corner, my guess is we'll be invited to spend the night."

Conor looked relieved, as if he had expected Kim to argue for pushing on. They wouldn't help Lucky Anne by getting lost. Kim had already resigned herself to another delay, although she had no doubt that Lucky Anne was in more danger than ever.

The drink made from manioc was white and tasted bitter, but she thanked the elderly woman who handed it to her, receiving a sweet smile in return. A dozen children surrounded her, laughing and pointing while she drank.

Conor spoke with the headman, who gestured upriver. She heard the name Chimu, but that was all she understood. She sat on a small stool watching Conor. He would never fail to amaze her, this man in a bush hat conversing in his host's aboriginal language. She remembered when she'd first seen him—in the Hamptons, oozing good looks and easy sophistication.

She had never really doubted him, she realized now; just her own good luck in finding such a man. A tremendous mixture of hot desire and lusty greed raged through her.

He came back to her smiling. "We can stay. It's not exactly the Hilton, but we'll get an early start in the morning. And here's the good part," he added. "This river feeds into the Chimu. It's swift moving and they're going to give us a ride right through. Meanwhile are you hungry?"

She gave him a silly grin. "For a lot of things, but I could settle for some food and maybe a swim."

He took her by the hand and led her to a communal house built on stilts. "A couple of hammocks and our hosts for company are about all I can offer," he said, regret coloring his voice. "No privacy tonight."

Chapter Eighteen

Michimu, main village of Chimu

Nightfall brought with it a prattling of insects and animals, sustained sounds as meaningless as static from some alternate universe. The air was still, moist and scented heavily with the fragrance of late-blooming jasmine that grew everywhere around her *palafita*. La Divina sat quietly on her porch above the river. The newspaper from Rio lay discarded at her feet.

She sat in darkness, the slatted blinds pulled down to keep the insects at bay. Through the blinds she stared unseeing at lights wavering like luminous moths from other houses, as villagers completed the last of their daily tasks. Playing along the river's edge, youngsters screamed with laughter. At the sound of their joy, an expected melancholy swept over her, a melancholy so complete she couldn't bear it.

In a moment time had changed and been given a new shape, a shape too terrible to behold. Her only child—the heir to the Dalrymple empire, which had invested heavily in Brazil—had been murdered in faraway New York. So stated *Jornal do Brazil*, the frayed copy of the Rio newspaper that had arrived in Michimu, as always, a week late. All around her the world snapped, buzzed, rubbed, laughed, swayed, intent upon its own business, immune to her unhappiness.

La Divina started from her trance. The sound of strange voices put her on the alert. She waited, her breath drawn in. As shadowy figures passed by, she recognized her nearest neighbors and let her breath out slowly.

And so it had begun, the fear. They would find her, those other, unknown shadowy figures who had murdered Benjamin and now her son. She had no doubt. The amulets would eventually tell the tale, one given in a moment of whimsy to her nephew, Benjamin, the other to her son, Tony, on that fateful day. Such gestures of sentiment were sometimes like drops of very lethal poison.

"Benjamin, I beg you by all that's holy, keep my secret."

"The Dalrymple fortune belongs to you and your son! You must make them suffer."

"But my husband is dead. I'm happy in this little corner."

"You won't have to hide anymore. You'll have your son, and you won't have to hide."

"He is better off not knowing."

Then the triumphant news that Benjamin had won the Berriman Prize. He had come for her in Chimu and had collected her, and together they'd gone to New York. As they neared the city, however, he'd become increasingly agitated. He wouldn't explain why.

He'd said, "I've booked us into the Waldorf Astoria." The hotel, he expected, would be the venue of the many media interviews he expected to have following the award.

There had been no convincing him then. He'd puffed with pride, and alternately had seemed troubled. She'd decided she had no choice but to meet her son, and to talk some sense into Kim Killian. And on that day of many decisions, when her happiness, after all, was most complete,

Benjamin had been murdered. The Berriman Prize had been the beginning of the end.

Without fanfare the rain began, a heavy sheet of water vengefully pushing insects to earth. Minutes later it stopped, as quickly as it had begun. La Divina got heavily to her feet and pulled the slatted porch blinds up.

Around her house, steam rose, haunting the forest. A pale, smoky shape drifted up from the river and drew her back in time to the island of Marajó, a time that had ended in fire and pale wisps of smoke.

The events of thirty years before lay in her mind as though imprinted there only yesterday. The early evening on Marajó had been silken. Her mood had been good, anticipatory. It was the start of winter, when the air cleared and fresh winds swept the island.

Cantering on horseback along the river edge, no longer underwater from the summer rains, Lucky Anne had come upon a ragtag group of Indians camping in the dry fields near the shore. She'd established at once that they were not islanders, nor were they from Belém. Their mode of dress, their narrow, high-bridged noses, long faces and prominent cheekbones would have made them more at home in the Andes. They were accompanied by their head woman, an elderly creature, bent and clearly in some pain, who spoke Portuguese.

"Who are you? Where do you come from?"

"Ah, *senhora,* if you please."

They were from Chimu, she'd explained, and they had left their home weeks before, traveling by boat down the Amazon to Marajó. Lucky Anne knew of Chimu only as a tiny spot between Peru and Brazil on an aerial map, an independent land of no value to anyone.

The story Lucky Anne heard was extraordinary.

They had only to ride the mighty river to its mouth, they had been told. There would be work and riches on the great island or in Belém, work that would lift them from a life of poverty forever.

"And who told you such a thing?" she had asked.

"Friends. An American who spoke Portuguese, for one."

"And did this American tell you to come to his ranch on Marajó?"

"We are waiting to see him, *senhora.*"

"I'm afraid he is not here. But he will come soon. You see, I'm waiting for him, as you are."

She had fed the small group and housed them in an unused stable. She had no idea what Anthony, her husband, had in mind for them, but knew they would not find work on Marajó, nor, she believed, in Belém. She tried to convince them to return to Chimu, but they said they would wait for the *senhor.*

She waited with them, for the return of her husband and son from the States. Until that day thirty years later, when the newspaper from Rio arrived, there had never been a moment when she did not wait for her child.

SHE KNEW EVERYTHING about her son, had watched him grow up from afar. She was like a visitor to a silent-movie house, leaving Chimu far behind several times a year merely to catch a glimpse of him. She had never again heard his voice.

The shop, a New York landmark, specialized in fine old books and maps. Tony frequented the place on upper Madison Avenue and usually stopped by every Monday morning following a meeting nearby. Lucky Anne had held her breath a moment, then spoke.

"Tony?"

He'd turned, surprised to hear his name. He held a book in his hand and gazed curiously and rather kindly at her. For a moment Lucky Anne was speechless. She could smell the musty bindings of old leather, the lemony scent of polished wood; hear the soft whispers of salespeople and customers.

"Excuse me," Tony had said politely, "do I know you?"

"My name is Anne Dalrymple. I wonder if I might speak with you."

He smiled, not at all surprised at her name. "Oh yes, cousin Lallie's mother?" He nodded, as though she had answered him in the affirmative. He reached out and shook her hand vigorously. "You're from the San Diego branch, am I right?"

She smiled, without answering.

He put the book down and offered her his arm. "Drinks. I know just the place. A little early perhaps, but a celebration is in order." He jauntily escorted her from the shop. "My treat, of course. How is Lallie, anyway? Last time I heard, she was on her way to Hong Kong. Talked about manufacturing shoes there. She's something."

"Yes, isn't she?" Perhaps the time wasn't quite right, after all. Anne, who had always been so adventuresome and forthright, was frightened of this handsome young stranger.

"Incidentally, how's the rest of the family?"

Was it a trap? Did he guess she was lying?

"As usual," she said.

"I only really know Lallie. Dalrymples are certainly spreading their joy all over the world." They walked along Madison Avenue. The day was particularly fine, sunny and warm, with a friendly breeze heading along the canyon made up of some of the finest buildings in the city.

Soon the world would know that she was alive. No, she would tell him now, end the unbearable waiting. Helpless to prevent Benjamin from revealing her whereabouts in Chimu, she must reveal herself to Tony; tell him he was in danger, too; ask him to stop Benjamin. In spite of all she had learned about him, she remained uncertain of the kind

of man her son had become. But she did know DeeDee
Ealing controlled Dalrymple's assets. A spare wife suddenly surfacing, possibly in possession of a marriage license could be a formidable enemy, especially when aligned
with her natural son.

That DeeDee was cold, hard and ambitious, Anne had
no doubt. She also had no doubt that DeeDee would do
anything to protect her inheritance.

They settled for a small outdoor café on Madison Avenue. "I'm afraid I'm not Lallie's mother, after all," she
said, once their drinks had been served.

Tony looked more amused than alarmed. "Ah, the accent, of course. You married a Dalrymple. Leon, wasn't
it?" He examined her openly. "But you're somehow familiar. The family look, I think."

"My name is Anne Severance Dalrymple," she said.
"Your father, *everyone,* called me Lucky Anne."

He dropped his glass of vermouth to the ground, and
when it shattered, he laughed.

HE HAD LAUGHED, his eyes, murky with drink and disappointment, suddenly shining on that last day of his life. But
there were things she had not mentioned to him then, and
now he would never know. About the nights she'd lain
awake, longing to hold her child in her arms; how she had
watched him from afar, but hadn't had the courage to approach him; how she had read about him in the newspapers, keeping the clippings until they rotted in the jungle
heat.

She had not given him back the mother he had known for
only three years of his life so much as warned him of the
danger that lay ahead, and asked him for help. He had listened, his face alight with purpose, and had agreed to do
what he could.

When Benjamin was murdered, she left New York without ever seeing her son again, for she thought Tony was the murderer. Now Tony was gone and she would have to live with the terrible knowledge that she had been complicit in her son's death.

TONY HAD BEEN LITTLE MORE than a baby when his father came for him and took him back to the States, a lively, sturdy child of three whose dark, defiant gaze would fade over the years. But she hadn't known it then; she had trusted his father to rear their son, and now he was dead, this child she had borne and had barely had time to know.

Anthony Dalrymple was not the first man she had loved, but he was the last. He was handsome, rich, autocratic, capable of bridling the wild streak that pulsed through her like a demon. She had found rest in his powerful arms; she'd wanted to hide with him forever in some dark and remote place.

And for a while she'd thought such dreams were possible. She was young, she was foolish, she'd thought the world revolved around her. She did not think of ecosystems or carbon dioxide levels or of indigenous peoples who had a right to their lands. She thought of her body, of love, of obsession with another person, that was all.

She knew he was ruthless and cunning—he had told her so often enough. He explained to her that the Amazonian basin was the last wild place in the world that could be harvested for the riches it held, both on its surface and below.

She bought his enthusiasm and made it her own. And when she became pregnant, Anthony took her pregnancy as an omen, marrying her before their son was born. They celebrated the marriage at the Dalrymple ranch, with half the island of Marajó present.

"He looks like you," Anthony had said, cradling the baby in his arms. She wasn't certain whether she read disappointment or wonder in his voice.

"*Your* ears," she had said, laughing. "And look at those tough little fists. He's going to be as determined and stubborn as you are."

He had cast her a glance she never forgot, an appraising look, as though she were a prize animal whose fertility was suddenly in question. Then he kissed her, and the next day was gone on the first of many separations, back to the States.

She'd never doubted his love. Managing his ranch, watching their son grow and never doubting Anthony's love filled contented days and dreamy nights.

"I'm taking Tony back with me this time," Anthony said when the boy was three years old. "This weather isn't doing him any good." He had returned from New York during the height of the summer season. The rains had been particularly harsh, but not harsh enough to subdue the clouds of insects and parasites that filled the air. Tony had been bitten by a minute insect that had left huge welts along his back. Running barefoot had given him another infection from the parasite *bicho de pé*.

"For the summer, then," she said, acquiescing almost immediately. The Dalrymple camp in the Adirondacks would do the child good. She offered to go along.

"You're needed here." His tone was peremptory, his manner unfamiliar and cool. "You dote on the child too much."

Their son *was* too much in her company; she agreed about that, too. He'd be back when the weather cooled.

Summer passed. The weather cooled. The island was swept by delicious breezes. She awaited their return with increasing joy, as the Indians from Chimu waited.

A week later, her husband appeared without their son. He had changed—grown thinner, looked elegant and dressed as though his life had become citified. He flew in with half a dozen similarly dressed men, American and Brazilian. They held meetings in her small office and talked about clear-cutting and government subsidies and allowances. She heard her first words about displaced Indians, the felling of stands of mahogany, the search for the elusive rosewood tree. She learned about iron mines and how the discovery of gold in the Amazon would open up the basin for further exploration, and how the Dalrymple empire was considered an asset by the Brazilian government, much favored.

He learned of the Indians from Chimu encamped on his land. His face grew red with fury. "They lie about how they came to be here. I told them that if they expected to be released from the poverty of their lives, they would do well to seek work in Belém."

But the problem could wait. She wanted to talk about their son. Later, when their guests were being given a tour of the *fazenda,* he had taken her by the hand and brought her into their bedroom. They made fierce love, and while she lay in his arms, he said, "I want this to go on forever."

"It will," she said. "Just you and Tony and me. Here, in the States, wherever you say."

"I want Tony with me," he said. "In New York. He's a young prince, the Dalrymple prince."

It didn't matter to Lucky Anne where she lived. "You'll have to hire a manager for the ranch."

"You're staying here, Anne."

She felt the blood drain from her face and pulled out of his arms. "I don't understand."

"You don't have to. I want you as my mistress, just as you've always been, but Tony needs a mother, not a half-domesticated wild woman whose greatest talent is riding herd on a bunch of buffalo.''

"Mistress?" The word stuck in her throat. She slipped out of bed. She went to the window and peered through the blinds, seeing figures moving around outside the stables. The Chimus, she had no doubt.

"You don't think that business of our so-called marriage was real, do you?" He came over to her and gripped her arms.

"I don't understand," she repeated thickly, as though she still lay with him, submerged in a dream.

"You don't believe that ceremony was genuine! How could you be such a fool? It was show, merely show for the locals."

She whipped around. "But we registered, signed papers, were duly married."

He shook his head. "What papers? What did we sign?"

"Anthony, don't joke."

"I don't joke. Where is it, that worthless piece of paper?" He bent over her. She thought for a moment that he was going to kiss her, tell her he *was* joking, but his veiled eyes and lips, stretched thin with purpose, convinced her otherwise.

She summoned all her strength to tell him the first lie of their marriage. "You have our marriage license, Anthony. You must remember. You insisted I give it to you. But then, at the celebration, you got drunk. You have it somewhere."

He stared at her for a long time. She felt impelled to whisper. "Where is it? You must know. Please tell me! It's proof that we were married. Please don't tease me."

"Nothing exists, not in the marriage registry and not on a license," he said. "Nor will any of the locals remember the celebration as anything but a party at the Dalrymple *fazenda*, where food and drink were plentiful."

"Why are you doing this to me?"

"Because I'm already married, to DeeDee Ealing, and she's going to raise our son."

"What? I'm sorry, but I thought you said..."

She stopped, confused, unable to take his words in.

"Nothing will change between us," he assured her.

"Our marriage was legal and binding. I won't let you do this to me."

His subsequent rage frightened her. He came charging at her, his hands closing around her neck. He had wanted to kill her. She broke away and rushed out into the night, to the stables, to the small group of Indians from Chimu. Because of his business associates, he could not come after her, could not drag her back, screaming. She hid in the stables and after a while heard the small Cessna they had arrived in start up.

"Go home," she said to the Indians who huddled around her. "You must go home. Tomorrow morning you must return upriver to Chimu."

The fire that began in the stables that night and raged on to the main house killed one person, the elderly Chimu head woman, who was hit by a falling beam as she tried to escape the blaze.

Lucky Anne took her place. They were going back to Chimu and she would lead them there. Though she could not speak their language, she would learn. When the fire started, she understood finally that her husband did mean to kill her, to destroy any evidence she might have of their marriage. Ealing Industries was the prize worth having; he could always find himself another mistress.

Anthony Dalrymple, in his arrogance, was wrong on two counts. Anne did not die in the fire, and their marriage certificate was safe and sound, and very real. It lay with some cash in a bank in Belém, along with her son's birth certificate, which stated that Tony was the son of Anthony and Anne Dalrymple, née Severance.

She had loved her husband. She had always trusted him, but those who have lived reckless and imprudent lives understand the importance of rainy-day investments.

THE SWEET SCENT of jasmine arose. The pale mists sank into the darkness. Tomorrow would be a celebration, the Feast of the Assumption. She must not allow her private sorrows to upset this yearly festival, this strange rite both Christian and Chimu. Her son's death would be her secret sadness.

She thought of Raf Mello. He was the first man she had allowed into her life in thirty years. She had told him everything, and perhaps she should tell him this, also.

Chapter Nineteen

"Where is everybody? This place is totally deserted."

The boat that had brought them to the village of Michimu moved slowly and unalterably downstream. Kim, standing on the floating dock tethered to shore, shaded her eyes and watched it go. "Maybe we should've asked him to wait," she remarked to Conor.

"He kept his end of the bargain," Conor said.

"It's a little spooky, though. If this is Michimu, where's the welcoming committee? I mean, I don't think visitors drop by everyday."

"It's midmorning," Conor said. "Maybe they know a thing or two about siesta."

"Children don't take *siestas*. Where are *they*? I don't hear them, don't see them."

Conor dug his hands into his pockets and stood surveying the shoreline. The river curved off to the left, and he had no doubt that if they followed it they'd come upon small enclaves surrounding pools and inlets. River floods during the rainy season precluded building close to shore. He was surprised, in fact, to find a *palafita,* a thatched house on stilts, about a hundred yards back, on a slight rise of land. It was situated to command a view of the dock and of the beautiful meandering river beyond.

He had to admit the silence around the dock was puzzling. Kim was right. Kids should be flocking around, chattering away, wide-eyed and giggling at the arrival of strangers. The only life they saw were birds trolling the nutrient-rich waters. He was pleased to catch sight of rare white jabiru storks with black faces and red throats wading through the shallows, reason enough to fight the bulldozers that were carving up the rain forest a dozen miles away.

"You're sure this is Michimu?" Kim asked.

He faked a laugh. "In the Amazon, one can't be sure of anything."

"Maybe..." Kim began and stopped.

"We'll find her," Conor said. "Come on, the place is a backwater. Don't expect town squares and mini-White Houses, or Big Macs."

"She's in trouble, I know it." Kim ran impatiently down the dock and along the path toward the *palafita*. "Anybody here?" A dog barked and came running out from under the house, a skinny brown mutt with tail wagging. Kim bent to pet him. "Where is she—where's Lucky Anne?"

Conor, coming up the path, tilted his head, then stopped. He heard another sound from a long way off: music. "Listen." The elusive, mournful sound of pipes and drums floated on the still air.

Kim got to her feet, her forehead creased with worry lines. "Indian pipes. Sounds funereal. I don't like this, Conor, I don't like it one bit."

He went over to her and put a comforting arm around her shoulder. "Don't get ahead of yourself. We're in Chimu, all right. Music like that is straight from the Andes. Just a little out of synch in the rain forest."

"Out of synch and chilling. I'm scared. Maybe we're too late."

"It's a religious ceremony of some sort. And headed this way. What we need is a good reviewing spot, where we can see and not be seen."

"The porch," Kim said. They took the half-dozen steps two at a time, the dog right behind them. The slatted blinds that enclosed the porch would hide them well enough. The height of the *palafita* also produced a dividend—a view of other stilt houses that ringed a small lagoon to the left, perhaps a hundred yards back.

"Hey, look." Kim pointed out a wooden hut with a tin roof, from which a wisp of smoke rose. "Let's go and ask some questions."

"No," Conor said. "Not yet." The door to the *palafita* stood open. He peered in. The one room, simply furnished, had a shortwave radio on a small desk.

"La Divina?" Kim asked, standing tentatively at his shoulder, looking in.

"Probably."

A statue of the Chimu bird stood alone on a small shelf above a narrow table. "There's the connection between Benjamin, Tony and the woman who calls herself La Divina," Kim said.

"A connection, but not the story of why they died." Conor noted a pile of magazines and books, with a copy of the Rio newspaper *Jornal do Brazil* on top. Even in this backwater at the end of time the lady was curious about the world outside. He idly picked up the Rio paper and found it open to an article concerning Tony Dalrymple's death. Damn, so she knew. He wondered how she was taking it, this news of a son she had long ago been forced to give up. Perhaps the music . . . Funereal, Kim had insisted.

The music was growing louder, the drums sharp and monotone. "Conor, I'm getting nervous."

"Take it easy." He put the paper down and placed a magazine over it. No use adding to Kim's worry.

"I'm not crazy about trespassing on someone else's property. Even if they don't have a police force, just poisoned bows and arrows."

"Wrong culture," Conor said. "And incidentally, I don't think they speak Portuguese."

"What do they speak?"

Conor shook his head. "Anybody's guess."

"Know how to use the shortwave? Can you call for help?"

Conor looked the system over. "No sweat. La Divina's up on the latest technology. My guess is it's used more to keep people out than to let the world in. I can probably get through to New York if I have to."

"Well, at least it's there if we need it. My opinion is we need it, but try someplace closer." She stalked out to the porch to gaze once more through the slatted blinds. The dog curled up at her feet and went to sleep.

Conor continued to study the shortwave, and was about to flick it on when Kim called out, "Hey, look. Someone's coming out of the hut, the one with the smoke, and he's no native. He's just standing there."

"Good sign. Maybe he's the ambassador from Brazil." Conor joined her, pushing the blind aside for a closer look. Dark-haired with an impressive mustache, khaki pants and a white shirt, the man stood still, arms across his chest, as if listening to the haunting music. A very civilized cigar was stuck in his mouth.

The sound was even closer now. Kim and Conor waited side by side in suspense, not speaking, not touching. After a while a parade of Indians came slowly into view along the river's edge. In spite of the heat, they were dressed in raiment that spoke of ancient rites practiced high in the Andes—colorful handwoven capes and flat, fringed caps. Several costumed dancers at the front had smeared their faces with paint. Behind them came the musicians, then a double line of natives carrying an elaborately decorated statue of the Madonna.

"Ah!" Conor remembered now. "The Feast of the Assumption. They were talking about it in Manaus."

Another group of marchers, dressed in black, followed the Madonna. As they came abreast of the *palafita*, Kim grabbed Conor's arm. "Emma Lambert, there! The woman I met in Central Park."

Walking alone behind the marchers was a dark-haired woman wearing a long, multicolored robe. Around her head, woven into a black braid, was a gold chain that ended in a gold amulet that lay against her forehead.

"La Divina." Conor felt Kim shaking with excitement.

"Lucky Anne Severance."

"Mrs. Anthony Dalrymple. Maybe." She was alive, this possible thorn in DeeDee's side.

"I'm laying bets the amulet is a Chimu bird. C'mon." Kim took his hand. "Let's go."

Conor looked over to see that the stranger they noted earlier was still there in front of his hut. He had been joined by two others. "Hold it, we're not going anywhere."

Just then La Divina cast a glance toward the *palafita* and faltered, as though she could see right through the slatted blinds.

"She knows," Kim said.

"Don't move, don't breathe."

After a moment La Divina turned away. The parade continued on, made up of hundreds of people who followed in no particular order, some wearing simple cotton clothing, others in Andean costume.

"The entire population of Chimu," Kim said. "How are we supposed to find her assassins?"

"That's the idea." Conor continued to keep his eyes on the three men outside the hut. If they had trouble on their minds, then they had timed it well. They would kill Lucky Anne with or without a festival to cover them.

He thought of the bulldozers and the rare storks, the felled mahogany and the long, straight road being cut through the middle of the rain forest. He thought of his father, and knew without a doubt that Lucky Anne was part of a larger plan. The three men went back into the hut. Perhaps he was wrong about them, but he didn't think so.

"Come on," he said to Kim. "I think we'd better stick close to your friend. We'll take a parallel route."

Just past the precincts of the village, they came upon an empty helicopter landing site. "I wonder why she doesn't have a chopper of her own," Conor said. "After all, the lady was a pilot."

"Perhaps that's why she doesn't. You can't keep a low profile piloting your own helicopter. She manages to get around, but with easy transportation maybe she'd begin to move a little too fast than is good for her." Kim glanced at the parade, still moving steadily onward. "Where do you suppose they're headed?"

"My guess is a shrine. I suppose if they had a sacred mountain they'd be climbing it."

"Sacred mountain around here? Not likely."

The parade continued on along the river until it reached a bare bulge a couple of acres in circumference, no more than a dozen yards high at its summit, where a small shrine was visible. Conor recognized the bareness of the *morro* as possibly signaling the presence of iron ore. Such anomalies weren't rare in unique and forbidding Amazonia, and might indicate far greater riches lying beneath the earth— another reason for the bulldozers.

At the river's edge, small fishing boats were tied up at a primitive dock. He had noted the skill of the Indian oarsmen as they'd made the journey that morning upriver from the Javari village. Here the rapids increased in fury, and he could hear the formidable crash of water where the river curved downstream. The dock was crowded with onlookers. The assassin might be any one of them, careful in his— or her—disguise. He meant to ask Kim where she'd gotten her shooting skills.

"We're going to have to position ourselves more closely," Kim said as La Divina moved slowly and solemnly up the incline toward the shrine. "Push our way through the crowd without making them mad."

Halfway to the top they discovered a goat being hauled up the hill, bleating and fighting with every step. The Madonna was already being steadied in place near the summit. The Chimu weren't particular about the distinctions between Christian and pagan beliefs.

"Sacrifice!" Kim said, grasping his arm and looking pained. "I don't think I want to see this. You keep an eye on Lucky Anne. I'll circle the crowd below."

But Conor had his eye, not on the goat or on Lucky Anne, but on the motorboat that was tied up at the dock.

"I see it, too," Kim said. "It wasn't there five minutes ago."

"No. Neither were they." He indicated the three men they'd seen in the village, now twenty or thirty yards apart, edging determinedly up through the crowds toward Lucky Anne. All three had decided bulges in their pockets, Conor noted. They weren't taking any chances. "I don't care how you do it," he told Kim, "but get her out of the way."

"Three men? You're taking them on alone?"

"Piece of cake. They may figure we're just a couple of tourists who've lost our way, or better, anthropologists."

She gave him a skeptical but trusting smile that said they had come all this way to rescue Lucky Anne and there was no backing down now. Then she turned and began to push through the crowd.

Conor had his hand on the Beretta. The gunmen were obviously counting on the crowd to create a diversion. There were enough people around for a major stampede. That could work two ways. One shot straight up should do it. People would be confused just enough, with no real harm done.

He saw Kim move in close and grab Lucky Anne. He saw the look of recognition and shock on the woman's face. The three men began to move in. Conor raised the Beretta.

"Aaieh, deu mio." The voice, a woman's, was close to his ear. He turned, distracted. A young woman in a fringed hat and wearing an embroidered apron over a cotton dress stared at him in horror. She grasped two youngsters tightly and began backing away.

The shot when it rang out didn't come from his gun. He saw Kim go down, taking Lucky Anne with her. His heart seemed to burst in his chest. All bets were off, Conor decided, as he raced toward Kim. He pushed his way through the panicking mob that was heading down the hill, fear etching their faces. He found Kim dazedly trying to get to her feet. Lucky Anne was gone. He pulled Kim up and held her close, his lips against her hair. For a long moment the world around him seemed calm and good.

The goat blissfully nibbled at a bowlful of corn that had been brought for the ceremony. The statue of the Madonna had been taken from its shrine. He could see it bobbing down below, being rushed back to the village.

"I'm okay," Kim assured Conor. "The shot went over our heads, but two goons grabbed Lucky Anne."

Conor came to his senses. "The motorboat! They figured on a fast escape!" He took Kim's hand and raced down the hill, neatly avoiding the last of the rushing mob. Halfway down, another shot rang out.

"My God, Lucky Anne," Kim cried out.

They reached the dock just as the motorboat took off, spewing water and knocking through native craft as it sped out.

"One of them's shot," Conor said. There were only two men in the boat, one with a shirt already bloodied. "And no Lucky Anne. Get down!" Without fanfare he threw Kim to the dock.

With a grimace, the wounded gunman took aim at them but then fell back, the shot harmlessly hitting the water.

Conor sighted down his Beretta, then shook his head. "That boat won't make it through the rapids, not at the rate they're going. One of them's wounded and can't shoot worth a damn, and the other doesn't know the first thing about boats. And to top it off, they don't have Lucky Anne. What the hell was that all about?" They watched as the boat disappeared down the river. Conor heard one long shout for help over the rush of the river, then nothing. He got to his feet. "We promised to send someone to help Hector Ramos. Add these two gents to the list. I think it's time we cranked up the shortwave."

"If Lucky Anne wasn't in the boat," Kim asked, "where is she?"

"We're short one gentleman, a man with a black mustache who smokes cigars," Conor said. "My guess is he has Lucky Anne."

"Or," said Kim hopefully, "she has him."

Chapter Twenty

"La Divina, do you know where she is? *Dove, donde, ou?*"

"*Aaiehh, La Divina! Meu dio.*" A wavery finger pointed in the general vicinity of the village.

They raced toward the village, past a stream of men, women and children heading purposefully in the same direction. Kim called breathlessly to Conor, "I figured it out. They're speaking a mix of Portuguese and Spanish."

"That's diplomacy for you—probably why they've managed to keep Peru and Brazil at bay."

"All I can say is, I hope they'll understand us, if we have to explain who we are and why we're here."

"Ssh, hold it." Conor stopped, his hand on her arm. "Listen."

The sound of a chopper just beyond the mangrove swamp across the river was unmistakable. "That's no mosquito," Kim said. "Do you suppose Ramos..."

"Ramos is out of action, Kim."

A small helicopter came into view and headed low over the river. The Dalrymple logo was clearly visible on its side.

"The landing pad—let's go!" Kim said, starting off at a near run. "Just what we need right now."

The chopper was already on the ground when they reached the clearing, its rotating blades sending currents of air into the surrounding vegetation. Waiting for the door to open were Lucky Anne Severance and the mustached stranger they had seen earlier.

Conor pulled Kim back to a thick grove of trees and ferns. "Let's not play our last card. Either DeeDee expects to walk in and take over, or she's come to talk peace. Whatever her plan is, I don't trust her."

"You're sure it's DeeDee?"

"I can smell the smoke from here."

The chopper door opened. Its pilot stepped out, a big, heavyset fellow in fatigues, carrying a holstered gun.

"Look familiar?" Kim asked.

Conor nodded. "American. Purely background stuff. Name's Joe Turbon. He's her bodyguard, pilot, you-name-it, here and in the States."

"Not to worry?" Kim asked.

"Never gave him a serious thought," Conor said, "until now."

Turbon nodded at the welcoming committee, took their measure, and then ducked under the blades to help his passenger, DeeDee Dalrymple, descend.

"So that's what a billion dollars looks like." Kim stared at her, as at an apparition. She had seen pictures of DeeDee in the magazines from time to time, formal photographs of a brunette with a pretty face, touched up to emphasize a youth that was no longer hers. She wore a camouflage suit, heavy boots and a sun hat with a wide brim. A bandanna was wrapped around her neck. Jungle chic, Kim thought, taking in the differences and similarities between the two women in Anthony Dalrymple's life. Both had the same aristocratic, self-possessed carriage. But it was DeeDee who seemed hard and leathered, where as Lucky Anne was feminine and earthy.

Conor suddenly gripped her arms. "Turbon's keeping his hands carefully away from his gun. He doesn't seem to notice that Lucky Anne's friend is also packing one."

"Is it going to get sticky?" she asked.

"Not at the moment. Call me a third, interested party. I still have the Beretta, remember. Right now I think both women have been curious about each other for too long to let the opportunity pass."

"Maybe, just maybe, DeeDee hasn't connected La Divina with Lucky Anne Severance."

"She has. She's looking into Tony's eyes."

"All along DeeDee has been following the trail of Lucky Anne Severance, only to be confronted by La Divina, alive and well."

"She was behind the assassination attempt," Conor said. "And now realizes it failed."

La Divina stepped forward. Kim caught the expression on her face, wry, imperative and questioning. She was Lucky Anne Severance, confronting the woman who had taken the man she loved, raised Tony, and with Anthony Dalrymple's death, now commanded an immense and powerful empire.

And Lucky Anne wasn't afraid. She might have lived with her fear until this moment, but it had finally washed away.

"She knows her son is dead," Conor said calmly.

"Yes, of course. She has nothing to lose."

DeeDee stared at Lucky Anne for a long moment without speaking. She seemed faintly rattled.

Lucky Anne was the first to speak. She did not introduce herself. The two women, enemies for so long, had no need of introductions. "Welcome to Chimu, Senhorina Ealing. This is Ambassador Raf Mello," she added, referring to the man at her side. "Of Brazil."

DeeDee scarcely gave Mello a glance. Her face had grown
pale with fury. "*Senhorina Ealing?* Thirty years is a long
time to cling to a story that was a lie to begin with."

"Never a lie, *senhorina,* I assure you."

"If you have any proof that you and my husband were
married, I'd like to see it."

Lucky Anne gave her a courteous smile. "Come," she
said, gesturing toward the village. "I think we have a few
matters to discuss."

DeeDee, her face rigid with indignation, walked for-
ward without giving Lucky Anne another glance. Kim and
Conor kept back a reasonable distance as La Divina and
Mello led their visitors to the village.

"I'd keep Turbon in clear view," Kim said. "I've got a
feeling he's more than her pilot."

"I knew she cast a wide net," Conor said, "but now I
understand how she was able to move so fast. She needed
somebody able to act on three minutes' notice, someone
who was never far away. He taught Tony to fly."

They arrived back at the *palafita.* The dock and shoreline were empty but for a small boat heading downstream.
The area was heavily trampled and some discarded flowers
lay on the ground. The sun had settled behind the trees on
the far shore, and the persistent chirp of some small creature had taken the place of pipes and drums.

Lucky Anne paused at the bottom step and gestured to
DeeDee, as though offering her entrance to a far grander
establishment.

DeeDee's mouth turned up in derision. "I'm only here
out of respect for your son. I'm willing to concede that he'd
want you to receive a fair share of his estate." She went
quickly up the steps, but when they all entered the *palafita*'s large single room, she at last caught sight of Conor and
Kim. "Well," she said with a small laugh. She took her sun
hat off and threw it onto a chair. "I should've known.

Conor. And Kim, isn't it? We've been playing hide-and-seek all along, haven't we?"

"I haven't been hiding," Kim said, "although you've been seeking."

"Exactly what are you up to?" DeeDee asked, squinting curiously at her. "What's your stake in all this?"

"Stake?" Kim was astonished. "This isn't about money, it's about truth."

"You know nothing of the truth, either of you. I married Anthony Dalrymple without even knowing of his liaison with this woman. He dragged his little son up from Marajó and thrust him on me, and that's the first I learned about her. She's haunted me throughout my married life, and even after my husband died. 'Lucky Anne. That was a woman,' he told me. 'A woman to love your whole life.' He killed her!" she cried. "He killed her but he never stopped loving her!" She turned on Lucky Anne, her faced twisted and ugly with anger. "But you're not dead, are you? What would he have done if he'd known you were still alive? Lucky Anne Severance in Chimu all this time!" Her laugh had an edge of hysteria. "And you don't know, do you?"

Lucky Anne, her face impassive, merely waited, as though DeeDee's fury, like a storm, would abate. Her very silence seemed to enrage DeeDee more. "This land, this Chimu, is owned from border to border by Dalrymple Enterprises."

"What the devil are you talking about?" Conor asked.

"My husband bought the entire piece of land thirty years ago, that's what I'm talking about."

Lucky Anne started, then reached for Mello's arm for support.

"That's right," DeeDee said. "One acquires land at the right moment and then waits. I'm afraid the waiting is over. How amusing to think that you've been here all this time. Anne Severance. Lucky Lady, indeed."

Lucky Anne had paled, and her eyes seemed a little feverish. "Did you know about this?" she asked Mello.

"Yes."

"I see." She stepped back, away from him. "Yet you rescued me from an assassination attempt."

"Yes."

She faced DeeDee. "I understand everything now. The picture becomes quite clear. Select your goal as you would a piece of chocolate from a candy store. No need to consume it, however—just put it aside for the time being. But of course, certain precautions might have to be taken, such as lying to the head woman, who so innocently signed a piece of paper. Send her and her closest advisors to Belém with promises of riches. Destroy the colony as you would an ants' nest. Once the queen bee is gone, the rest will disappear or die."

"I have no idea what my husband did or didn't do," DeeDee said. "I only know this—we've come to claim what's ours. Dalrymple Enterprises is now ready to begin exploring Chimu."

"Exploiting it, you mean," Conor put in.

DeeDee scarcely bothered to look at him. "I'll deal with you later," she said curtly.

"Oh, I've no doubt you'd like to."

As though in a dream, Lucky Anne went over to her desk, opened the drawer and lifted out a small metal box.

"Ordinarily this was kept in a safe in an air-conditioned bank in Belém," she said, addressing no one in particular. She might, in fact, have been only recounting events to herself. "The tropical climate isn't particularly kind to documents of this sort. The change is slow, insidious and irrevocable. But I had a dream of my son coming to Chimu to stay, and I wanted him to have this." She took a key from a chain around her neck and opened the box. Inside lay a single piece of paper, somewhat yellowed. "For the last couple of days, I thought this of such little value I almost destroyed it." She took the paper out and unfolded it. "Here," she said, offering the document to Kim. "This was what your friend Benjamin was looking for."

"Your marriage license." Kim took the document as though she had just been handed the original *Constitution of the United States.* "Anne Severance and Anthony Dalrymple sealed as husband and wife."

"Lies. Give me that." DeeDee lunged for it, but Raf Mello pushed her roughly out of the way.

"All right, everybody stay calm. I'll take the license and make you all happy." Turbon, gun drawn and cocked, smiled and held his hand out. "Right now."

Mello started forward, but the pilot shook his head. "Uh-uh, I wouldn't if I were you." He nodded at Kim. "I said hand it over."

Kim, in a sidelong glance, caught Conor's eye. He nodded at the license, then at the floor.

Right. Diversion. From the expression on Lucky Anne's face, it was possible she'd caught Conor's meaning as well. Kim dropped the license and watched it flutter to the floor. DeeDee made a grab for it.

"Got it. Just so much trash," she said. "And to think you've been hanging on to it all this time. Pity you didn't show this to Anthony, but then you couldn't, could you? You were dead."

"Hand it over, Mrs. Dalrymple," Turbon said, smiling at her.

"Kill them, Joe, all of them. Now."

The pilot smiled. He held his hand out. "I'll take the license."

"Are you questioning my authority?" DeeDee said.

"I don't recall asking any questions," Turbon said. "Hand it over."

DeeDee turned on Turbon. "You fool, you damn fool. Just where do you think you'd be without me? I'll have you hung for my stepson's death."

"Don't talk. Just give me the license."

"Sorry, fella, drop it." Conor was behind him.

Turbon raised his gun, then saw Mello reach for his. Outside, high in the canopy, a monkey suddenly screamed, the sound human and shattering. The dog, which had been on the porch when they came in, now lumbered heavily into the room, sat down and began to scratch his fleas.

Kim, her heart battering in her chest, felt as though the world had turned a corner into another universe, where time had slowed and everything was preternaturally clear.

"Drop the gun."

Turbon understood the pressure of the Beretta at his neck. He dropped his gun to the floor.

"Nice and easy now," Conor said. "Kim, pick up the gun and watch our friend Turbon here. And DeeDee, I won't hesitate to rearrange your beautiful kneecaps. Just hand me the license."

"It won't be worth a damn in court," she said. For a moment she held it up, both hands on it, as though she would rip it to shreds.

"Don't," Conor said. He held his hand out.

"Take it," she said imperiously. "I'm glad it's all in the open now."

Conor glanced over the license. "This is clearly a bona fide reason why Senhora Anne Dalrymple, known locally as La Divina, holds clear title to the lands bordered by Brazil and Peru, known now and forever after as the Independent State of Chimu. Any questions?" He looked around the room. "None?" With a smile he handed the document to Lucky Anne.

"Thirty years," she said quietly to DeeDee, a note of compassion in her voice. "We were both victims of Anthony Dalrymple."

"I wasn't his victim," DeeDee said coldly.

"Perhaps he was yours," Conor said. "I doubt I'd forgive you anything, but I might have, considering whose shoes you're wearing. To have cold-bloodedly ordered Tony's death because you no longer had any use for him..."

"He threatened me," DeeDee broke in. "He said he had proof that his mother was alive, that I'd lose everything."

"Oh, dear God," Lucky Anne cried, her hand to her mouth. "It's true. I told him and sealed his death warrant."

"What the hell am I doing in this hot, godforsaken place?" DeeDee headed for the door, hesitated, then whipped around. "I'll break you," she said to Lucky Anne, "here and in the States. As for you, Conor, I'll see your career is finished forever. And I hope you have a long, long life."

Conor laughed and waved her back in. "Sit down, DeeDee, you've got no place to go. What we need now is a little help from La Divina. She may have to use her troops to move us out of Chimu."

Lucky Anne Severance went to the shortwave radio. "I'll signal for help," she said. "I believe the Brazilian government will be happy to hear from the president of Chimu. I believe the time has come to open up honest areas of communication," she added with a fond glance at Raf Mello.

"And for Lucky Anne to come out of hiding," Kim said. "Now and for all time."

Chapter Twenty-One

"Here, let me do that." Kim removed Conor's fumbling fingers from his bow tie and tied it herself. "There," she said, fondly kissing him on the cheek. "How'd you ever manage without me?"

"I didn't." He stepped back from the hotel-room mirror and examined himself critically.

"Darn right." Kim tucked her arm through his, and for a moment they stood before the mirror, husband and wife, aglow with a deep and profound love. What a long way they'd come, what a complicated route, to stand quietly locked arm in arm in a hotel room one serene September night in Geneva.

"I seem to remember someone on a beach in the Hamptons, pants rolled up, bow tie undone," she said. "I thought you were a pretty classy guy then, and you're even more so now." She raised on her toes to kiss him.

He pulled her close and deepened the kiss. "You were wearing something filmy," he said in a voice husky with emotion. "I'd been thinking about you, telling myself not to get involved, that I had no time for love. And there you were out of nowhere, standing stock-still. I recall a soft night breeze, the moon disappearing behind a cloud. I'd been staring out to sea, and for no good reason at all, turned around to find you."

"Did you think I was a ghost?"

"Not even out of my past. Ghost*writer* as it's turned out. I'd begun to think I was suffering from jungle fever when you turned and ran. You were real, all right."

"I'd been spooked myself. The Blackfoots and I figured you knew more than was good for you. When you said you wanted to get to know me, I didn't trust you one bit." She laughed. "How I wanted that ice-cream soda."

"I didn't trust myself," he said. "I was committed to one thing only, one half hour in Geneva...."

"About to come up," Kim said in a sudden attack of efficiency, pointing to her watch.

"Not exactly a time for sentimentality, is it?" He kissed her once again, a brief, wistful kiss that would have to do.

Kim turned back to the mirror. She wore pale blue silk, a sliver of a dress that showed off a complexion touched by the sun of faraway places. No, not exactly a time for sentimentality. "Definitely out of order," she mused, "when the DeeDees of this world hire expensive lawyers and go about their business as usual. She'll never stand trial for anyone's death."

"She always had Joe Turbon to run her errands for her," Conor said.

"Well, he won't be running errands anymore."

"The courts could take years to decide exactly who owns Dalrymple Enterprises," Conor said. "Tonight's speech might give them a jump start." He gathered together the pages of the speech he had been studying all that day, and then threw them aside. "I knew what I was going to say a long time ago," he told his wife. "Nothing's changed. The world needs a strong agenda on the environment, not a spineless one, and I'm going to hand it to them tonight.

Straight from the heart. Straight from Conor Stark, Sr.'s only son."

"And Lucky Anne's protector," Kim reminded him. "You started out wanting to avenge your father's death and then Tony's, and ended up with a tiny, defenseless little country no one even knew existed."

He grinned. "And a wife."

A wife, Kim thought with a smile, whose pocketful of adventures had turned her into a pretty lucky lady, after all.

As though Conor were charging himself up for the speech ahead, he said, "But what hasn't changed are governments and individual corporations operating with a free hand and without an eye to the future, with murderers as allies. And the bigger the country and bigger the corporation, the more they ply their trade with immunity. I'm not going to give them a chance with places like Chimu."

"Lucky Anne won't let that happen," Kim said. "Tourism's the way to go. Even she knows that." She held up her silk wrap for Conor to drape around her shoulders and for a moment leaned into him. Then she said briskly, "Come on, she's waiting for us downstairs—the president for life of Chimu on the arm of the ambassador from Brazil. I think Chimu is safe for the next millennium."

Fifty red-blooded, white-hot, true-blue hunks from every
State in the Union!

Beginning in May, look for MEN MADE IN AMERICA!
Written by some of our most popular authors, these
stories feature fifty of the strongest, sexiest men, each
from a different state in the union!

Two titles available every other month at your favorite
retail outlet.

In May, look for:

FULL HOUSE by Jackie Weger (Alabama)
BORROWED DREAMS by Debbie Macomber (Alaska)

In July, look for:

CALL IT DESTINY by Jayne Ann Krentz (Arizona)
ANOTHER KIND OF LOVE by Mary Lynn Baxter
(Arkansas)

You won't be able to resist MEN MADE IN AMERICA!

WIN-A-FORTUNE • MILLION DOLLAR SWEEPSTAKES
OFFICIAL RULES • MILLION DOLLAR SWEEPSTAKES
NO PURCHASE OR OBLIGATION NECESSARY TO ENTER

To enter, follow the directions published. **ALTERNATE MEANS OF ENTRY:** Hand-print your name and address on a 3"×5" card and mail to either: Harlequin Win-A-Fortune, 3010 Walden Ave., P.O. Box 1867, Buffalo, NY 14269-1867, or Harlequin Win A Fortune, P.O. Box 609, Fort Erie, Ontario L2A 5X3, and we will assign your Sweepstakes numbers (Limit: one entry per envelope). For eligibility, entries must be received no later than March 31, 1994, and be sent via 1st-class mail. No liability is assumed for printing errors or lost, late or misdirected entries.

To determine winners, the sweepstakes numbers on submitted entries will be compared against a list of randomly preselected prizewinning numbers. In the event all prizes are not claimed via the return of prizewinning numbers, random drawings will be held from among all other entries received to award unclaimed prizes.

Prizewinners will be determined no later than May 30, 1994. Selection of winning numbers and random drawings are under the supervision of D.L. Blair, Inc., an independent judging organization whose decisions are final. One prize to a family or organization. No substitution will be made for any prize, except as offered. Taxes and duties on all prizes are the sole responsibility of winners. Winners will be notified by mail. Chances of winning are determined by the number of entries distributed and received.

Sweepstakes open to persons 18 years of age or older, except employees and immediate family members of Torstar Corporation, D.L. Blair, Inc., their affiliates, subsidiaries and all other agencies, entities and persons connected with the use, marketing or conduct of this Sweepstakes. All applicable laws and regulations apply. Sweepstakes offer void wherever prohibited by law. Any litigation within the province of Quebec respecting the conduct and awarding of a prize in this Sweepstakes must be submitted to the Régies des Loteries et Courses du Quebec. In order to win a prize, residents of Canada will be required to correctly answer a time-limited arithmetical skill-testing question. Values of all prizes are in U.S. currency.

Winners of major prizes will be obligated to sign and return an affidavit of eligibility and release of liability within 30 days of notification. In the event of non-compliance within this time period, prize may be awarded to an alternate winner. Any prize or prize notification returned as undeliverable will result in the awarding of the prize to an alternate winner. By acceptance of their prize, winners consent to use of their names, photographs or other likenesses for purposes of advertising, trade and promotion on behalf of Torstar Corporation without further compensation, unless prohibited by law.

This Sweepstakes is presented by Torstar Corporation, its subsidiaries and affiliates in conjunction with book, merchandise and/or product offerings. Prizes are as follows: Grand Prize—$1,000,000 (payable at $33,333.33 a year for 30 years). First through Sixth Prizes may be presented in different creative executions, each with the following approximate values: First Prize—$35,000; Second Prize—$10,000; 2 Third Prizes—$5,000 each; 5 Fourth Prizes—$1,000 each; 10 Fifth Prizes—$250 each; 1,000 Sixth Prizes—$100 each. Prizewinners will have the opportunity of selecting any prize offered for that level. A travel-prize option if offered and selected by winner, must be completed within 12 months of selection and is subject to hotel and flight accommodations availability. Torstar Corporation may present this sweepstakes utilizing names other than Million Dollar Sweepstakes. For a current list of all prize options offered within prize levels and all names the Sweepstakes may utilize, send a self-addressed stamped envelope (WA residents need not affix return postage) to: Million Dollar Sweepstakes Prize Options/Names, P.O. Box 7410, Blair, NE 68009.

For a list of prizewinners (available after July 31, 1994) send a separate, stamped self-addressed envelope to: Million Dollar Sweepstakes Winners, P.O. Box 4728, Blair NE 68009.

SWP-H493